Under the Autumn Leaves

Under the Autumn Leaves

Morgan McDonnell

TABLE OF CONTENTS

ACKNOWLEDGMENTS

Writing this book has been an incredible journey, one that I could not have completed without the support, guidance, and encouragement of many people.

First and foremost, I would like to thank my family. Your unwavering belief in me, patience, and love provided the foundation I needed to pursue this story. I am eternally grateful for your support.

A very special thank you to Cherry, my Crimepedia podcast co-host. I wouldn't be where I am without you. Your energy, enthusiasm, and unwavering support have been a guiding light throughout our friendship, and I am beyond grateful to have you as my true crime partner.

To the readers—thank you for taking a chance on this story. Your willingness to immerse yourselves in the world I've created is the greatest gift I could ask for. I hope this book resonates with you as much as it has with me.

This story exists because of all of you, and for that, I am forever grateful.

With all my thanks,

Morgan

PROLOGUE

The night in Blendon Woods, was eerily still. A thick, oppressive fog draped over the quiet forest, swallowing the familiar landmarks and muffling the faint sounds of life. It was as if the entire city had been silenced, holding its breath, waiting for something to emerge from the mist.

On the edge of Columbus, Ohio, the park—normally peaceful in the daylight—seemed to pulse with a dark, watchful energy. The trees, half-hidden by the dense fog, stood like sentinels guarding a secret. Deep within those shadowed depths, a figure moved, deliberate and invisible. Each step was slow, controlled, as if rehearsed a thousand times before.

Sarah ran this path nearly every evening, finding solace in the steady rhythm of her footsteps. But tonight, something was wrong. The woods seemed different, the air heavier, thick with tension. Her steps faltered, unease prickling at the back of her neck. The path ahead dissolved into the fog, the blackness almost suffocating.

She wiped the sweat from her brow, feeling a tremor in her fingers. It's nothing, she told herself. Just the fog playing tricks. But the thought did nothing to calm the rising panic in her chest. Something was wrong. The quiet wasn't right. The woods were too still, as if the entire world was waiting, watching.

She stopped and glanced over her shoulder. Nothing. The same pale mist, the same impenetrable shadows.

But the feeling wouldn't leave her. The sensation of being watched clung to her skin, raising the tiny hairs on the back of her neck. She forced herself to breathe, tried to steady her pounding heart. You're being ridiculous. But even as she whispered the words, she couldn't shake the dread curling in her gut. Something was out there. Waiting.

Then it came.

A twig snapped somewhere behind her.

Sarah froze, her heart suddenly hammering against her ribs. She told herself it was nothing—just a squirrel or maybe a deer. The woods were full of wildlife, especially at dusk. But the prickling sensation intensified, spreading down her spine like ice water.

Someone was watching her.

She'd felt it for weeks now, that crawling sensation of eyes following her every move. At work, at home, even here on her evening runs. She'd tried to convince herself it was paranoia, the natural result of digging too deep into old case files and connecting dots that others had missed. But standing here in the gathering dark, with fog wrapping around her ankles like cold hands, she knew better.

The air felt different suddenly—heavier, charged with something beyond the natural stillness of evening. Sarah turned slowly, scanning the misty woods around her. The trees had become silhouettes, their branches reaching toward a sky she could no longer see through the fog. Everything looked wrong, twisted by fear and failing light into shapes that seemed to move when she wasn't looking directly at them.

Another snap, closer this time. Deliberate.

Her muscles tensed, ready to run, but something kept her rooted to the spot. Movement caught her eye—a shadow darker than the others, sliding between the trees with terrible purpose. Her mind screamed at her to move, to flee, but her body wouldn't respond. The fog had thickened, making it impossible to tell which direction led to safety.

"Hello?" The word came out barely above a whisper, immediately swallowed by the mist. She knew she shouldn't have called out—every instinct warned against revealing her position—but the silence was worse than any response could be.

The shadow moved again, and this time Sarah caught a glimpse of something that made her blood run cold. A face in the fog, features indistinct but somehow familiar. Someone she knew. Someone she trusted.

That's when she ran.

Sarah's lungs burned as she pushed herself harder, veering off the trail in desperate hope of losing whoever was following her. But even as she crashed through the underbrush, she knew it was useless. They weren't chasing her— they were herding her, driving her exactly where they wanted her to go.

A root caught her foot, sending her sprawling. The ground rushed up to meet her, knocking the air from her lungs. Pain shot through her knees, her palms. She tried to push herself up, but her arms shook too badly to support her weight.

That's when she felt it—a hand on her shoulder, gentle almost, a horrible parody of comfort.

"Shh," a voice whispered, terrifyingly familiar. "Don't fight it. That only makes it worse."

Panic exploded in her chest. "No! Please!" Her voice cracked, raw and desperate. She tried to crawl away, but her body was betraying her, limbs sluggish from the fall. The needle glinted in the faint light as the figure brought it closer with eerie calm, as if this moment had been rehearsed countless times. There was no hesitation, no rush—just precision. Control.

The needle pierced her skin, and Sarah gasped, feeling the icy burn of the drug as it seeped into her bloodstream. Her body began to shut down, her muscles weakening, vision swimming in and out of focus. She could still think, could still feel, but her body no longer obeyed her. She was trapped inside her own skin, helpless.

As the paralysis spread, the figure knelt beside her, their presence a cold shadow looming over her. Even in her numbed state, Sarah's mind screamed in terror, but she couldn't move, couldn't fight back.

The figure leaned in close, so close that Sarah could feel the cold brush of their breath against her cheek. "This is just the beginning," the voice said, clinical and detached. "You should have left the past alone."

Controlled. It wasn't a threat—it was a statement, a fact. The killer had already decided what came next, and Sarah's fate was just another part of their plan.

The darkness closed in, her vision fading, her body going slack. But the figure didn't leave. They lingered, as if savoring the moment, watching her slip away with the same detached curiosity of a scientist observing an experiment. This wasn't about rage or passion—this was about control. About watching the life drain from her, knowing they held the power.

The last thing Sarah saw before the darkness swallowed her whole was the vague outline of the trees above, their branches reaching out like skeletal fingers, stretching toward the sky. And then, finally, there was nothing.

CHAPTER 1
THE BODY IN THE WOODS

As Jessica laced up her running shoes and stepped outside, the morning chill clung to her skin. The leaves rustled in the tall trees above, filling her nostrils with the familiar scent of pine and damp earth. She jogged down the path, carefully avoiding the muddy patches left by last night's rain. Ahead, her golden retriever, Max, darted forward, his nose tracing invisible lines along the forest floor.

"Max!" Jessica called, her breath hitching slightly from the incline. She glanced at her watch and frowned—it was 8:30 a.m., much later than her usual morning run. The woods were shrouded in thick fog that muffled the sounds of nature and cast an eerie glow. Jessica squinted, struggling to see through the mist as it seemed to swallow the light. She pushed on, determined to meet her goal for the day. "Just a little more," she gasped, her legs burning with each step.

Max's ears perked up when he heard another dog barking in the distance. Without warning, he lunged forward, yanking the leash from Jessica's hand. She stumbled, struggling to regain control.

"Max, no!" She tightened her grip, trying to reel him back. "Stay on the trail."

Max's nose hovered inches above the forest floor as he prowled through the dense vegetation. Jessica trailed behind, her heart racing as she watched him.

She couldn't shake the unease in her stomach—a sense that something was wrong.

"What is it, boy?" she muttered, loosening her hold on the leash. Maybe he'd found a wounded animal or something else that needed help. Despite the gnawing feeling of dread, she allowed Max to lead her deeper into the woods.

Max surged forward, his nose twitching as he followed a faint scent. Jessica struggled to keep up, slipping on the slick leaves covering the forest floor. The trees closed in around them, branches like skeletal arms blocking the sun. The air felt heavy and damp, making it harder to breathe as they pressed further into the thick woods.

"Max, slow down!" Jessica's voice felt small, swallowed by the sudden quiet of the woods. She realized with a start that even the birds had fallen silent, as if the forest was holding its breath.

Max's ears perked, and he froze. His fur stood on end, a low growl rumbling deep within him. He cautiously approached a brush pile, his nose quivering as he sniffed at something hidden beneath the autumn leaves.

Jessica's pulse quickened as she crouched down beside him. With shaky hands, she pushed aside the tangled branches, a mixture of dread and curiosity churning in her stomach.

At first, it was just a pale shape, barely visible under the leaves. Jessica's heart raced as she tried to rationalize what she was seeing. A discarded mannequin? Garbage? But deep down, she knew it was something more sinister. Max let out a sharp bark, shattering her denial.

Her body jolted as her eyes widened in horror—a pale, lifeless arm stretched out from beneath the leaves. The fingers were contorted as if frozen in a final, desperate struggle. Jessica's breath caught in her throat as the grim realization settled: this was a real human arm.

"Oh my God," she gasped, trying to steady herself as she took in the sight. A chill ran down her spine as she realized she had stumbled upon a dead body, lying forgotten among the leaves.

The woman's lifeless body lay on the ground, limbs bent at unnatural angles. She looked like a discarded doll, her bruised wrists and neck a stark contrast against her pale skin.

Jessica's heart pounded as she stumbled backward, her vision tunneling as she fumbled for her phone. Her hands trembled violently as she punched in the numbers.

"9-1-1, what's your emergency?"

"I—I found a body," Jessica stammered, her voice barely audible. "A girl. She's dead. Blendon Woods."

The next hour passed in a blur of sirens and voices. Police cruisers arrived first, their lights cutting through the fog in alternating flashes of red and blue. Officers secured the scene with yellow tape, creating a barrier between the normal world and the horror that lay within. Jessica sat in the back of an ambulance, a shock blanket around her shoulders, answering questions on autopilot while Max pressed against her legs, refusing to leave her side.

John sat at his kitchen table, his gaze fixed on the half-empty mug of lukewarm coffee before him. The low hum of the refrigerator provided the only noise in his sparsely furnished apartment. His eyes drifted to the photo on the counter—a snapshot from his daughter Sam's eighth-grade graduation. In the photo, she beamed with happiness, her bright eyes full of hope and dreams for the future.

His fingers trembled as they rested on the smooth surface of the phone. He couldn't bring himself to listen to Sam's last voicemail. The weight of regret hung heavy in his chest, knowing their final conversation had ended with sharp words and a deafening silence. Now, all he had left was that voicemail, waiting like a bookmark he couldn't turn past. But he couldn't bring himself to press play. Not yet.

A sudden buzz pulled him back to the present. The precinct.

"DiMatteo," he answered, his voice gravelly, worn from too many sleepless nights.

"Detective, we've got a body in Blendon Woods. Patrol says it's bad."

John closed his eyes, inhaling the familiar earthy scent of the park in his mind. He remembered the case that had brought him here—a young woman's body found in the woods. His hand clenched around the phone, a physical reminder of his duty pulling him away from haunting memories.

"I'm on my way."

He reached for his coat, the rough wool scratching his skin. The chilly morning air seeped through his shirt and jacket, making him shiver as he stepped out the door. A heavy weight settled in his chest as he made his way to the park in his car, an unshakable sense of unease lingering within him, one he couldn't quite place.

John arrived as the fog began to lift, his presence changing the atmosphere among the first responders. He moved with purpose, his experienced eyes taking in every detail. The medical examiner's van pulled up shortly after, its arrival marking the shift from discovery to investigation.

"Morning," Ramirez muttered, his tone flat. He glanced up briefly, meeting John's eyes before returning to his notes.

"What have we got?" John asked, tugging on his gloves. His voice was calm, steady—a practiced facade.

"Female, mid-twenties. No ID yet. Jogger found her about an hour ago." Ramirez gestured toward the body, his expression tight.

John inched closer, trying to steady his trembling hands. His eyes widened as the gruesome scene unfolded before him—a lifeless body hidden under a pile of leaves, her limbs twisted at odd angles. Deep purple bruises stood out against her pale skin, evidence of the restraints that had once bound her. But now, she appeared to have been posed with malicious intent, contorted into a grotesque display for whoever might stumble upon her.

A chill crept down his spine, and he swallowed hard. This place felt all too familiar. In a split second, a vivid flashback flooded his mind: a dead body lying in a similar spot. He closed his eyes and took a deep breath, pushing the image away. He had a job to do, and dwelling on the past wouldn't help.

"Cause of death?" John asked, his stomach churning despite his steady tone.

"No obvious trauma," Ramirez replied. "Looks like asphyxiation from the bruises around her neck. The ME will confirm."

John knelt down next to the body, his latex gloves snapping against his skin as his fingers hovered over the pale flesh. He noticed faint cuts tracing along her torso, each one a careful and calculated wound. A sour taste rose in his mouth as he realized this was no random act of violence. It was a deliberate and brutal attack that left him feeling sick to his stomach.

"This wasn't just an attack," John muttered, more to himself than to Ramirez. "It's controlled."

Ramirez knelt and ran his hand along the rough ground, feeling the deep grooves in the dirt. "Whoever did this took their time," he said. "See these drag marks? They dumped her body here after she was already dead."

John's eyes scanned the deep purple bruises on both wrists, the limp and twisted limbs. A surge of fear and dread coursed through him as he stepped closer. Memories flooded his mind, sending his heart racing and his throat constricting. It was like reliving a nightmare he thought he had escaped. But this time, it was different. This couldn't be happening again, could it?

"DiMatteo?" Ramirez's voice cut through his thoughts.

John cleared his throat, shaking off the feeling. "Right. Anything else at the scene?"

Ramirez glanced at him but didn't move. "I know where your head's at," he said, hands sliding into his jacket pockets. "Don't get ahead of this."

John clenched his jaw, a flicker of irritation passing through him. "I'm fine."

"Just don't let it cloud you," Ramirez cautioned. "Not this time."

The sun climbed higher, burning away the last of the fog, but the chill in the air remained. As the crime scene team worked, the woods began to feel less like a natural space and more like a violated sanctuary. Yellow evidence markers dotted the ground like malevolent flowers, each one representing another piece of a puzzle that would consume the investigators in the weeks to come.

John stood at the edge of the scene, his weathered face set in grim lines as he watched the investigation unfold. He'd seen too many scenes like this, too many lives ended in violence. But something about this one felt different—the careful positioning of the body, the methodical concealment, the location itself. None of it felt random.

"Detective?" An evidence technician approached, holding up a sealed bag containing what looked like a scrap of dark fabric. "Found this snagged on a branch about twenty feet from the body. Looks fresh."

John nodded, his eyes narrowing as he examined the evidence through the clear plastic. "Log it and get it to the lab. Priority analysis." Something about the fabric tugged at his memory, but he couldn't place it. Not yet.

As the morning wore on, the woods filled with more personnel—FBI evidence technicians, K-9 units sweeping the surrounding area, drone operators preparing for aerial photography of the scene. Each new arrival added another layer to the organized chaos of a major crime scene.

Jessica watched it all from her seat in the ambulance, unable to leave, unable to forget what she'd found. Max stayed pressed against her, his earlier agitation replaced by protective stillness. Together, they witnessed the transformation of their peaceful morning running trail into ground zero of what would become one of Columbus's most haunting investigations.

The autumn breeze carried the sound of more sirens approaching, and with them came the first news vans, their satellite dishes rising above the trees like modern totems. The world beyond the woods was waking up to the horror found in their midst, and soon the quiet tragedy would become a public spectacle.

John turned away from the cameras, his mind already building the framework of the investigation to come. Behind him, Dr. Whitman continued her examination, her quiet voice recording observations that would soon become evidence in a case that would change everyone involved.

The woods had given up their secret, but many more remained to be discovered. As the autumn day warmed, the sense of unease that had first drawn Max off the trail settled over the scene like a shadow—a warning that this was only the beginning.

CHAPTER 2
THE HARDEST WORDS

The forensics lab hummed with its usual morning activity. Matt Lawson, one of the department's technicians, stood at his workstation reviewing preliminary findings. His workspace was organized with the meticulous efficiency expected of lab personnel, manila folders stacked neatly beside his computer.

John set down his half-finished report as he entered the lab. The morning light streaming through the windows cast harsh shadows across the sterile space, making everything look slightly washed out under the fluorescent lights. He'd gotten used to the lab's atmosphere over the years, though the overly clean smell still bothered him sometimes.

"You have something for me?" John asked, approaching the workstation. The sooner he got the results, the sooner he could get back to the investigation.

"Preliminary results from the Thompson scene," Matt said, handing over a folder. "The lab's still working on a full analysis, but there are some patterns you might want to see." He gestured to the relevant pages as he explained the findings.

John flipped the file open, scanning the first few pages. Most techs showed some reaction to brutal cases like this—a tremor in their hands, a flinch when discussing details, something that proved they were still human underneath the professional veneer. But Matt's hands remained perfectly steady, his eyes clear and focused, as if death was simply another puzzle to solve.

"Anything interesting?" John asked, though something told him Matt had already prepared his response, probably rehearsing it before calling him over.

Matt shrugged lightly, his face maintaining a careful neutrality. "It's early, but we found traces of paracord fibers on the body. Military-grade—the kind you'd find in surplus stores or serious camping gear. High tensile strength, perfect for…" He paused, choosing his words with deliberate care. "Perfect for restraint."

The way he said it made John's stomach turn. Not because of the words themselves, but because of the clinical detachment behind them, like someone describing a particularly fascinating experiment.

"No signs of defensive wounds either," Matt continued, his voice taking on an almost contemplative tone. "She was subdued before the bindings were tied. Professional work, really. Someone who knows what they're doing." His eyes met John's for a moment, empty as still water. "Pretty methodical for a random attack."

John felt his pulse quicken. There was something about the precision of it all that tugged at old memories, a case he'd rather forget. But this wasn't the time to go down that road. Not yet.

"The lab found something else too," Matt added, flipping to another page. "A substance we're still analyzing—might be a sedative. Need more time to confirm, but the preliminary markers are interesting." His eyes flickered briefly to the crime scene photos spread across John's desk, lingering a half-second too long on the images of Sarah's body. "It's a pretty rough one, huh?"

"Yeah," John said quietly, his voice heavy with the weight of all the cases that had come before, all the grief he'd witnessed. He closed the file, unable to shake the feeling that something was off about this whole interaction. "Thanks, Matt. Keep me posted."

Matt gave a brief nod, precise and measured like everything else about him. "Will do. If anything else comes up, I'll let you know." He turned back toward his lab, his movements fluid and controlled, fading into the background hum of the precinct like he'd never been there at all. Just another shadow moving through the halls, collecting evidence, watching.

John's attention shifted as movement caught his eye. An officer was leading Benjamin and Kathleen Thompson toward the interview room, their steps slow and painful, as if each movement cost them something vital. Kathleen clung to Benjamin's arm, her knuckles white against his sleeve, her steps unsteady as if she'd forgotten how to walk in a world without her daughter. The fluorescent lights cast harsh shadows under her eyes, highlighting the dark circles that spoke of sleepless nights and endless tears. Her face was pale, almost translucent, with tear tracks carved into her cheeks. Her gaze seemed to look through things rather than at them, as if searching for Sarah in every empty space.

Benjamin moved like a man carrying an impossible weight, his shoulders hunched, his jaw clenched so tight John could see the muscles jumping beneath his skin. His grip on Kathleen's hand betrayed a desperate need to hold onto something, anything, that might keep him from falling apart. The corridor seemed to bend around their grief, other officers and staff instinctively giving them wide berth, as if their pain was something tangible that might spread through casual contact.

John had witnessed this scene more times than he cared to count—families being led into sterile rooms, carrying burdens too heavy for any heart to bear. Their unimaginable loss filled every silent space, pressing against the walls, making the air itself feel thick and hard to breathe. It never got easier, watching people struggle under the crushing weight of having their world torn apart. The hollow look in their eyes, the way their hands trembled as they reached for support, how they moved as if the very act of existing had become a monumental task—it all hit too close to home.

He could almost feel their pain settling onto his own shoulders, a familiar weight he knew too well. The kind of loss that breaks people, that reshapes them into something different, something harder. No words could touch it, no gesture could ease it. Watching the Thompsons struggle to stay upright under their burden, John felt a deep, unspoken empathy that went beyond the professional boundaries of his job. He knew their wound would never truly heal—it would only become a part of them, like his had become a part of him.

John nodded to the officer, a silent acknowledgment of the Thompsons' arrival, before following them into the interview room. The space seemed to shrink as they entered, the fluorescent lights casting an unforgiving glare across the metal table that separated them. The room held the stale scent of old fears and broken promises, the kind of place where truth and tragedy mixed until you couldn't tell them apart.

Kathleen sank into her chair like her legs could no longer support her, her hands immediately finding and gripping a tissue until her knuckles went white. Benjamin remained standing a moment longer, as if sitting down would make everything too real, before finally lowering himself into his chair. His eyes stayed locked on the tabletop, studying its scratched surface with an intensity that suggested he was trying to avoid looking at anything else, as if by not acknowledging their situation, he could somehow keep it from swallowing him whole.

John cleared his throat, the sound seeming too loud in the confined space. He leaned forward, carefully modulating his voice to project calm and steadiness, though his own heart ached for them. "Mr. and Mrs. Thompson, I'm so sorry for your loss. We're doing everything we can to find out who did this to your daughter." The words felt inadequate, as they always did, but they were all he had to offer.

Kathleen's lip trembled as she fought back a fresh wave of tears. "She was such a good girl." Her voice barely rose above a whisper, fragile as spun glass. "Always helping others. But something changed. She wasn't herself anymore." The last words caught in her throat, as if saying them aloud made the change more real, more final.

John tilted his head, watching her carefully. "What do you mean? How did she change?" He kept his tone gentle, encouraging, though his instincts were already alerting him that something important lay buried in Kathleen's observation.

Kathleen dabbed at her eyes with the crumpled tissue, her fingers twisting it into increasingly tighter knots. "She started pulling away from us. Canceling Sunday dinners. She seemed distracted, distant." She paused, swallowing hard. "I thought it was just stress from school. But now, I don't know." The uncertainty in her voice spoke volumes about the questions that would now forever go unanswered.

John let her words settle in the heavy air between them. The gradual pulling away, the subtle shifts in behavior—he'd seen this pattern before, too many times. Victims slowly withdrawing, their world shrinking as someone else's influence grew. He leaned forward slightly, his voice staying steady despite the familiar dread building in his chest. "Did she mention anyone new in her life? A friend or someone she was spending time with?"

Kathleen's gaze drifted to the wall, as if searching for answers in the institutional beige paint. "Not a friend, really…" Her voice faded for a moment before finding strength again. "But she talked about Jason. He wasn't anyone from school or work. He was… different."

John frowned slightly, pen hovering over his notebook. "Jason?"

Kathleen hesitated, her eyes seeking Benjamin's face for support, for permission, for anything to help her continue. "Jason Newsome," she managed finally. "A homeless man, mid-thirties. Sarah—" Her voice caught on her daughter's name. "Sarah had this habit of trying to fix everyone, even when they didn't want to be fixed. She'd give him rides, help him find food. She was too kind, always seeing the good in people." The last words came out like an accusation against the world that had punished such kindness.

Benjamin's jaw clenched, his voice coming out harder than his wife's, rough with barely contained anger. "She should've left him alone. But Sarah wouldn't turn anyone away. Couldn't stand to see anyone hurting." His fist clenched on the table, then slowly uncurled, as if he were forcing himself to release something he couldn't afford to hold onto. "That's who she was. Always trying to help, even when it put her at risk."

John wrote the name in his notebook, the letters precise and dark against the white paper. "Did Jason start spending more time around her?" He kept his tone neutral, professional, though every instinct was screaming that this was important.

Kathleen nodded slowly, her movements almost mechanical. "At first, she'd just give him rides. Said he didn't have anyone, that everyone deserves a chance." She twisted the tissue tighter, reducing it to worried shreds. "He seemed harmless, she thought. But then he started showing up more, and it got… strange."

"Strange how?" John's pen hovered over the page, waiting.

"He started following her," Kathleen whispered, her voice dropping as if saying it too loudly might make it more real. "Even when she wasn't offering help. She moved to Chicago for a few months, thinking maybe…" She swallowed hard. "But somehow, Jason found her there too. He slept behind the coffee shop where she worked. She tried to laugh it off, like it wasn't a big deal, but I knew." Her eyes met John's, filled with the particular agony of a mother who had seen the danger too late. "I knew it scared her."

John's grip tightened on his pen as he processed the details, his mind already constructing the familiar pattern. Jason Newsome—another lost soul whose obsession had twisted something innocent into something dark. "Did she ever say she felt threatened by him?"

"She never used that word," Kathleen said, dabbing at fresh tears. "But she told me she felt like someone was watching her. She just didn't know if it was him or…" Her voice trailed off, leaving the alternative unspoken but heavy in the air between them.

Benjamin shifted in his chair, speaking up with a voice thick with frustration and self-recrimination. "She asked me once—" He stopped, collecting himself. "She asked if I thought someone could hurt another person without meaning to. Like she was trying to understand something she couldn't quite see."

John's gaze sharpened, his pulse quickening. "What did she mean by that?"

Benjamin shook his head, his expression darkening. "She wouldn't explain. Said I wouldn't understand. It was like she was afraid of pushing him away, like she thought she could handle it herself." His voice cracked slightly. "She always thought she could handle everything herself."

John leaned back in his chair, letting the weight of their words settle around him. Sarah had been trying to help, reaching out to someone in need, but this man—Jason—had taken that kindness and twisted it into something possessive, dangerous. That much was clear. Whether or not he was directly involved in her death, they needed to bring him in. The pattern was too familiar to ignore.

After a long pause filled only by the soft hum of fluorescent lights and Kathleen's quiet sniffling, John closed his notebook with a deliberate gentleness. "I know this is difficult," he said, his voice carrying the weight of years spent delivering similar words to other grieving families. "But we'll do everything we can to find out what happened to Sarah."

Kathleen nodded weakly, fresh tears spilling down her cheeks, catching the harsh overhead light. "Please," she whispered, the word carrying all the desperate hope of a mother who had lost everything. "Please find who did this."

John offered a quiet thank you to the Thompsons, his voice barely cutting through the thick atmosphere of the room. As he stood, the chair scraped against the floor with an uncomfortable screech that seemed to emphasize the awkwardness of the moment—that point where professional duty collided with human empathy, where no words could bridge the gap between those left behind and those tasked with finding answers.

As he stepped out of the interview room, the weight of their grief clung to him like a physical presence, heavy and suffocating. It settled in his chest like a stone, pressing against his ribs with each breath. He'd seen this kind of pain before, witnessed it too many times to count, but it never softened with repetition. If anything, each new case dug deeper, carved new channels in his conscience, left fresh scars alongside the old ones. Some things never got easier—they just got harder to carry.

Ramirez was waiting for him in the hallway, fresh from the crime scene, his notepad tucked under one arm like a shield. His shoes were still muddy from the search site, leaving faint impressions on the polished floor. He looked up as John approached, his expression expectant but tempered with the kind of professional patience that came from years of working together.

"Caught most of the interview," Ramirez said, his tone carefully balanced between professional detachment and personal concern. "Sounds like you got as much out of them as you could." He studied John's face, reading the subtle signs of strain that most people would miss.

John gave a slight nod, though his eyes remained distant, still processing the weight of the conversation with Benjamin and Kathleen. Their pain had stirred something in him, awakened old ghosts he'd rather keep buried. Ramirez studied him closely for a beat, then cleared his throat, shifting gears with the practiced ease of someone who knew when to push and when to redirect.

"We need to bring in Jason Newsome," Ramirez continued, his voice taking on a more focused edge. He flipped open his notepad, scanning his notes. "From what they said, things got strange between them. The stalking, following her to Chicago—that's not normal behavior. We should get ahead of it before the trail goes cold."

John hesitated, a flicker of doubt crossing his mind like a shadow. He should've agreed immediately—Newsome was the obvious first move, the logical step that any investigator would take. But something about the whole thing felt off, familiar in a way that gnawed at his gut. Something about the precision of the crime scene, the careful planning, didn't match the profile of a homeless man acting on obsession.

"Newsome…" John muttered, narrowing his eyes as he stared down the empty hallway. "You sure that's the play?"

Ramirez raised an eyebrow, a knowing smirk tugging at the corner of his mouth. "You got someone else in mind? Or should I just guess?" The words carried a hint of challenge, of familiar territory they'd covered before.

John's jaw tightened, the familiar knot of frustration building in his chest. He didn't need to say it—Ramirez knew exactly where his mind had gone, could see him fighting the urge to make the same connections he always did. But he couldn't go down that road. Not yet. Not without more evidence.

After a long pause that seemed to stretch the fluorescent-lit hallway into infinity, John gave a curt nod. "Newsome first."

Ramirez chuckled softly, pushing off the wall as he flipped open his notepad with practiced efficiency. "Figured as much. Alright, let's bring Newsome in and see what shakes out." His tone was light, but his eyes held a warning—a reminder of paths they'd gone down before, of obsessions that had led nowhere.

John's gaze drifted, already lost in thought as he started down the hall, his footsteps echoing in the institutional silence. Behind him, Ramirez watched for a moment, the tension thick between them. He knew this case was pulling at something deep in John—something neither of them wanted to face again. A darkness they'd thought was behind them.

But it was too late for that now. The case had its hooks in them, and there was no going back. Only forward, into whatever shadows awaited.

CHAPTER 3
FLIGHT RESPONSE

Jason Newsome's apartment was the kind of place where hope went to die. Yellowed wallpaper peeled from the corners like old scabs, and the single window let in just enough gray morning light to make the shadows seem alive. He sat on the edge of his bed, a spring digging into his thigh through the thin mattress, staring at the water stains that spread across the wall like disease. His fingers wouldn't stop trembling, no matter how hard he pressed them together.

Sarah Thompson was dead.

The truth hit him in waves, each one threatening to drown him. He'd heard it first from the news—her name falling from the broadcaster's lips like just another headline. But Sarah had never been just another anything. She had been the only person who looked at him and saw something worth saving.

Now, she was gone. Murdered.

The word echoed in his mind, mixing with older memories: Sarah's smile when she'd first offered him a ride, how she'd remembered how he liked his coffee, how she'd listen—really listen—when he talked about his life before everything fell apart. She'd treated him like a person when the rest of the world saw right through him.

The cops would come. Jason knew this with the bone-deep certainty of someone who'd spent his life being blamed for things—some he'd done, most he hadn't. They'd look at his record, his situation, the way he'd followed Sarah around, desperate for just one more moment of kindness. They'd see an obsession. A motive. They wouldn't understand that his need for her presence had been about survival, not possession.

His breath came in short bursts, each one shallower than the last. The walls of his tiny apartment seemed to pulse inward with each exhale. They were probably already watching the building. Gathering evidence. Building their case. Who would believe him? Sarah had been his only advocate, the only person who might have vouched for his character. But Sarah was lying on a cold metal table somewhere, and his alibi felt as fragile as tissue paper in the rain.

Jason stood, unable to stay still, and began to pace. Seven steps to the kitchenette, turn, seven steps back. The floor creaked beneath him, each sound making him flinch. What if they didn't believe him about that night? The memory felt solid enough—the clatter of dice, awkward laughter, the decisive click of his friend's door lock when he left. But doubt crept in like smoke under a door. Had it really happened that way? Were the others even his friends or just people who tolerated his presence?

His phone sat on the nightstand, its screen cracked but still functional. Sarah's number was still in his contacts. He'd never delete it; he couldn't bear to erase that last tangible connection. His fingers twitched toward the device, muscle memory urging him to call her, to hear her tell him everything would be okay. Instead, he found himself checking bus schedules, his hands shaking so badly he had to type "Cincinnati" three times to get it right.

Just for a few days, he told himself. Just until things calm down. Until he could think straight. Until the panic stopped and his breath eased enough to figure out what to do next. It wasn't really running—it was a tactical retreat. Self-preservation.

The lie tasted bitter, but he swallowed it anyway.

His backpack was already packed. It had been since he'd first landed on the streets years ago. Old habits died hard. He needed a few changes of clothes, basic toiletries, and medications he couldn't afford to replace. His hands moved on autopilot, checking the zippers and testing the straps. The familiar routine should have been comforting, but it felt like surrender instead.

He pulled his hood up, a futile attempt at invisibility in a world where he already felt like a ghost. The hallway outside his apartment stretched before him like a gauntlet—flickering fluorescent lights, garbage someone had left to rot, the distant sound of a neighbor's TV bleeding through thin walls. Each step felt like walking through quicksand, his legs heavy with the weight of what he was about to do.

The night air hit him like a physical blow as he stepped outside. The street was empty, but shadows seemed to move at the corner of his vision. Every parked car could hide watching eyes; every darkened doorway could conceal someone waiting. The paranoia wasn't new—it had been his constant companion since childhood—but tonight, it felt sharper, more real. His skin crawled with the certainty of being watched.

The bus station was a fifteen-minute walk, but it felt like hours. Each passing car made his heart stutter, and each distant siren sent ice through his veins. The few people still out at this hour gave him a wide berth like they always did. Usually, this invisibility was a comfort. Tonight, it felt like judgment.

Sweat beaded on his forehead despite the cool night air, his breath coming in shallow gasps when he reached the station. The fluorescent lights inside buzzed like angry insects, casting sickly shadows across tired faces. He approached the ticket counter, fingers fumbling with wrinkled bills and loose change he'd been saving for laundry.

"Cincinnati," he managed, the word barely audible. "One way."

The clerk's eyes slid over him with practiced disinterest, probably used to people running from something. The ticket felt like a confession in his hands, damp from his sweating palms.

"Last call for Cincinnati," the driver's voice echoed through the terminal, startling Jason badly enough that he nearly dropped his backpack.

The bus interior smelled of stale cigarettes and desperation. Jason slumped into a seat near the back, pulling his hood lower, trying to make himself smaller. The engine rumbled to life, the vibrations traveling through his feet into his bones. They felt like tremors before an earthquake.

His mind wouldn't stop replaying moments with Sarah: the first time she'd stopped her car, offering him a ride during a rainstorm; how she'd insisted on buying him coffee, treating him with the dignity he'd almost forgotten he deserved; how she'd listen to his stories without judgment, her eyes full of genuine interest rather than pity.

"Everyone deserves a chance," she'd told him once. "Everyone deserves to be seen."

His fingers curled into fists in his lap, nails biting into his palms. He hadn't killed Sarah. He knew that with the same certainty he knew his own name. But the doubt was there too, a poisonous whisper in his mind. What if he'd blacked out? What if his need for her attention and kindness had twisted into something darker without him realizing it?

No. The memory of that night was real. It had to be. The game night at Mike's apartment—the cheap beer, the rolling dice, the bad jokes. He remembered leaving at eleven, the lock clicking behind him. He remembered walking home in the cool air, feeling almost normal. He had to hold onto that memory. It was all he had.

Dawn was breaking as the bus rolled into Cincinnati, the city emerging from the darkness like a monster from the sea. The windows were streaked with grime, making the early morning light look diseased. Jason's stomach churned with exhaustion and fear as the bus pulled into the terminal.

He waited until most passengers had filed out before rising on shaky legs. His muscles ached from holding himself tense for so long. The terminal was starting to fill with morning commuters, their faces blurring together as he scanned for exits, escape routes, for—

His heart stopped.

A police officer stood near the main entrance, his stance casual but alert. He was scanning the crowd with the practiced eye of someone who knew what to look for.

They found me. They found me already.

Jason's mind raced, thoughts skittering like cockroaches under sudden light.

Stay calm. Act normal. Just another traveler. Just another invisible person that no one looks at twice. But his body betrayed him—sweat rolling down his back, pulse thundering in his ears.

The officer's gaze swept the terminal. Their eyes met.

Time stretched like taffy, reality bending around that single moment of recognition. Jason saw his future collapse into a single point: handcuffs, cells, accusations he couldn't fight. His legs tensed, ready to run even as his mind screamed for control.

"I just need to get out," he whispered, a desperate prayer. "Find somewhere else. Head west. Stay low." But his thoughts fragmented, spinning faster and faster until they became white noise.

The officer took a step forward.

Something in Jason snapped.

He ran.

His feet barely seemed to touch the ground as he bolted, his backpack slamming against his spine with each stride. He heard shouts behind him, the chaos of overturned luggage, and his own ragged breathing. But it all seemed distant, unreal, like sounds from another world.

Then hands grabbed him from behind, reality crashing back with brutal force. The concrete rushed to meet him, knocking the air from his lungs. Pain bloomed across his chest, his face, and everywhere the ground connected.

"Stop resisting!" The officer's voice seemed to come from very far away.

Was he resisting? He didn't think so. But then—a flash of memory: his elbow connecting with something solid, a grunt of pain that wasn't his own. Had he fought back? He couldn't remember. Everything was fragments, pieces that wouldn't fit together.

The officer's knee pressed into his back, forcing another wheeze from his lungs. Cold metal circled his wrists, ratcheting tight. The handcuffs' click seemed to echo through his entire body, a sound of finality, of endings.

"I didn't kill her," he gasped, his voice breaking. "I didn't… I couldn't…"

But the words dissolved into the morning air, meaningless as breath on a cold window. Around him, travelers moved past, their shoes appearing and disappearing from his limited view like a strange dance. None of them stopped. None of them looked. He was invisible again, but not in the way he wanted to be.

Sarah's face floated in his mind—her kind smile, her gentle eyes. She had been the only one who truly saw him. And now she was gone, and he was facedown on dirty concrete, and nothing would ever be right again.

The cruiser's back seat smelled of stale sweat and old fear. Jason closed his eyes against the growing light as the door slammed behind him. The doubt gnawing at his edges finally broke through, flooding his mind with terrible possibilities.

What if he had done it? What if everything he remembered was a lie his mind had created to protect him from the truth?

No. No, I didn't hurt her. I couldn't have.

But as the cruiser pulled away from the terminal, carrying him back to face whatever awaited, Jason wasn't sure he believed himself anymore.

CHAPTER 4
FRAGMENTS OF TRUTH

John DiMatteo had seen enough men run from guilt to know this was something different. The security footage from Cincinnati's bus terminal played on his screen for the fourth time, each viewing deepening his unease. Jason Newsome—the quiet shadow who'd haunted Sarah Thompson's final months—hadn't just tried to escape. He'd fought with a desperate violence that transformed him from prey to predator in the space of heartbeats.

Three officers had been needed to subdue him. Jason, who'd spent years perfecting the art of invisibility, who flinched at raised voices and crossed streets to avoid confrontation, had left one officer with a bloody nose and another nursing cracked ribs. The footage showed him wild-eyed and snarling, a cornered animal who'd chosen violence over capture.

Something wasn't right.

"Still looking for answers in those pixels?" Ramirez's voice cut through John's thoughts. His partner stood in the doorway, jacket slung over one shoulder, the weight of twenty years on the force evident in the silver threading his temples. "Or are you hoping the fifth viewing might show something different?"

John rubbed his eyes, the hours of staring at the screen catching up with him. "Look at his face, Luis. That's not guilt driving him. That's fear." He froze the frame on Jason's expression—a mask of pure terror that made John's instincts scream. "I've known him for years. The man's a ghost, not a fighter. Something happened. Something that scared him more than jail ever could."

"Maybe killing Sarah Thompson had that effect." Ramirez dropped a manila folder onto John's desk, its contents spilling out like accusations: crime scene photos, witness statements, the carefully documented evidence of a life brutally ended.

But John couldn't shake the feeling they were missing something crucial. He'd seen killers run—watched guilt drive them to desperate acts. This was different. This was the kind of fear that came from knowing too much, from witnessing something you weren't meant to see.

The question that haunted him wasn't why Jason ran. It was what he was running from.

The interrogation room felt colder than usual, the overhead lights casting stark shadows across metal surfaces that reminded John of autopsy tables. His fingers drummed restlessly against the table, leaving shallow dents in its worn surface. The air felt charged, like the stillness before a storm.

When they brought Jason in, John barely recognized him. Gone was the timid man who used to duck his head and hug walls. This Jason moved like damaged prey, every movement sharp and jittery, his gaze flicking from corner to corner as though he expected to see someone lurking in the shadows. The bruise from his arrest had bloomed across his jaw in violent purples and yellows, his split lip crusted with dried blood. His hoodie—probably the same one he'd been wearing for days—hung from his frame like a shroud, dark with sweat despite the room's chill.

Jason's eyes darted to the two-way mirror, then to the door, then to John, each glance quick and full of suspicion. He flinched at the faint hum of the air conditioning, as though every sound could be a threat.

"Water?" John kept his voice soft, the same tone he'd use with a spooked animal. Jason's gaze snapped to the paper cup, but he didn't reach for it. His hands, resting on the table, were clenched so tightly his knuckles were bone-white.

"I didn't kill her." The words tumbled out before John could even start the interview, too fast, too desperate. "I wouldn't—I couldn't hurt Sarah. She was…" His voice cracked. "She was the only one who saw me. Really saw me."

John studied him, noting every tick, every micro-expression that might betray deception. But all he saw was raw fear—a fear that seemed to crawl just beneath the surface of Jason's skin, like it might tear him apart from the inside. "Then help me understand, Jason. Why run? Why fight the officers in Cincinnati?"

Jason's whole body trembled, his fingers drumming an erratic pattern on the metal table, a nervous rhythm with no clear beat. He kept glancing over his shoulder, toward the camera in the corner of the room, as if he could feel unseen eyes on him. "I thought—I thought they were coming for something else. Not Sarah."

"Something else?" Ramirez's voice cut through the tension as he pushed off the wall, his casual stance belying the predatory focus in his eyes. "What exactly did you think we were coming for, Jason?"

Jason's breathing grew quicker, his fingers digging into the table as though he were bracing for impact. He cast another look at the camera, then the mirror, before finally meeting John's gaze. "I don't know." His eyes darted back to the door. "I just—I saw things. Things I shouldn't have seen."

John leaned forward, the chair creaking beneath him. "What kind of things?"

Jason's hands twisted together, knuckles white with strain. His gaze flickered between John and Ramirez, as if he couldn't decide which of them was safe to look at. "She knew someone was watching her. Not me—I mean, yeah, I checked on her sometimes, but that's not…" He swallowed hard, his throat bobbing visibly. "Sarah told me she felt eyes on her. All the time. Like someone was studying her."

The air in the room grew heavier. John exchanged a quick glance with Ramirez, catching the subtle shift in his partner's stance. "When did she tell you this?"

Jason hesitated, his gaze darting around the room again, like he was searching for a trap. "About two weeks ago. She was…" His voice dropped to barely a whisper. "She was scared. Really scared. Said things had started disappearing from her apartment—little things, stuff you might not notice at first. Hair ties. Coffee mugs. Then bigger things. Like someone was taking pieces of her life, bit by bit."

John's pulse quickened. None of this had been in the initial reports. "Did she report it?"

Jason laughed, a bitter sound that was almost a sob. "To who? She tried telling her friends, but they said she was being paranoid. Working too hard. Stressed about school." His eyes found John's, bloodshot and wide, like a trapped animal's. "But I believed her. I knew what it was like to be invisible, to see things others missed. So, I started watching. Trying to catch whoever was stalking her."

"And did you?" Ramirez's voice cut through the tension. "See anyone?"

Jason's face drained of what little color remained. His hands began to shake so badly he had to grip the edge of the table to steady them. "I thought—maybe once. A shadow that didn't belong. Movement when there shouldn't have been any. But every time I got close…" He shook his head, his voice dropping lower. "It was like trying to catch smoke."

"The night she died," John pressed, leaning forward. "Where were you?"

"Playing games at my friend Mike's place. Board games." The words came out in a rush. "I can prove it. There were five of us there. We ordered pizza, took pictures. I saved the receipt because—" He stopped abruptly, color flooding back into his face, like he'd said too much.

"Because what?" John's voice hardened.

"Because I knew." Jason's voice dropped to a whisper, his eyes darting to the door, the mirror, the camera. "I knew something bad was going to happen. I could feel it. So, I made sure I had proof of where I was." His breathing grew ragged, shallow. "But it didn't matter, did it? I couldn't protect her. I failed her, just like I fail at everything else."

Tears spilled down his cheeks, but Jason didn't seem to notice. He was staring down at his hands, fingers twisting together, trembling. John felt the familiar twist in his gut—the instinct that told him when someone was telling the truth, even if it wasn't the whole truth.

"What aren't you telling us, Jason?" The question hung in the air like smoke. "What were you really running from in Cincinnati?"

Jason's breathing grew erratic, his chest rising and falling in quick, shallow bursts. His eyes darted to the one-way mirror, then back to John, his face taut with fear. "I saw—I saw someone coming out of her apartment. The night before they found her."

The room seemed to grow smaller, the air thicker. John forced his voice to remain steady. "Why didn't you tell us this before?"

Jason's fingers traced invisible patterns on the table, his voice dropping to a hoarse whisper. "I wasn't sure. It was dark. They moved like they belonged there, you know? Professional. Like they had every right to be there at three in the morning."

Ramirez straightened, his casual demeanor evaporating. "You got a look at them?"

"No, not really. Just—a shape. Dark clothes. The way they moved…" Jason's voice cracked. "The way they checked over their shoulder, like they were making sure no one was watching. But someone was. I was."

John leaned forward, every instinct on high alert. "And then?"

"They saw me." The words came out like a confession, dragged from somewhere deep and terrified. "Just for a second, our eyes met across the street, and I—I knew." His voice broke, and he started to shake. "I knew if I said anything, if I told anyone what I saw…"

"This person," John kept his voice steady, "did they seem… comfortable? Like they'd done this before?"

Jason's hands clenched together, knuckles white. "Yeah. That's what scared me most. They moved like… like it was routine. Like they were just going through the motions of something they'd done a hundred times before."

The silence that followed felt thick enough to cut. John could feel pieces shifting in his mind, forming a picture he wasn't sure he wanted to see. "Is that why you ran? Because you recognized them?"

"Not exactly. More like…" Jason's hands twisted in his lap, knuckles white. "More like they recognized me, like they knew I was going to be there." His eyes met John's, full of terrible certainty. "I'm sure that, for a brief second, they gave me a smirk."

The implication hung in the air like smoke. John felt Ramirez shift behind him, a subtle movement that spoke volumes. Every instinct John had developed over fifteen years of detective work screamed that Jason was telling the truth— or at least his version of it.

"That's why you panicked at the bus station," John said quietly. "You weren't running from us. You were running from them."

Jason's face crumpled. "You don't understand. They're everywhere. They know exactly what they're doing." His voice cracked. "Sarah figured something out. Something big. That's why she started feeling watched. That's why she—" He cut himself off, fear closing his throat.

"We're done here," John said abruptly, standing. "Officer Jenkins will process you out. But Jason?" He waited until the other man's eyes met his. "Stay close. And stay alive."

Outside the interrogation room, Ramirez grabbed John's arm. "You buying his story?"

John stared through the one-way glass at Jason, still hunched in his chair like a man carrying an impossible weight. "I think we're looking in the wrong direction. Whoever did this has killed before." He turned to his partner, his voice hardening. "We need to start looking into some old friends."

CHAPTER 5
A FATHER'S BURDEN

The Paradise Diner sat like a tired sentinel on the corner of 5th and Main, its neon sign flickering weakly against the oppressive evening sky. Rain tapped against the streaked windows, transforming the city lights outside into bleeding watercolors. Inside, John sat alone in a worn vinyl booth, pushing cold eggs around his plate as darkness settled over Columbus like a burial shroud.

The memory hit him without warning—Sam's last phone call. He'd been sitting in this same booth that night, hiding from an empty apartment and a stack of case files that seemed to multiply like cancer cells. Even now, months later, he could recall every detail with devastating clarity.

His phone lit up with her name, making his heart stutter—she hadn't called in days, not since their argument about her slipping math grades. Guilt had surged through him even then, knowing he'd never followed up on his promise to help her study.

"Hey, kiddo." He'd forced warmth into his voice, trying to mask the exhaustion that had become his constant companion.

"Hi, Dad." Sam's voice had been small but steady. In the background, he'd heard the domestic sounds of her other life—television murmuring, dishes clinking, the normal evening routine at her mother's house that had become increasingly foreign to him.

"More coffee, John?"

He startled from his memories as Michelle appeared beside the booth, coffeepot in hand. She'd been serving him late-night eggs and sympathy for what felt like years now, since back when Sam was still alive and he'd bring her here for Saturday morning pancakes.

"Thanks, Michelle." He pushed his cup forward, watching the steam rise from the fresh pour. "Slow night?"

"You know how it is." She settled into the booth across from him with the familiar ease of long acquaintance. The move reminded him of Sam—she used to slide into booths the same way, all teenage confidence and grace. "Though honestly, I prefer slow to whatever's got you looking like you haven't slept in a week."

John managed a weak smile. "That obvious?"

"Please. I've been feeding you coffee and pie through every major case since you made detective." She studied him with the shrewd insight of someone who'd spent decades reading people across diner tables. "This is about the Thompson girl, isn't it?"

His jaw tightened slightly. "You heard about that?"

"Hard not to. That true crime podcast—you know, True Crime Garage? — just did an episode about it." Michelle leaned forward, lowering her voice conspiratorially. "They're saying that Jason Newsome guy definitely did it. Had a whole timeline and everything about how he stalked her."

John felt a familiar irritation curl in his gut. Armchair detectives and podcast hosts, turning real tragedy into entertainment. Sarah Thompson wasn't just another true crime story to be dissected over morning commutes. She was a young woman whose future had been stolen, whose parents still woke every morning to the fresh hell of her absence.

"You can't believe everything you hear on podcasts," he said carefully, keeping his tone neutral. Michelle meant well—she always did.

"Maybe," she conceded, rising as the cook's bell chimed. "But from what they laid out, seems pretty clear to me. Sometimes the obvious answer is the right one, you know?"

If only it were that simple, John thought, watching her head back to the counter. If only solving murders was as straightforward as piecing together a podcast narrative. But twenty years of detective work had taught him that truth was rarely obvious and never simple.

He stared into his coffee, the memories of Sam threatening to pull him under again. How many people had turned her death into content too? How many amateur sleuths had picked apart his failures as a father, analyzing them between ad breaks and promotional codes?

The rain intensified outside, drumming against the windows like impatient fingers. Somewhere in this city, Sarah Thompson's killer walked free. And despite what Michelle and her podcasts might think, John wasn't convinced Jason Newsome was their man. Something about this case nagged at him, an echo of old wounds and older doubts.

Michelle's footsteps faded into the ambient diner noise—the soft clink of silverware, the hum of conversations, the steady drum of rain against glass. John's reflection stared back at him from the window, fragmented by raindrops and neon light. The same window he'd stared through that night, when his phone had lit up with Sam's name.

Strange, how certain moments burned themselves into memory. He could still recall the exact way his stomach had knotted when he saw her name on the screen, how the vinyl cushion had creaked under him as he shifted to answer. Even the song playing from the kitchen radio—some old Eagles tune that Michelle always hummed along to during her closing routine.

The vinyl cushion beneath him wheezed now just as it had then, a small detail that pulled him deeper into the memory. He'd been sitting in this same booth, running from an empty apartment and a stack of case files that seemed to multiply like cancer cells. Even now, years later, he could recall every detail with devastating clarity.

"I've been thinking," she'd said, her voice carrying an edge of uncertainty that had made his police instincts flare. "About... living arrangements."

The words had hit him like a physical blow. He'd straightened in the booth, his hand tightening around his coffee mug. "Living arrangements?" Each syllable had felt like glass in his throat. "What do you mean?"

Even now, sitting in the same diner under the same flickering fluorescent lights, the pain of what followed felt fresh as an open wound. The late-night regulars hunched over their own solitary meals faded away, replaced by the echoes of his daughter's voice.

"I want to live with Mom full-time."

The world had tilted beneath him. His reflection in the rain-streaked window—then and now—showed a man being hollowed out from the inside, watching his failures catch up with him in real time.

"What?" His voice had emerged rougher than intended. "Sam, where is this coming from?"

"It's not sudden, Dad." Her tone had carried a maturity that startled him— when had his little girl grown so old? "I've been thinking about it for a while now."

The accusations had come then, each one striking with devastating accuracy: missed soccer games that seemed unimportant at the time, forgotten birthday dinners replaced by hasty apologies, promises broken in the name of justice. He'd sat in this same booth, pressing fingers against his temple, fighting the headache building behind his eyes.

"I don't understand," he'd managed. "I thought things were okay between us."

"They're not." The gentleness in her voice had somehow made it worse. "You're always at work, Dad. And even when you're home, you're... somewhere else. Like you're just waiting for the next call, the next case. We don't talk anymore—not really."

"I know work's been demanding lately, but it's important. You understand that, right?"

"I do understand." Frustration had edged into Sam's voice, cracking her careful composure. "But it's always important, Dad. Every single time. More important than coming to my games, more important than my school events, more important than—" She'd caught herself. Still, the unspoken words had hung between them: More important than me.

The night air pressed against the diner windows, dark and heavy with rain. John stared at his reflection, seeing not the man he'd become but the father he'd failed to be. A plate clattered in the kitchen, the sound sharp as breaking glass, like the way his world had shattered two weeks after that call.

Sam's last words to him played on repeat in his mind: "I love you, Dad. But I need more than empty promises."

That was the last time he heard her voice.

Two weeks later, they found her body.

The eggs on his plate had long since gone cold, congealing in the harsh diner light. Outside, the city continued its endless rhythm, unaware that somewhere in its darkness lurked the monster who'd stolen his daughter's future. His badge sat heavy in his pocket, no longer a symbol of justice but a reminder of all he'd sacrificed for it—including, ultimately, his daughter.

John dropped a few crumpled bills on the table, enough to cover his untouched meal and Michelle's endless refills of coffee. The vinyl cushion protested as he stood, shrugging on his coat against the rain and his own dark thoughts.

He had a promise to keep now, one last vow to his daughter's memory. He would find who did this. He would make them pay. It wouldn't bring her back or erase his failures as a father, but it was all he had left to give her.

The diner's bell chimed weakly as he stepped out into the rain, leaving behind the warmth and light for the cold embrace of his mission. Somewhere in this city, a killer walked free, unaware that they'd created something far more dangerous than a grieving father—they'd forged a man who would stop at nothing to find justice, even if it cost him whatever remained of his soul.

CHAPTER 6
A KILLER'S SIGNATURE

The forensics lab existed in its own peculiar bubble of reality—a sterile shrine to science where even the air felt filtered, scrubbed clean of everything except the sharp bite of antiseptic and the metallic whisper of stainless steel. Kate Whitman stood at her workstation, her back straight, her fingers gloved and steady as they manipulated a series of test tubes. Jazz trickled softly from her speakers, the mellow notes of a trumpet battling to bring warmth to a space that felt incapable of holding it. But to John, the music only heightened the surrealness of the room, as if it were mocking the brutal truths they sought to uncover here.

John leaned against the counter, arms crossed over his chest, watching Kate as she meticulously worked. Ramirez stood a few feet away, absently fidgeting with the strap of his watch. The silence between them wasn't comfortable—it was the kind born from unanswered questions and nagging suspicions. And on the far side of the lab, Matt Lawson sat at his own workstation, his movements as efficient and precise as a machine, logging evidence into the department's digital system.

Matt didn't look up, didn't acknowledge them, his focus unbroken. The rhythmic tapping of his keyboard filled the space between the occasional clink of glass and the jazz's muted melody. It was easy to forget Matt was even there, blending seamlessly into the clinical monotony of the lab.

"Let's get to it." Kate's voice cut through the artificial calm as she snapped the file shut. She carefully removed her glasses, placing them on the table like pieces of evidence. Her expression remained professionally neutral, but something in her eyes tightened John's stomach. The weight of what she'd found was visible in every careful movement.

"I couldn't sleep after reviewing these results," Kate said, her voice uncharacteristically soft. Her usual crisp professionalism wavered, letting exhaustion creep into her tone. She spread the folder open, the papers inside catching the unforgiving fluorescent light. "The level of precision here—it's not just intentional. It's..." She hesitated, searching for the right word.

"Sadistic," Ramirez offered, his voice low.

Kate nodded grimly. "Yes. Exactly."

John crossed his arms, trying to ward off the perpetual chill of the lab. He'd always hated these spaces—the morgues, the labs, the sterile rooms where death was dissected and cataloged. Every answer only seemed to breed more questions, like bacteria in a petri dish. "What killed her?" The words came out clipped, sharp.

Kate's eyes flicked to the whiteboard on the far wall. Sarah Thompson's crime scene photos stared back at them, her neck marred by deep, angry bruises. The autopsy photos were even worse, the paracord burns etched into her flesh like an artist's cruel signature.

"Cause of death was strangulation," Kate said, her tone taking on the practiced neutrality of a medical professional. But her hands weren't as steady as usual—they lingered on the edges of the photos as if reluctant to touch them. "But it wasn't your typical ligature strangulation. The pattern of bruising tells us the killer used a specific knot. A constrictor knot."

In the corner, Matt's typing slowed almost imperceptibly.

"What do you mean?" Ramirez frowned, leaning forward.

Kate moved to the whiteboard with measured steps, her finger tracing the lividity patterns on Sarah's neck. "These marks tell us something specific. They're inconsistent with standard ligature strangulation. The paracord was tied using a particular knot—a constrictor knot."

Ramirez frowned. "A constrictor knot?"

Behind them, the rhythmic clacking of Matt's keyboard faltered for just a moment.

Kate nodded, moving to the whiteboard. She picked up a marker and began sketching the knot in question, her movements fluid, almost artistic. The pattern she drew was deceptively simple—a loop tightened by pulling on its tail. "The constrictor knot is designed to tighten under tension. The more the victim struggled, the tighter it became. Her survival instincts worked against her, accelerating the process."

"Jesus," Ramirez muttered, running a hand over his face.

Kate glanced at him briefly before turning her attention back to the diagram. "This isn't a knot you stumble across. It's specialized. It's used in sailing, rock climbing, and certain types of industrial work. Someone learned this deliberately—it's not a skill you'd acquire accidentally."

John felt a cold weight settle in his stomach. He stared at the knot, at the brutal efficiency it represented. "So she did this to herself by struggling?" His voice was quieter now, as though he wasn't entirely sure he wanted the answer.

"Yes," Kate said, and her voice cracked slightly for the first time. "She would've been aware of what was happening. She would've felt it tightening, knowing she couldn't stop it."

"Whoever did this," she continued, her voice regaining its steel edge, "wanted her to feel powerless. To feel that every action she took to save herself was only bringing her closer to death."

Ramirez exhaled sharply, stepping away from the table as if he could distance himself from the horror of what she was saying.

John's jaw tightened. "This wasn't their first time. Someone who goes to this level of detail... They've done this before."

Kate nodded grimly. "I agree. The killer knew exactly what they were doing. The knots, the drug, the timing—it's all too precise. Too calculated." She hesitated, then flipped to a toxicology report. "And then there's this."

She pointed to a section of numbers, Dexmedetomidine bolded near the top.

"What's that?" Ramirez asked, leaning over her shoulder.

"Dexmedetomidine," Kate explained. "It's a veterinary sedative. It's not commonly used in humans except in highly controlled medical environments. In Sarah's case, the dosage was exact—enough to paralyze her but not enough to make her unconscious."

John's frown deepened. "She was aware the whole time?"

Kate nodded. "She couldn't fight back, couldn't move, but she was conscious. She would've felt everything."

The weight of her words hung in the air like a noose tightening around all of them.

"Where would someone even get this stuff?" Ramirez asked.

"It's not impossible to obtain," Kate admitted. "A veterinarian could order it, or someone with the right connections to a medical supply chain. But this dosage suggests familiarity. Whoever administered it knew exactly what they were doing."

Matt's fingers had resumed their steady rhythm on the keyboard at his workstation, the sound almost hypnotic in its regularity. John barely noticed him, his mind already spinning, assembling the implications of this new information.

"Whoever did this," Ramirez said, his voice dropping lower, "they're experienced. This isn't some crime of passion or opportunity."

Kate nodded. "Everything about this was measured, controlled. The drug dosage, the knotwork, and the timing all speak to someone who planned carefully. Someone who wanted to maintain complete control over every aspect of Sarah's death."

"We need to dig into Sarah's circle," John said finally, his voice harder now. "Anyone with ties to climbing, sailing, veterinary work—anyone who could've learned how to tie that knot or get their hands on this drug."

"I'll run a search for known climbing gyms, sailing schools, and related industries in the area," Ramirez said, already pulling out his phone. "We'll narrow it down."

Kate nodded but didn't look reassured. "This wasn't impulsive. This person planned every step, from the sedative to the ligature. They knew how to avoid leaving forensic evidence—no fingerprints, no skin cells, nothing to trace."

"And that takes experience," John muttered.

The quiet clicking of Matt's keyboard paused again. He stood, a file held precisely in both hands, and approached the group with the careful efficiency that marked all his movements. "Dr. Whitman," he said, his voice professionally neutral. "I have analyzed the fabric we found near the body."

Kate took the folder from him, flipping it open as Matt spoke.

"The weave suggests older workwear—industrial, likely used in outdoor environments. It's durable, designed to withstand heavy use."

Kate frowned. "A specific manufacturer?"

"Nothing definitive yet," Matt said. His tone was casual, almost disinterested, but his eyes briefly met John's. "But it's not designer. This is the kind of material you'd find in a contractor's jacket or an outdoor worker's gear. Functional. Practical."

Ramirez exchanged a glance with John. "Like something Mick Garrett would wear?"

John didn't answer. His thoughts were already racing, pieces of the puzzle clicking together in a way that felt too neat, too convenient.

Mick fit the profile—a contractor who worked with his hands and knew how to handle tools and materials. The pieces clicked together in John's head, even if some edges felt rough. The fabric, the methodical nature of the scene, and the precision were tinged with brutality—it all pointed toward someone who understood efficiency and knew how to get things done without concerning themselves with clean lines.

Matt had already returned to his workstation, his presence fading back into the background hum of equipment and soft jazz. His movements had the calm, practiced efficiency that was almost comforting in its predictability.

Kate cleared her throat, professional focus returning to her voice. "I'll have the team do a more detailed analysis of the fabric and see if we can match it to specific manufacturers or suppliers."

John nodded, but his thoughts were already racing ahead. Every piece of evidence, every dead end, somehow led back to Mick Garrett. The fabric was just another breadcrumb on a trail he'd followed for too long. A trail that refused to go cold.

Kate closed the folder decisively, her gaze moving between John and Ramirez. "I'll update you as soon as we have anything more concrete."

Ramirez acknowledged with a grunt, but John was already moving. His footsteps echoed against the tile floor as he headed for the door, each step heavy with purpose.

"Mick Garrett," he muttered, the name bitter on his tongue.

Ramirez caught up to him in the hallway, keeping his voice low. "You really think it's him?"

John didn't answer immediately. The familiar tightness was building in his chest—the same frustration that had haunted him since watching Mick Garrett walk free the first time. A killer might slip through the cracks once, but twice? He couldn't let that happen. Not again.

"Even if it's not," John said finally, his voice harder than he intended, "I'm not taking chances." His pace quickened, determination setting his jaw. "We're bringing him in."

He didn't wait for Ramirez's response and didn't need to see his partner's concerned expression. His footsteps echoed down the hallway, a steady rhythm matching the certainty in his mind. Behind him, the lab door closed softly, sealing away the jazz music, the antiseptic smell, and the quiet, routine efficiency of the lab that felt, for now, just like another part of the job.

CHAPTER 7
THE LONG WAIT

The TV's glow flickered across Mick Garrett's living room like dying fireflies, casting shadows that seemed to breathe. He sat hunched on the edge of his sagging couch, eyes fixed on the screen without seeing it. The news anchor's voice was just white noise—easier to focus on than the thoughts churning in his head. His calloused fingers traced the rough scar along his chin—an old souvenir from a bar fight he barely remembered. Over the years, the scar had become a kind of barometer, itching whenever storm clouds gathered on his horizon. Tonight, it burned.

Nine years.

The number echoed in his mind like a prison sentence, which, in many ways, it was. Nine years of sideways glances and whispered accusations. Nine years of watching people cross the street when they saw him coming, their eyes full of judgments their lips wouldn't speak. Nine years of living under the weight of what everyone thought he'd done, waiting for him to prove them right.

The memory of that night simmered beneath his skin like hot coals that refused to die. The courtroom materialized in his mind with perfect clarity: the hard wooden benches, the smell of lemon-scented cleaner barely masking decades of fear and desperation, the weight of all those eyes boring into him. The detectives with their certainty, the jury with their barely concealed disgust, even his own lawyer's carefully masked doubt. The evidence had been circumstantial at best—hearsay and coincidence woven together with the thread of his past mistakes. But that had been enough. In their minds, his history of violence had already written the verdict.

Mick drew in a slow breath, letting it out between clenched teeth. He leaned back, and the couch springs groaned beneath him, matching his weariness. The familiar itch had started at the base of his spine weeks ago—the same warning signal he'd felt before everything fell apart the first time. It had begun as a whisper, a shadow in his peripheral vision, but it had grown into something he couldn't ignore. Like knowing the blade was falling before you felt its edge.

"DiMatteo."

The name tasted like copper on his tongue, bitter and metallic. Detective John DiMatteo, the man who'd turned pursuit into obsession, who'd made destroying Mick's life his personal crusade. Mick could still see his face with perfect clarity—those cold eyes that seemed to look straight through him, already convinced of what they'd find. The hung jury and case dismissal had never mattered to DiMatteo. He'd kept watching, kept waiting, like a man who knew secrets the rest of the world hadn't caught up to yet.

Nine years since that night—since they'd found the body and dragged him from his house in handcuffs, neighbors watching from behind twitching curtains. They'd thrown him into an interrogation room like he was already guilty, already condemned. The press had seized on the story like wolves on fresh meat. A man with a history of violence, bar fights scattered through his past like landmines, rough around every edge. He'd been the perfect villain for their story. They didn't want him to be anything else.

He'd made mistakes—Christ, he knew that better than anyone. His temper had gotten the better of him more times than he could count. But murder? That was different. That line, he swore he hadn't crossed. Yet the questions lingered, worming their way into his mind during long nights when sleep wouldn't come. Even after walking out of that courtroom, a technically free man, the doubt had followed him like a shadow. He hadn't been cleared in their eyes—he'd just gotten away with it.

Mick pushed himself up from the couch, too restless to stay still. The TV droned on about weather patterns and local politics, meaningless background noise to the storm in his head. He paced the cramped living room, nine steps in each direction, like marking time in a cell. The isolation of his home had been a choice—a refuge from prying eyes and whispered accusations. But sometimes the quiet pressed in too close, made the walls feel like they were watching him.

His gaze fell on a half-empty beer bottle, leaving sweat rings on his table. The urge to finish it tugged at him, but something held him back. His nerves were already too raw, his senses too sharp. That crawling sensation between his shoulder blades was getting worse, like phantom fingers tracing his spine, warning him.

He should have seen this coming. DiMatteo wasn't the type to forget; he wasn't built to let go. Even during the quiet years, Mick had felt him out there, circling like a shark that had caught the scent of blood. Mick had done everything right—kept his head down, stayed out of trouble, tried to become invisible. But he'd somehow known it was only a matter of time. You couldn't escape a man like DiMatteo. Not really.

The flash of headlights swept across his walls like searchlight beams, and Mick's heart stumbled in its rhythm. Instinct tightened his muscles; he knew what this was even before he registered it fully. Time was up.

Two sets of headlights. Not a casual visit, then. Mick's mouth went dry even as his palms began to sweat.

Through the thin walls of his house, he could hear it all with perfect clarity—car doors opening with measured care, the crunch of boots on gravel, the soft murmur of voices trained to carry authority. The red and blue lights started their rhythmic dance against his walls, turning his living room into something from a fever dream.

Mick swallowed hard against the pulse hammering in his throat. His mind felt oddly calm, almost detached, like watching everything unfold from a distance. He'd been here before, after all. Been living in this moment for nine years, waiting for it to circle back around.

The knock, when it came, was sharp and official, brooking no argument. Mick stood there for a moment, staring at the door, feeling the weight of inevitability settle over him. Part of him had rehearsed this scene since the last time, knowing it would come again.

He opened the door with deliberate slowness, his face carefully arranged into a mask of indifference. The porch light caught the badges of two uniformed officers, their stance rigid with practiced authority. The younger one shifted his weight, eyes scanning the shadows behind Mick, while the senior officer maintained steady eye contact.

"Mr. Garrett?" The words carried the weight of procedure, of things set in motion that couldn't be stopped. "We need you to come with us for questioning."

Mick looked past them to the patrol car idling in his driveway, its lights painting the night in alternating flashes of crimson and cobalt. He kept his breathing steady, even as something in his chest twisted tight enough to snap. Nine years of waiting, of looking over his shoulder, had prepared him for this moment.

"Yeah," he said, his voice coming out rough, almost amused, though there was nothing funny about any of this. "Figured DiMatteo wasn't done with me yet."

The words hung between them, heavy with the weight of history about to repeat itself.

CHAPTER 8
PRESSURE POINTS

The interrogation room hummed with artificial light and a tension thick enough to choke. Mick Garrett sat across the steel table, arms folded over his chest, trying to project an air of casual indifference. But John could read the tells—the rhythmic tapping of Mick's fingers against his arm, the tight cords of muscle in his neck, the way his eyes kept darting to the room's exits, like a caged animal sizing up escape routes.

John stood against the wall, arms crossed, every muscle in his body coiled tight. The fluorescent lights cast harsh shadows, making Mick's face look skeletal, almost ghoulish. Each second in the room with him felt like throwing gasoline on the fire that had been smoldering in John's chest for years. Only the practiced control of a seasoned detective kept him from erupting.

Ramirez sat opposite Mick, his posture deliberately relaxed, his voice carrying an air of calm that belied the gravity of the situation. He slid a photograph across the table's scratched metal surface. Sarah Thompson's face smiled up at them—young, vibrant, alive—everything she wasn't anymore.

Mick barely glanced at the photo before his eyes found John's, a sneer twisting his lips. "Another dead girl you're trying to pin on me, DiMatteo?"

John's fists clenched involuntarily, but Ramirez stepped in smoothly before he could respond. "Just answer the question, Mick."

Mick's sneer faltered as he looked back at Sarah's photo. "No. I don't recognize her." His voice carried the practiced neutrality of someone who'd been in too many interrogation rooms.

"Interesting." Ramirez retrieved the photo, flipping through his notebook with methodical care. "Because her family mentioned she had a part-time job at the hardware store near your place. You're a regular there, aren't you? Never noticed her behind the register?"

Mick shrugged, leaning back in his chair. The metal creaked under his weight as he crossed his arms—a mirror of John's stance, whether intentional or not. "A lot of people work at that place. Maybe I saw her, yeah. But she was just another face. Just some girl at the register."

"Just another face," John muttered, the words sour in his mouth.

"Any issues with her?" Ramirez pressed on, pen hovering over his notebook. "Arguments? Run into her somewhere else? Outside the store?"

"Like I said," Mick's voice sharpened. "I don't know her. Never did."

John pushed off the wall, unable to hold himself back any longer. "Funny how that keeps happening, isn't it?" He took a step forward, watching Mick's shoulders tense. "How you're always right there, close enough to these women to be a suspect, but somehow you never 'know' them. Just another coincidence, right?"

Mick's eyes met his, cold as winter frost. "I don't know what you're implying, DiMatteo, but I'm not your guy. I didn't know her, and I sure as hell didn't touch her."

"Not what we've heard." John's voice dropped, carrying a hard edge. "Seems like every time a young woman turns up dead, your name finds its way into the conversation."

A bitter smile twisted Mick's face. "Is that what this is about? You think this is the same as before?" He leaned forward, the chair groaning beneath him. "You really can't let it go, can you? Still trying to pin everything on me because you couldn't handle the truth back then."

The air in the room grew heavier, thick with unspoken accusations. Ramirez shifted, sensing the powder keg about to blow. "Let's stick to the present, Mick," he said, his voice steady but firm. "Sarah's body was found in Blendon Woods. You spend any time out there?"

Mick scoffed, but something flickered in his eyes. "I haven't been near that park in years. The only thing I do is stay home and mind my own business." His gaze slid back to John. "Some of us learned our lesson about being in the wrong place at the wrong time."

John stepped closer, his shadow stretching across the table. "You ever see her in your neighborhood? Maybe during her morning runs?"

Mick's eyes flashed with something—anger, fear, satisfaction—before his face smoothed back into careful neutrality. "I don't even know where she lived."

"Sure you don't," John muttered, close enough now to see the faint scar on Mick's jaw from some long-ago fight.

Ramirez leaned forward. "So, where were you the day Sarah was murdered?"

"Home." Mick ran a hand over his face, stubble scratching against his palm. "Same as always."

"Anyone who can verify that?" John's voice cut through the air like a blade. "Anyone who can say for sure you were home all day?"

Mick's jaw tightened, a muscle twitching beneath the skin. When he spoke, his voice was laced with bitterness. "Who the hell would corroborate it, DiMatteo? You made damn sure I don't have anyone left." He gestured sharply with one hand. "Since you ruined my life, nobody wants to be around me. Can't even get a pack of smokes without people looking at me like I'm some kind of monster." His eyes locked onto John's. "Wonder whose fault that is?"

John's hands curled into fists at his sides. Ramirez shot him a warning glance, but the rage was already building, a pressure behind his eyes. "You want to talk about ruined lives?" His voice came out as a growl. "You did that, Mick. Not me."

Mick leaned forward, his voice dropping to a mocking whisper. "Did I? You sure about that?"

Something inside John snapped, like a wire pulled too tight, finally breaking. The next few seconds happened in flashes: his body moving before his mind could stop it, his fist connecting with Mick's jaw, the sharp screech of the chair across the floor. Mick stumbled back, blood already welling from his split lip.

But it was Mick's eyes that stopped John cold. Instead of fear or anger, they gleamed with satisfaction. Like this was exactly what he'd been waiting for.

Ramirez was there instantly, strong hands gripping John's shoulders, pulling him back. "John!" His partner's voice cut through the red haze of rage. "Get out of here! Now!"

John struggled against Ramirez's grip, his breath coming in hard gasps, pulse thundering in his ears. Through it all, he could see Mick wiping the blood from his mouth, that damned smirk still in place despite the injury.

"Same asshole as always, huh, DiMatteo?" Mick's words dripped with contempt, with triumph.

Ramirez muscled John toward the door, his voice low and firm in John's ear. "You're done. Go."

The rational part of John's mind knew Ramirez was right. He couldn't let this continue; he couldn't give Mick more ammunition. But his body still thrummed with the need to finish what he'd started, to wipe that knowing smile off Mick's face.

"That temper's gonna get you one day." Mick's voice followed him as Ramirez pushed him through the door. "You know that, right?"

The words burned like acid in John's mind. He let Ramirez guide him out, leaving Mick behind with his bloodied smile and his victory. The door slammed shut with a finality that echoed down the hallway.

In the corridor, the fluorescent lights felt harsher, amplifying every sound. John's hands were still shaking, his breath coming too fast. He barely registered

Chief Harrison's presence until the man stepped directly into his path, arms crossed, face set in granite.

"DiMatteo," Harrison's voice was low, but carried the weight of authority. "What the hell was that?"

John couldn't find words immediately. His chest still heaved with the force of everything that had just happened. Sweat trickled down his temple as he tried to steady his breathing. Harrison's cold stare made it impossible to think clearly.

"I asked you a question." The Chief's voice was clipped, dangerous. "You want to explain why you just assaulted a suspect during questioning? Because last time I checked, we're supposed to interrogate people, not beat them."

John shook his head, still fighting to push down the anger. "He's not a suspect." The words came out rough. "He's a killer. We both know it."

Harrison's eyes narrowed. "That's not the point, John, and you damn well know it." He stepped closer, voice lowering. "If you can't control yourself, I'll pull you off this investigation faster than you can blink. You understand me?"

Panic flared beneath the anger. John couldn't get pulled, not now. Not when they were so close. "Chief—"

"Don't 'Chief' me." Harrison cut him off. "You're letting your emotions run this investigation, and it's going to blow up in all our faces." He jabbed a finger toward the interrogation room. "Garrett pushed your buttons, and you gave him exactly what he wanted."

The truth of it hit John like a blow. Mick had played him, known exactly which strings to pull. And John had taken the bait.

Harrison sighed, some of the anger easing from his posture. "Look, John, I get it. This case... it's too close to home. But you need to get your head on straight." His tone softened slightly, though the steel remained. "Pack it in for today. Go home. Get some rest. I don't want to see you back here until tomorrow morning."

John started to protest, but Harrison held up a hand. "I'm serious. I'm not pulling you off yet, but I will if you come back tomorrow in this same headspace."

Ramirez stood silently beside John, his presence a steady reminder of reality. When John looked at him, there was no judgment, no pity—just quiet agreement with Harrison's words.

The fight slowly drained out of John, leaving exhaustion in its wake. "Fine," he muttered, hating how defeated the word sounded. "I'll go."

Harrison nodded, but his eyes never left John's face. "We'll regroup tomorrow. But next time?" He paused, making sure the message landed. "Keep it together. We need you on this case, but we need you in control."

John nodded numbly and turned away, his footsteps echoing down the empty hallway toward his desk. His hands trembled slightly as he pulled his jacket off the chair. Harrison was right—he needed rest, to think, and to get his head straight.

But as he exited the precinct and got into his car, Mick's words followed him like shadows.

Same asshole as always, huh, DiMatteo?

He slammed the car door and gunned the engine, tires squealing against wet pavement as he backed out of his spot. His mind was so clouded with rage that he barely registered the headlights in his rearview mirror until the last second. John slammed on his brakes, his car skidding sideways on the slick asphalt.

The other vehicle swerved, missing him by inches. In that brief moment, as the cars passed each other, John caught a glimpse of the driver's face through the rain-streaked windows.

Matt Lawson.

Their eyes met for just a split second, and Matt's lips curled into that familiar, knowing smile that made John's blood run cold. Then he was gone, his taillights disappearing into the precinct parking lot as John sat frozen behind the wheel, his heart hammering against his ribs.

CHAPTER 9
NEW PERSPECTIVE

The precinct was controlled chaos—phones ringing in staccato bursts, keyboards clattering like anxious insects, voices weaving through the air in urgent whispers. But John barely registered any of it. His mind was trapped in a loop, replaying the interrogation with Mick Garrett over and over, Mick's smug face taunting him from the edges of memory. Every time he thought of that knowing smirk, his fists clenched, as if tightening around an invisible neck.

The hinges of Chief Harrison's office door creaked. Harrison's face appeared, his expression grave and resolved. "DiMatteo. Get in here."

John pushed himself off the wall where he'd been brooding, exhaling sharply as he stepped into Harrison's cramped office. The room was a cluttered landscape of case files and half-finished paperwork, scattered like fallen leaves across the desk. In the corner, a woman stood with her arms crossed, observing him with a focus that was almost clinical.

"John," Harrison said, tone carefully neutral, "this is Dr. Claire Harper. Forensic psychologist. She's consulting on the Thompson case."

The woman's gaze sharpened as she took in John's stance, her eyes assessing in a way that made him feel more exposed than he liked. She looked exactly like what she was—someone who preferred analyzing people from behind a glass wall, who'd spent more time in lecture halls than crime scenes. Everything about her was precise, from her perfectly pressed blouse to the way she held her hands, fingers loosely interlocked as though even her gestures were measured.

"Dr. Harper." John kept his voice professionally neutral, though his jaw tightened. He'd dealt with these types before—outsiders with their neat profiles, trying to turn raw violence into tidy psychological patterns. Meanwhile, he was out in the field, dealing with the aftermath in all its blood and ugliness.

Claire's nod was polite, undented by his skepticism. "Detective DiMatteo." Her voice carried the calm certainty of someone used to dealing with resistance. "I've reviewed the case files. There are things we need to discuss."

Harrison muttered something about an urgent call and slipped out, leaving them alone in the cramped office. The silence settled thick between them, charged and prickling.

Claire didn't waste time. "The Thompson case," she said, each word delivered with a precise, almost surgical detachment, "isn't what it appears to be on the surface. The body positioning, the method—it's too controlled, too deliberate. This wasn't an impulsive killing. Whoever did this knew exactly what they were doing."

John bristled at the implication that he'd missed something obvious. "You think I don't know that?" His voice carried an edge of defensive heat. "We've got the body, suspects, motive. What else is there to see?"

Claire tilted her head slightly, studying him like he was a puzzle she was piecing together. "There's more here than a simple murder, Detective. The way the body was staged—it speaks to a need for control. Whoever did this didn't just want Sarah dead; they wanted to send a message, to make a statement. This killer is experienced. They've done this before."

The words landed like a punch, striking a nerve he hadn't wanted to examine. He'd sensed it too, deep down—that the scene had been too precise, too calculated. But following that thread meant confronting questions he wasn't ready to face.

The door's hinges groaned softly as Matt Lawson entered, a manila folder tucked precisely under his arm. "Sorry to interrupt," he said, glancing between John and Claire with a practiced neutrality. "The toxicology report just came in."

John seized on the interruption, grateful for something that might break the tension. "Matt, come in for a second." He gestured vaguely. "This is Dr. Claire Harper. She's consulting on the Thompson case."

Matt nodded politely, his face a mask of professionalism. "Dr. Harper," he acknowledged, voice steady.

Claire extended her hand. "Nice to meet you, Matt. I look forward to working together."

"Likewise." Matt's handshake was brief and businesslike. Then, without another word, he handed the folder to John and stepped back toward the door.

John flipped open the file, grateful for the excuse to look away from Claire's unblinking gaze. He skimmed the report, though his mind remained half-focused on the psychologist beside him, still bristling from her insinuations.

Matt slipped out as quietly as he'd entered, leaving them alone again. Claire didn't miss a beat, turning back to John with renewed intensity. "The way Sarah's body was left—it wasn't random. This was about control. The killer wanted her to feel powerless, to understand that her life was in their hands."

John's jaw tightened. He didn't like how she was pulling at threads he'd been carefully ignoring, unraveling certainties he'd clung to. "And you're saying Mick Garrett doesn't fit that profile?" The question came out more challenging than he'd intended.

Claire regarded him with that maddening, steady patience. "Garrett has a history of violence, yes," she said. "But his crimes were impulsive, emotional outbursts. This killer is methodical. Calculated. They plan every move."

"So you're saying Garrett's not capable of planning?" John's fists clenched at his sides.

"I'm saying you might be too focused on Garrett," Claire replied, her eyes unwavering. "There may be other suspects you're overlooking because you're locked into a theory."

John felt the sting of her words as they hit their mark. Garrett wasn't just another suspect; he was a figure from John's past, someone who'd haunted his career. But Claire's analysis was peeling back layers he didn't want to examine, forcing him to confront the possibility that he might be missing something crucial.

"I'm not ruling anything out," John said, his voice steeling. "But Garrett isn't just a theory. He's got a history, a pattern. You think it's coincidence he's on our radar again?"

"I'm not saying it's coincidence," Claire answered, her calm persistence unsettling him more than he cared to admit. "But this killer is experienced. They've done this before, maybe multiple times. If we focus too narrowly, we could miss the bigger picture."

John felt the walls of the office closing in, the air thick with the weight of her words. She wasn't wrong, and that was what burned the most. He'd sensed it too—the meticulousness, the control. It was unlike any of Garrett's prior crimes, and it gnawed at him.

"You're suggesting this isn't just about Sarah," he said, his voice tight.

Claire's gaze held his, unflinching. "I'm suggesting there may be a pattern here. Whether it's Garrett or someone else, we need to dig deeper. This wasn't their first kill."

John's chest tightened. He hated how much sense she was making, how her analysis was stripping away the layers of certainty he'd wrapped himself in. But he wasn't ready to let go of Garrett—not yet.

"Alright, Dr. Harper," he said, forcing control into his voice. "You want to look for patterns? Fine. But I'm not dropping Garrett. He stays on the list."

"I wouldn't expect you to," Claire replied smoothly. "But remember—this killer is patient. They'll strike again, and if we don't stay open to all possibilities, we could miss our chance to stop them."

John opened his mouth to argue, but the words caught in his throat. Her logic was unassailable, and that realization settled like a stone in his gut. The control, the precision, the deliberate positioning of Sarah's body—it painted a picture he didn't want to see. This wasn't just about Garrett anymore. The killer had a plan, and if they didn't figure it out soon, someone else would die.

With a curt nod, he pushed away from the wall, frustration mounting with each step toward the door. The tension in his shoulders had become almost unbearable, a physical reminder that the case was slipping through his fingers. What he'd thought would be a straightforward path to justice was transforming into a maze of psychological analysis and hidden meanings.

And with Claire Harper peeling away his certainties, exposing cracks in his perspective, the walls felt like they were closing in faster than he could escape.

CHAPTER 10
THE MAN ON THE APP

The notification buzzed on Sarah's phone, a slight vibration breaking through the quiet hum of her apartment. She glanced down, half-expecting another alert about some deal at the local running store. Instead, the screen lit up with a dating app message: "You've matched with Aaron!"

Sarah tapped the notification, and the app opened to reveal his profile. Aaron had dark hair and a neatly trimmed beard, and he wore glasses that gave him an approachable, thoughtful look. In one photo, he stood at the edge of a cliff, a sprawling national park stretching out behind him. Another showed him crouched next to a scruffy golden retriever, his smile wide and unguarded. His bio was short but inviting: "Big fan of hikes, indie bookstores, and bad puns. Let's trade travel stories."

He seemed... normal. This was refreshing after a string of lackluster dates, where "normal" seemed to be asking too much. No shirtless gym selfies. No cryptic quotes about success or women. Just a guy who looked kind and genuinely interesting. She swiped through his profile one more time before opening the chat.

"Why not?" she said aloud, typing her first message.

Their conversations started light. Aaron's easy humor put her at ease, and soon, they were trading stories about awkward high school moments and embarrassing first dates. When he asked her about her favorite place to travel, she admitted that she hadn't been to many national parks.

"That's criminal," he replied, his messages arriving almost as quickly as she could read them. "Yellowstone? Grand Canyon? Not even Zion?"

"Maybe I just don't include those in my profile pics," she wrote back, grinning.

"Well," he answered, "if we ever meet, you owe me your favorite hike story. And I'll tell you mine. Deal?"

She hesitated for a moment before typing, "Deal."

The coffee shop Aaron suggested was the place Sarah loved—a hole-in-the-wall with mismatched chairs and the smell of roasted beans so rich it practically hugged her as she walked in. Aaron was already there, sitting by the window, his head bent over a book.

He stood as she approached, smiling warmly. "You're early," she said, setting her bag on the chair beside her.

"First dates are like job interviews," he replied. "You always want to show up prepared."

His voice was steady and calm, the kind that put her at ease. As they talked, Sarah found herself laughing more than she had in months. Aaron asked questions that made her feel interesting—about her favorite books, her worst date stories, and what got her into running.

Aaron was open but not overly forthcoming when she turned the conversation toward him. He grew up out west, worked freelance IT gigs, and had a thing for photography. He didn't have siblings and hadn't been in a serious relationship for years, which he chalked up to "bad timing."

Sarah was intrigued enough to agree to a second by the time the date ended.

Over the next few weeks, Aaron slipped into her life as if he had always been there. He planned thoughtful dates—a hike through Blendon Woods, a visit to an art exhibit she'd mentioned in passing—and always seemed to remember the smallest details about her. Sarah wasn't used to this kind of attention. After a few weeks of knowing him, she felt herself softening, her defenses lowering.

Then came the afternoon at his apartment.

Aaron's place was small but meticulously organized, with just enough personality to make it feel lived-in: framed black-and-white photos of mountains and forests, a stack of books on true crime and psychology by the couch. They'd spent the morning hiking, and now Aaron was in the kitchen, rummaging for snacks. At the same time, Sarah flipped through magazines on his coffee table.

A corner of a manila folder poked out from under the pile. Something about it caught her attention—maybe the way it was tucked away but not hidden. Curiosity got the better of her, and she pulled it free.

On top was a newspaper clipping, the headline jumping out at her: "Still No Leads in Emily Reardon's Disappearance ." As she continued thumbing through the folder, newspaper clippings and handwritten notes filled page after page. The notes were meticulous, detailing Emily's routines, habits, and places she frequented. The handwriting was familiar.

"Find something interesting?"

Sarah jumped, clutching the folder awkwardly. "I—sorry, I didn't mean to snoop. I just... I'm really interested in true crime cases."

Aaron stepped closer, his expression unreadable. He held his hand, and Sarah hesitated before letting him take the folder.

"She was someone I knew," he said after a moment, his voice calm but clipped. "Not well, but we ran in the same circles. Her disappearance hit close to home."

"That's awful," Sarah said softly, watching his reaction.

Aaron gave a slight shrug. "I guess it's one of those things you can't stop thinking about. I've looked into her case a little, but it's not like I've found anything." He chuckled a bit too quickly. "Probably just my morbid curiosity. You know how it is."

Sarah forced a smile, but an unease thread wound through her. His explanation seemed reasonable, but his tone—so practiced and smooth—unsettled her.

That night, back in her apartment, Sarah couldn't shake the feeling that something was off. She'd pulled up Emily's name on her laptop and scanned through articles about her disappearance. Still, none of them mentioned Aaron or anyone fitting his description.

She opened Facebook and typed "Aaron Blake" into the search bar on a whim.

The first few results were generic—unrelated profiles and a local business page. Then she spotted a post in a private group titled "Are You Dating This Guy?"

Her stomach twisted as she clicked it.

The photo was unmistakable. Aaron standing in front of what looked like the same coffee shop where they'd had their first date. Only the post called him "Nate Harris."

The comments below sent chills racing through her.

"He's super charming at first, but trust your gut. Something's off about him."

"RUN. He was so controlling, I had to block him on everything."

"I think he followed me home after our third date."

Sarah's fingers hovered over the keyboard before she sent a private message to the woman who'd posted it. "Hi, I saw your post about Nate. I think I've been seeing him too. Can you tell me what happened?"

The reply came almost immediately.

"Be careful," the woman wrote. "He's not who he says he is. I'm pretty sure he's dangerous."

Sarah stared at the message, her hands trembling. In the quiet of her apartment, every creak and rustle seemed louder, closer. She stood and walked to her door, checking the lock twice before returning to her laptop.

The pieces clicked into place—Aaron's vague past, his detailed notes about Emily, his perfect apartment with everything just so. Sarah's mind raced through their conversations, finding new meaning in his careful questions and seemingly coincidental appearances at places she frequented.

The cursor blinked on her screen as she composed the email to Detective Frank Hargrove. Each word felt like crossing a line she couldn't uncross:

"Detective Hargrove,

I recently learned about Emily Reardon's disappearance, and I have information you need to hear. I've been seeing someone who knows details about her case that I don't believe were made public. He kept extensive notes about her movements before she vanished. Please contact me as soon as possible.

Sarah Thompson"

She hit send before she could lose her nerve. Outside her window, shadows stretched across the street like reaching fingers. For the first time, Sarah wondered if one of them belonged to Aaron, watching, waiting, knowing she'd discovered his secret.

The cursor continued to blink, marking time in an empty inbox. Sarah pulled her curtains closed, but she couldn't shake the feeling that somewhere in the darkness, someone was smiling.

CHAPTER 11
DEADLY SIGNS

The dead speak in fragments, but tonight, they were screaming.

Sarah Thompson's text and email messages stretched across John's screen like a digital autopsy, each message a clue to her final days. Her voice emerged in casual mentions of coffee dates and study groups, then disappeared into strange gaps of silence that spanned days. These weren't the typical patterns of a young woman's life—they were the fingerprints of someone being watched, isolated, and gradually drawn into a dark orbit.

Another dead girl, he thought, bitterness rising in his throat. Another life reduced to evidence logs and witness statements.

A message from three weeks ago caught his attention. "Everything's fine," Sarah had written to her mother. "Just busy with school. Don't worry so much." Simple words, but John recognized the familiar lie. People who were truly fine didn't need to say it so often.

Ramirez's knock cut through his dark thoughts. John looked up to find his partner's face set with the kind of tension that meant pieces were finally starting to fall into place.

"I got something," Ramirez said, clutching a manila folder. His usual easy manner was gone, replaced by tightly controlled intensity. He dropped the folder onto John's desk, papers spilling out like accusations—crime scene photos, witness statements, fragments of Sarah's life reduced to grim documentation.

"She reached out to a retired detective named Frank Hargrove," Ramirez explained, leaning against the desk. "A series of emails about a cold case from Chicago—college student disappeared six years ago. Emily Reardon. Sarah discovered someone who knew non-public details about Emily's case. Her messages started professional, methodical, but grew more urgent over time. The final email came three days before she died, mentioning evidence logs with critical inconsistencies. Hargrove never replied."

John felt the name settle in his gut like a stone. "Why was she looking into a six-year-old disappearance?"

"Look at this." Ramirez pulled out another document, this one bearing the Chicago PD letterhead. "Sarah requested copies of Emily's original case file. Standard procedure, right? But three key pieces went missing in transit. Crime scene photos, witness statements, lab reports—all vanished."

"You think this connects to Sarah's murder?" John asked, though skepticism edged his voice. His mind circled back to Mick Garrett—the anger, the history. But this connection to Emily Reardon threw everything into question, complicating his certainties.

Ramirez shrugged, but his expression remained grim. "It's our best lead. Sarah was digging into the past, pulling on threads someone wanted left alone. Maybe she found something she wasn't supposed to. Maybe someone decided to silence her." He tapped the file meaningfully. "Smart people don't just vanish, John. Not without leaving traces."

John sat back, letting the weight of it all sink in. Sarah wasn't just a college kid poking around in things she didn't understand. She'd gone out of her way to track down a retired detective, to reopen a six-year-old disappearance. What had she found? What had put her in the killer's crosshairs?

"I'll talk to Hargrove," Ramirez said, pushing off the desk. "There's got to be more here. Sarah wouldn't chase a cold case without a reason."

John nodded absently, his mind racing, trying to reconcile this new information with his existing theory. Mick Garrett still felt like the key—his violent history, his rage. But this new lead with Emily Reardon pulled at loose threads in his mind, challenging the picture he'd so carefully constructed.

Through the glass partition of his office, John caught a glimpse of Matt Lawson heading toward the lab, case files tucked precisely under his arm. The forensics tech moved with his usual quiet efficiency, almost invisible against the precinct's background noise.

"Keep me posted on Hargrove," John said to Ramirez, the tension in his voice betraying his growing unease. "I need to talk to Claire."

He found her in the conference room, surrounded by stacks of case files. The fluorescent lights cast harsh shadows across her face, highlighting her focused, unsmiling expression. As he stepped inside, Claire looked up, her gaze calm and sharp, her composure as steady as ever.

John shut the door behind him, crossing his arms as he leaned against the frame. His patience was wearing thin. He was running on fumes, caffeine, and the gut-deep conviction that they were close to something—something he could almost feel slipping through his fingers.

"We need to talk," he said, his voice carrying an edge honed by too many sleepless nights. Claire set down her pen, a small, deliberate movement that told him she was ready.

"Alright," she replied, her gaze never wavering. "What's on your mind?"

How she said it—calm, collected—made his jaw tighten. He felt scrutinized, cataloged, like he was another piece of evidence to be analyzed. The last thing he needed right now was to be psychoanalyzed by someone who hadn't spent a single night on the streets chasing monsters.

"Let's get one thing straight," he began, his tone clipped. "This is my case. I don't need you derailing it with theories. We go after real leads, not profiles."

Claire's expression remained neutral, though her eyes sharpened, studying him. "I'm here to help solve this, Detective," she replied evenly. "And right now, it looks like you're missing things. Big things."

The words hit like a slap, striking a nerve he hadn't expected. "You think

I'm missing something?" he shot back, his voice rising. "I've been doing this for over twenty years. I don't need some desk-bound psychologist telling me what I am or am not seeing."

But Claire didn't flinch. If anything, his anger seemed to fortify her calm. "You think I don't understand the stakes here? I know exactly what's at risk." She leaned forward, her voice dropping. "And I can see what's happening to you, John. You're so focused on Garrett, so sure he's the answer, that you're ignoring other possibilities."

Her words landed like punches, each one dismantling the certainty he'd built around himself. Part of him wanted to lash out, to push her away, but another part—the part that still carried the weight of every victim he hadn't saved— knew she was right.

"Let's get something clear," he said, voice cold as steel. "This killer isn't playing mind games. They're a real threat, a real danger. I don't need theories. I need action."

Claire met his anger with an unsettling steadiness. "Then let's take action. But you need to start seeing the bigger picture. If you're right about Garrett, fine—but what if there's more here? What if Sarah found a connection that goes deeper than Garrett?"

The words struck a chord he hadn't wanted to acknowledge. "You're suggesting…what? That this goes beyond a single murder?"

"I'm saying we need to dig deeper," Claire replied. "Sarah was onto something, and if we don't figure out what, we're never going to catch her killer."

John's fists clenched, but the fight was draining out of him, replaced by a cold, gnawing dread. "Fine. Look into it. But remember—this is still my case."

"I wouldn't dream of taking it from you." Claire's voice softened, almost in understanding. "But if we don't understand why she was killed, we'll never get ahead of this."

John turned on his heel, leaving the room without another word. As he walked back through the precinct, the noise and movement around him faded into a blur. The certainty that had fueled him for so long was unraveling, replaced by questions he hadn't thought to ask.

Through the glass walls, he saw Matt Lawson moving quietly through the lab, methodically logging evidence. He was so much a part of the scenery that John almost overlooked him—but something made him pause. What else was he missing? What other pieces were hiding in plain sight?

As he pushed through the doors, he felt the weight of the case pressing down harder than ever. The real work was just beginning, and he knew that this time, the answers would demand more than he was prepared to give.

Somewhere in the city, a killer was watching, knowing exactly how this game would play out. And John DiMatteo was starting to realize that he'd only just begun to see the board.

CHAPTER 12
INVISIBLE INK

Evening shadows crept across Ramirez's desk like spilled ink, the dying sunlight turning his Venetian blinds into prison bars. His third coffee of the night had gone untouched since the call came in. Frank Hargrove's voice crackled through the speaker, weathered and rough as old leather. Even through the static, Ramirez could hear the exhaustion of a man who'd carried too many unsolved cases for too long.

"Emily Reardon," Hargrove said, dragging the name out slowly, like pulling something from a deep well. "Yeah… six years ago. That was my last case before I retired." A pause, heavy with unspoken weight. "Should've stayed on longer. Maybe if I had…"

Ramirez straightened in his chair, pen hovering over his notepad. Something in Hargrove's tone set off warning bells. "Your last case—was that your choice?"

A bitter laugh crackled through the line. "Let's just say some cases cost more than others, Detective. Sometimes the price is your whole damn career."

"What happened with Emily, Frank?" Ramirez kept his voice steady, though his fingers tightened around the pen. "Walk me through it."

"College student at Loyola. Bright kid, full of potential." Hargrove's voice caught slightly. "Then one day, she was just… gone. No body. No trace. Like she'd never existed at all." Another pause. "The kind of disappearance that doesn't happen by accident."

Ramirez's eyes skimmed over the spread of files before him—Sarah Thompson's increasingly urgent emails, her frantic questions, the record of her meetings with Hargrove. Each document felt like a breadcrumb leading somewhere dark. His pen tapped an unconscious rhythm against the paper.

"And Sarah Thompson," he prompted carefully. "When did she first contact you about Emily?"

"Couple of months back," Hargrove replied, his puzzlement evident even through the static. "Met with me more than once. Couldn't figure out why she cared so much about an old case like that. Didn't make sense—not until now, anyway."

The fluorescent lights overhead buzzed faintly as Ramirez's pen stilled against the paper. "Did she mention why? What drew her to Emily's case specifically?"

"Not directly. But she was persistent—kept pushing about missing evidence and inconsistencies in the timeline. Details that don't add up unless..." Hargrove trailed off, and Ramirez could almost picture him rubbing his face, wrestling with old ghosts. "Maybe she dug too deep. Maybe she saw something she wasn't supposed to see."

"Was there ever a suspect?" Ramirez pressed, his voice hardening. "Anyone close to Emily who raised flags?"

"There was a student." Hargrove's words came slower now, more careful. "Spent time around Emily at Loyola. Can't remember his name now—too many years gone by." The pause that followed was heavy with unspoken knowledge. "He was on our radar, but nothing stuck. All circumstantial. We had whispers, rumors... but evidence would vanish every time we got close. Witnesses would change their stories. Files would go missing."

Ramirez's jaw tightened, his grip on the pen tightening. Another dead end. "You think someone inside the Chicago PD might've been covering for him?"

"All I know is, it wasn't anyone on our side pulling those files," Hargrove said, his voice rough with a defensive edge. "We tried to pursue him, but every time we started building a case, pieces of evidence would disappear. Not just physical evidence—reports, witness statements, even lab results. And this wasn't just sloppy work; it was intentional. Someone was scrubbing this kid's tracks."

Ramirez leaned back in his chair, feeling the familiar burn of frustration settle in his stomach. A nameless suspect, a case gone cold—yet something about it had caught Sarah's attention, strongly enough that she'd kept digging until… what? Until someone decided to stop her?

"You think Sarah found something new?" he asked. "Something in the old case files?"

"I don't know," Hargrove replied, his voice softening, carrying the weight of resignation. "But whatever it was, it got her killed."

A chill ran up Ramirez's spine. He gathered his notes, movements sharp with purpose as he headed for John's office. The hallway seemed longer than usual, each step carrying him closer to something they weren't ready to face. Through the glass partition, he could see John at his desk, still buried in Sarah's notes, trying to make sense of the Chicago connection.

Ramirez pushed open John's door, his face tight with focus. The air in the office was heavy with tension, the late afternoon light casting strange shadows across John's desk. John didn't look up from Sarah's notes, but his shoulders tensed at Ramirez's entrance.

"What did Hargrove say?" John's voice came out gravelly, worn from too many hours of chasing dead ends.

Ramirez dropped into the chair across from him, running a hand across his face. The leather creaked beneath him, too loud in the quiet office. "Emily Reardon was his last case before retirement. Student at Loyola Chicago." He paused, watching John's reaction. "Same profile as Sarah—bright, driven, full of potential. Then, one day, she just vanishes. No trace, no body. Nothing."

John finally looked up, the fluorescent lights catching the shadows under his eyes. Something in Ramirez's tone had caught his attention. "Anything solid? Suspects?"

Ramirez shook his head, frustration evident in the sharp movement. "There was a guy—another student. Hargrove couldn't remember his name." He tapped his notepad where he'd scribbled the sparse details. "They were interested in him, but everything was speculative. Not enough to build a case, so he dropped off their radar."

"A person of interest should be named in the investigation file." John's fingers drummed against his desk, a rhythm that spoke of mounting tension. "If this guy circled around Emily, we need to know who he is."

"That's what I figured," Ramirez said, reaching for the thin folder he'd brought. "I got Emily's file from Chicago. Thought we could go through it together."

John opened the folder, eyes scanning the pages with the intensity of someone looking for ghosts between the lines. Witness statements, timelines, theories—all there, but something felt off. Too thin, too neat, too… sanitized. His frown deepened as he flipped through the pages faster.

"Where's the full report?" The edge in John's voice matched the knot in Ramirez's stomach. "This can't be everything."

"It's not." Ramirez leaned forward, catching the concern in his partner's tone. "Look—" He pointed to the page numbers. "Thirty-nine jumps to forty-four. Five pages just… gone."

John held up several sheets, his movements sharp with growing agitation. "No suspect profiles, no detailed interviews." His jaw tightened. "Nothing about the person of interest Hargrove mentioned. Someone sanitized these files during the original investigation."

"Exactly," Ramirez muttered. "Hargrove said every time they got close to this guy, pieces would vanish."

John leaned forward, eyes locking onto Ramirez's with intensity. "We need to find out who would have access to those file. Anyone with the reach to influence a police investigation."

Ramirez was already pulling out his phone. "I'll see if anyone at Chicago PD remembers strange activity on the case, but this was six years ago. If whoever did this covered their tracks well, we might have to dig somewhere else for answers."

As he dialed Chicago PD, John's fingers drummed against the edge of Emily's file, a restless rhythm that matched the tension building in the room.

"Someone went to a lot of trouble to erase those records," John said quietly, almost to himself. "First, Emily vanishes without a trace. Then Sarah starts asking questions, gets too close, and ends up dead. Now we find gaps in both case files—evidence that someone didn't want us to find."

"The question is why," Ramirez replied, phone still pressed to his ear. "What was in those missing pages that was worth killing for?"

The afternoon light faded outside, casting longer shadows across John's desk. Shadows that seemed to reach toward them like fingers, hinting at darker truths still hidden. The precinct bustled around them, phones ringing, officers moving through their routines, everyone playing their part in the machinery of justice.

But somewhere in this building—or perhaps somewhere in the city— someone knew exactly what those missing pages contained. Someone had orchestrated this elaborate dance of disappearance and death, and that someone was watching to see how close the detectives would get.

The records clerk finally picked up, her voice tinny through the phone. Ramirez straightened, pen poised over his notepad. "Yeah, this is Detective Ramirez. I need to know if anyone recalls discrepancies in the Emily Reardon file. Missing pages, strange access requests—anything like that."

John watched him, tension visible in every line of his body. They both knew they were venturing into murky territory, digging up ghosts from a case someone wanted buried. But Sarah's death demanded answers, and those answers seemed to lie in shadows that went all the way back to Chicago.

The hunt was just beginning. And this time, the prey might be watching them, waiting to see how close they dared to get to the truth.

CHAPTER 13
PRETENSES

Claire's apartment felt different at night. The familiar comfort of her living room had transformed into something darker, filled with shadows that seemed to shift when she wasn't looking. Case files spread across her desk like tarot cards, illuminated by a single lamp that cast more shadows than light. She'd been at this for hours, losing track of time as she searched for patterns in the darkness.

Sarah Thompson's preliminary report lay open in her lap, its clinical language reducing a life—and death—to mere facts and figures. Outside, a car passed slowly beneath her second-floor window, its headlights sweeping across the wall. She didn't notice how the light lingered a moment too long or the faint sound of the engine idling before it moved on.

The heating kicked on with a soft rattle, stirring the papers slightly. A wine glass sat forgotten on the side table, its deep red hue now dulled. Behind her, the curtains weren't fully drawn, leaving a sliver of glass exposed to the night. If anyone had been watching, they would have seen her hunched over the files, absorbed in her work, oblivious to anything outside.

But Claire noticed none of this. Her mind was deep in the killer's psychology, reading between the lines of reports and witness statements. This wasn't just murder—it was evolution, each crime more refined than the last. A progression that spoke of someone learning, adapting, perfecting their technique.

She leaned back, scanning her meticulous notes. The details coalesced into a portrait she'd seen before: paracord bindings applied with surgical precision, then removed post-mortem. The deliberate arrangement of the body, the obsessive attention to detail—too familiar, too practiced to be the work of an amateur.

"Evolution," she whispered into the stillness.

The profile crystallized in her mind, each element snapping into place with chilling clarity. Methodical. Precise. Pathologically intelligent. This wasn't someone driven by fleeting emotions; this was an artisan of death, viewing each murder as a stepping stone toward perfection. The removal of restraints post-mortem was telling—a signature intentionally withheld, allowing the work to stand on its own, shrouded in anonymity.

The psychology both fascinated and repelled her. This killer showed no interest in the chaos of death itself; the obsession lay in absolute control, in mastering both victim and circumstance. The deliberate erasure of physical evidence was like an artist wiping away brushstrokes to let the canvas speak in silence.

A familiar tension crept up Claire's spine—a warning honed by years of navigating the darkest recesses of the human psyche. This case demanded more than professional detachment; it tugged at personal threads she usually kept tightly secured. Memories stirred: another case, another time when understanding a killer had become painfully personal.

Her hand trembled slightly as she recalled the loss that had propelled her into this line of work. Few knew the true catalyst behind her relentless pursuit of justice—the personal tragedy that had forged her into the profiler she was today. The pain of watching someone she loved become another statistic had never dulled; it had merely sharpened, becoming the lens through which she examined every case.

That crucible of grief had transformed her, burning away uncertainty and leaving behind a steely resolve. The words of her mentor echoed in her mind: "The best profilers are those who've danced with their own demons." At the time, she'd dismissed it as a platitude. Now she understood. Her pain wasn't merely a burden; it was a tool—a means to see what others overlooked.

And it had made her damn good at what she did.

The third file nearly slipped from her grasp. Something about this one felt different; she sensed it before even opening the cover. Inside were crime scene photos of another young woman, displayed with haunting familiarity: the same paracord bindings, the same meticulous attention to detail that marked Sarah Thompson's murder. But this case was older, its pages yellowed and heavy with the weight of long-buried secrets.

Claire forced herself to breathe, to steady the whirlwind of thoughts threatening to overwhelm her. Methodically, she began dissecting each piece of evidence, laying them out like artifacts at an archaeological dig. Every detail was scrutinized, filtered through years of expertise, and compared against Sarah's case with precision.

The killer had been more careful back then, leaving fewer traces. Yet his signature was unmistakable—like discovering an artist's early work, the foundational strokes of what would become a chilling oeuvre.

Her pen moved swiftly across fresh paper as patterns emerged from the chaos. The victims were more than mere targets; they were carefully selected challenges. Strong women, fiercely independent, on the brink of significant milestones in their lives. The killer hadn't simply wanted to end their lives; he sought to extinguish their potential, to assert dominance over their strength.

Realization settled over her like a cold fog. Sarah Thompson had been chosen with deliberate intent. Her investigation—whatever she'd unearthed— had placed her squarely in the killer's sights. Claire's gut twisted with certainty: Sarah had discovered something in these old cases, something that had sealed her fate.

Her thoughts drifted to Detective John DiMatteo, and frustration bubbled beneath the surface. His resistance to psychological profiling was more than mere skepticism. John inhabited a world defined by tangible evidence— fingerprints, DNA, concrete proof. He was uneasy in the shadows where Claire operated, in the negative spaces where killers often left their most telling marks.

But there was more to it. She'd caught glimpses of a deeper turmoil within him—the way his jaw tightened at certain details, how his eyes clouded when specific names were mentioned. Mick Garrett's name, in particular, elicited a visceral reaction. She suspected that John's personal demons were not unlike her own, that his drive was fueled by wounds yet to heal.

Perhaps they were more alike than either cared to admit.

Claire's gaze returned to the array of files, but her mind remained on John—the tension in his voice, the guarded anger simmering beneath the surface. She sensed his struggle, watched how he clung to hard evidence as if anything less might slip through his fingers. Whatever haunted him had carved deep channels into his life, shaping the man he had become.

She shook herself mentally. This was not the time for introspection about her colleague. There would be time later to unravel the complexities of John's connection to the case. For now, she needed to focus on what Sarah had uncovered before it was too late.

Then she saw it—the word "paracord" leapt out from a crime scene report, stark and undeniable. The same material used to bind Sarah had appeared in another cold case years prior. Her heart skipped a beat as she realized the significance.

Reading the report anew, she caught details previously overlooked. The clinical precision, the methodical execution—it wasn't random. This killer had orchestrated every aspect, planned each moment with meticulous care. It mirrored the shadow that had loomed over her own nightmares.

The realization hit her hard.

The words on the page blurred momentarily, but Claire steadied herself. The killer was communicating through his methods, his precision, his evolution. She just needed to decipher the language.

Her hands trembled as she delved back into the old case file, seeking the victim's name. She hadn't connected the dots before, but now, with Sarah's case fresh in her mind, the parallels were unmistakable.

John wasn't tormented by this case solely because of its brutality. It cut much deeper than she'd initially perceived. Claire leaned back, the pieces coalescing with dreadful clarity as her fingers hovered over the final page of the report.

A slow exhale escaped her lips as understanding dawned. She grasped why John was so relentlessly driven, why this case gnawed at him from within. Yet even as she pieced together his pain, echoes of her own resurfaced.

This is why I'm here, she reminded herself. This is why I do what I do. Years ago, she'd endured her own descent into darkness, losing someone she couldn't save. That loss had become her compass, guiding her into the minds of killers in an unending quest to comprehend the incomprehensible.

But even now, the wounds hadn't fully healed. The ghosts of her past lingered, just as they did for John.

Claire rose and moved to the window, pressing her forehead against the cool pane. Below, the city sprawled in a maze of lights and shadows, each one potentially concealing secrets as dark as those haunting her files. She had channeled her grief into purpose, but the scars remained—a constant reminder of battles fought and those yet to come.

Her reflection stared back, and she saw in it a mirror of John's struggle. Both of them haunted, both driven by losses that refused to fade. She recognized the signs in him because she confronted them in herself daily.

"We're fighting the same war," she murmured, her breath misting the glass. "Just on different fronts."

Returning to her desk, Claire began packing the files with renewed determination. She couldn't push John too hard; his wounds were still raw. But they needed each other on this case—their intertwined demons might be the key to unmasking the killer.

She slipped the last file into her bag. The hour was late, and the silence of her apartment pressed in, but she felt a newfound resolve. Tomorrow, she would find a way to reach John, to show him that he wasn't alone in his battle against the darkness.

Because sometimes, the only way to defeat monsters was to confront them together—even if it meant facing the demons within themselves.

As she switched off the lamp, shadows reclaimed the room. But within that darkness, Claire felt a glimmer of hope—a fragile belief that perhaps their shared pain could become their greatest strength.

CHAPTER 14
BLURRED LINES

The words on Sarah Thompson's emails blurred before John's eyes as he hunched over his desk. His mind raced, assembling fragments of evidence like pieces of a shattered mirror, each shard reflecting part of a truth he couldn't quite grasp. Something dark and insistent gnawed at his gut—an instinct he'd learned never to ignore.

A sharp knock on his doorframe broke his concentration. Ramirez stood there, his face etched with determination, eyes shadowed with the same frustration that kept John awake at night.

"Got something," Ramirez said, striding in.

John's fingers felt heavy as he took the manila folder Ramirez handed him. The words hit him like a blow: Jason Newsome's alibi was solid. Multiple witnesses placed him at a board game night during Sarah's murder. The confirmation they'd been waiting for had arrived, but it brought no satisfaction.

"Damn it," John muttered, his jaw clenching. He'd expected this, but seeing it documented in black and white twisted his gut.

"He's clear," Ramirez said, crossing his arms.

John slammed the folder shut. "Something still doesn't add up. You've seen how obsessed Newsome was with Sarah—the way he followed her, watched her. A guy that unhinged doesn't just stop." His voice was edged with frustration, a blade that needed a target.

"Facts are facts," Ramirez countered, though doubt edged his voice. "Three witnesses put him across town, rolling dice and playing Monopoly when Sarah died."

John pushed back from his desk, the chair's wheels squeaking. Another name, Mick Garrett, rose in his mind, dark and inevitable as a storm cloud. The mere thought of Garrett sent a familiar surge of anger through his veins.

"I know that look," Ramirez said. "You're thinking about Garrett again."

John began to pace, his thoughts tangling around possibilities he couldn't quite articulate. Mick Garrett fit—the violence, the rage, the history—but something else nagged at him, a detail that refused to align.

Ramirez straightened. "Look, we can't ignore the cold case angle. Sarah dug into something dangerous—something that got her killed. Whatever she found, someone wanted it buried."

The weight of everything—Sarah's murder, Jason's obsession, Mick Garrett's looming shadow—pressed down on John's shoulders. He strode from his office, footsteps echoing down the hallway toward the briefing room. Tension coiled in his chest like a spring wound too tight.

Claire Harper's presence in the briefing room struck him immediately. She sat surrounded by case files, her sharp eyes scanning each page with focused intensity. She looked up as he entered, and something in her steady gaze made him pause.

"Got a minute?" The words came out rougher than he intended.

"Always." Claire pushed aside her papers, giving him her full attention.

John couldn't stay still. He paced the room's perimeter, his restless energy seeking an outlet. "The Emily Reardon case—I need you to dig deeper. Cross-reference everything with Sarah's murder. There has to be something we're missing."

Claire watched his movement, her expression thoughtful. "I'll look into it," she said, then paused. "But first, we need to address something else."

His steps faltered. The weight in his chest grew heavier.

"You're pushing yourself too hard, John. I see it wearing on you."

He turned to face her, crossing his arms defensively. "What exactly are you suggesting?"

"This isn't just another case for you." Claire's voice remained steady, but her words carried a concern that cut through his defenses. "It's personal. Something about this investigation has hooked into you, pulled you deeper than you should go."

The truth in her observation stung. John turned away, resuming his pacing with increased intensity. "I'm doing my job," he snapped.

"Are you?" Claire's calm question sliced through his anger. "Or is this case dragging up things you've tried to bury?"

John stopped, fists clenching at his sides. Every instinct screamed at him to shut this down, to push back against her insight. But something in her tone made him hesitate—not judgment or criticism, but understanding—maybe even empathy.

Claire's words hung in the air. John's chest tightened as memories he'd fought to suppress threatened to surface. She didn't know his story, but somehow, she'd seen through the walls he'd built.

"You don't understand," he muttered.

"Maybe not everything," Claire admitted, standing slowly. "But I understand enough. I'm not here to dissect you, John. I'm here to help."

He turned to face her, struggling to maintain his composure. The fluorescent lights cast harsh shadows across her face, but her eyes remained soft. It made it harder to push her away.

"I don't need help," he insisted, but the words rang hollow.

Claire closed the distance between them. "You're carrying a weight that's crushing you. I can see it in every move you make."

Her observation pierced his defenses. John tensed, preparing for the empty reassurances he'd heard too many times before. But Claire's expression held something different—a shadow of personal pain that matched his own.

"I know what it looks like," she continued, her voice just above a whisper. "When something marks you so deeply, it becomes part of who you are. It doesn't just leave scars—it changes how you see everything."

John's throat constricted. The truth in her words resonated with something deep inside him, something he'd tried to bury beneath years of casework and bourbon. She understood more than anyone else at the precinct, and that terrified him.

Silence stretched between them. Claire wasn't pushing or prying, but her pain showed through the cracks in her professional exterior. He saw it in how she held herself, heard it in the weight behind her words.

"I'm not trying to psychoanalyze you," Claire said softly. "But pain leaves traces. I recognize them because I see them in myself every day."

Their eyes met, and something shifted. John wanted to ask about her story, to understand what darkness she carried that let her see so clearly into his own. But the words stuck in his throat. He wasn't ready for that kind of vulnerability.

"I'll keep that in mind," he managed to say.

Claire didn't push further. She recognized the boundary they'd approached. She'd shared enough for now, letting the weight of their shared understanding settle between them.

"Look into the Reardon case," John said, his voice steadier. "We'll regroup when you have something."

Claire watched him turn to leave, noting how his shoulders carried less tension. The wall between them hadn't crumbled entirely, but she'd created a crack. This small opening might eventually let light through.

John returned to his desk, his mind churning with their conversation, when Matt Lawson appeared in his doorway. Something in Matt's posture made him straighten—an urgency that cut through his emotional haze.

"This came for you," Matt said, extending an envelope. "I ran it for prints already. Thought you should see it right away."

The envelope felt heavy in John's hands. The paper was expensive, and the handwriting precise. His fingers trembled slightly as he tore it open, unfolding the single sheet inside.

The message struck him like a blow:

You're getting closer, Detective. But just like last time, you're not close enough. I'm watching you. Always watching.

Ice spread through John's veins as he reread the words. The killer wasn't just taunting him—they were demonstrating control. His mind immediately jumped to Mick Garrett. The arrogance felt familiar, and the need to assert dominance matched Garrett's profile.

But something nagged at him. The precision of the handwriting and the calculated nature of the message didn't fit Mick's brutal, impulsive style. Garrett was a hammer; this felt more like a scalpel.

He glanced up at Matt, who watched him with an unreadable expression. "Thanks," he managed just as Ramirez entered the office.

"Take a look at this," John said, passing the letter to his partner. He watched Ramirez's face darken as he read.

"Son of a bitch is playing games," Ramirez growled. "Think it's Garrett?"

John's jaw tightened. "Who else could it be?"

But even as he said it, doubt crept in. Claire's earlier words echoed in his mind, warning him about letting personal history cloud his judgment. The letter felt wrong for Garrett—too controlled, too precise.

"We need to bring Garrett in," John said, his voice hardening. "Question him before whoever wrote this decides to strike again."

Ramirez studied the letter again, skepticism clear. "We need more than a hunch, John. If we move too fast, we risk losing him—again."

The air in the office grew thick with tension. John stared at the letter lying between them, Claire's warnings mixing with his instinct to act. The killer was watching, waiting, perhaps even planning their next move. Time pressed against him like a weight.

He ran a hand across his face, feeling the roughness of stubble. For the first time in years, he forced himself to pause, to examine his driving need to pin everything on Mick Garrett. Claire had seen something in him today—a blindness born of past pain. He couldn't afford that luxury anymore. Not with lives at stake.

"All right," he said finally, surprising Ramirez and himself with his measured tone. "We do this right. Build it clean. Every piece of evidence documented, every witness statement corroborated. No shortcuts."

Ramirez's eyebrows rose slightly. "You sure about this approach? It'll take time we might not have."

"I'm sure." John's voice carried a quiet intensity different from his usual driven fury. "We go after Garrett; it has to stick. No legal loopholes. Nothing he or his lawyers can use to slip away."

He picked up the letter again, studying the precise handwriting. Each curve and line seemed to mock him, challenging his assumptions. The killer was playing a game, but maybe it wasn't the game he'd thought it was.

"Get the lab to analyze every aspect of this letter," he told Ramirez. "Paper type, ink composition, linguistic patterns—everything. And pull surveillance from around the precinct. Someone had to deliver this."

Ramirez nodded, already reaching for his phone. "I'll put the team on it."

John turned to stare out his office window at the darkening sky. The city spread out below, lights twinkling like stars. Somewhere out there, a killer watched and waited. Whether it was Garrett or someone else, they were moving pieces on a board he couldn't fully see.

Claire's words from earlier resonated in his mind: "When something marks you so deeply, it becomes part of who you are." She was right. His obsession with Garrett had marked him and shaped how he viewed every case. But he couldn't let that blindness cost another life.

"We'll find them," he murmured, more to himself than Ramirez. "Whoever they are."

The letter sat on his desk, its message burning in his mind. The killer thought they were in control, thought they could manipulate him like before. But something had shifted today. In accepting his own wounds, in hearing Claire's insight, he'd gained something valuable: perspective.

This time would be different. This time, John would see clearly.

The office hummed with renewed purpose as Ramirez made calls and set the investigation in motion. Outside, the night settled over the city like a shroud, but John felt more awake than he had in years. The killer was watching, yes.

But now, finally, he was truly watching back.

CHAPTER 15
PRIVATE MATTERS

John stared out the rain-streaked window of his dimly lit office, the city's neon lights blurring into a kaleidoscope of color against the night sky. The weight of the recent developments pressed heavily on his shoulders. Mick Garrett was in custody again, but something about it felt wrong—too convenient. Doubt gnawed at him, whispering that they were missing something critical.

He closed his eyes, and memories surged forward unbidden, dragging him back to the courtroom of two years ago. The trial that had promised justice but delivered only frustration. The scene unfolded in his mind with vivid clarity, every detail etched into his consciousness.

Electric tension filled the courtroom, each rustle of paper sounding like a thunderclap. Light slanted through high windows, casting stark shadows across Mick Garrett's face at the defense table. His jaw was set like granite, eyes fixed ahead with unsettling calm. He exuded the confidence of a man who had danced with the devil and lived to tell about it.

John sat three rows back, gripping the wooden bench until his knuckles whitened. He couldn't tear his gaze from Mick—the slight twist of his mouth hinting at secrets John had spent years trying to uncover. The space between them buzzed with unspoken accusations and buried truths.

The prosecutor rose, drawing every eye in the room. His voice sliced through the air. "Ladies and gentlemen, the evidence speaks plainly. Mick Garrett is guilty." He stepped toward the jury, each footfall echoing. "The rope found near the scene. His documented history of violence. Witness testimonies. Every piece points to one man."

He paused, letting silence amplify his words. "This wasn't a crime of passion or chance. It was calculated. Methodical. Mick Garrett didn't lose control—he exercised it with chilling precision. Because of his deliberate actions, a young woman is dead."

John's chest tightened as images flashed in his mind—the crime scene photos, the body posed with unnerving care, a life extinguished too soon. The prosecution's case seemed airtight. Yet a splinter of doubt gnawed at him, one he couldn't dislodge.

The air conditioning hummed overhead, a cold counterpoint to the heat rising within him. He leaned forward, muscles taut, as the prosecutor continued laying out the evidence. Each fact landed like a hammer blow: the neighbor who saw Mick near the scene, the paracord matching what he kept in his truck, the violent past painting him as a man on the edge.

"I saw him that day," the neighbor had testified, voice steady despite trembling hands. "He looked... different. Like something had snapped inside. The way he moved, the look in his eyes—I was scared."

John watched the jurors absorb every detail—the slight shifts in posture, the furrowed brows. They were seeing what he'd seen for years: a predator hiding in plain sight.

Then the defense attorney stood, and the atmosphere shifted. He moved with measured calm, his voice smooth and dangerously reasonable.

"Ladies and gentlemen," he began, approaching the jury box slowly. "Anger isn't a crime. Suspicion isn't proof. Where's the evidence?" He let the question hang. "Yes, Mick Garrett has a temper. Yes, he's made mistakes. But mistakes aren't murder."

He looked each juror in the eye. "No fingerprints. No DNA. No direct link to this tragic death. The prosecution asks you to convict based on fear and assumption."

They're buying it, John thought, a knot tightening in his stomach. He's twisting the truth, and they're eating it up.

The defense attorney pressed on. "The prosecution weaves coincidences into a tale of guilt. They want you to see a monster because it's easier than accepting that sometimes, bad things happen without clear reason."

John's stomach churned. He saw doubt creeping into the jurors' faces, the way they glanced at Mick with less certainty. The defense was spinning reasonable doubt like a web, each word strategically placed.

Deliberations dragged on for days, each hour adding weight to John's shoulders. When the jury finally returned, their expressions told the story before the verdict was read. They looked worn, haunted by indecision.

The judge's voice cut through the heavy silence. "Ladies and gentlemen, as you are unable to reach a unanimous verdict, I declare a mistrial."

The words struck John like a blow. His vision narrowed, focusing on Mick. He caught a fleeting smirk—a flash of triumph before his face settled back into neutrality. John's blood boiled.

The prosecutor stood, voice strained. "Your Honor, given the severity of the charges and Mr. Garrett's history, we request he remain in custody pending retrial."

"Objection!" The defense attorney shot up. "My client has not been convicted. To hold him would violate his rights."

John watched the exchange, heart pounding. The judge deliberated, then delivered the decision.

"Mr. Garrett will be released under conditions: weekly check-ins, surrender of passport, and restricted travel."

John barely registered the specifics. He watched Mick adjust his suit jacket with deliberate care, a subtle smile playing at his lips. Their eyes met across the room. In that instant, John saw not relief but calculated control.

As Mick walked toward the exit, time seemed to slow. Each step echoed like a countdown. Passing John's row, Mick gave the slightest nod—a silent taunt.

Rage surged in John's chest. Muscles tensed, ready to act, but Ramirez's firm hand on his arm held him back.

"Not here," Ramirez warned quietly. "Not like this."

John's jaw tightened, but he sank back into his seat. The courtroom emptied slowly, the murmur of voices fading as people filed out. The prosecutor gathered his papers with a resigned sigh, already preparing for the next battle.

"We'll get him next time," Ramirez said, trying to sound optimistic. "The evidence is strong. We just need to present it better."

John stood, tension radiating from him. "There shouldn't have to be a next time," he muttered. "He's walking free because we couldn't make them see."

Sunlight streamed through the windows, casting long shadows. John stared at the empty defense table, replaying every moment, every misstep. Mick hadn't shown relief—he'd shown satisfaction. Like a man confident he'd beaten the system.

"This isn't over," John whispered, more to himself than Ramirez.

They stepped outside into the harsh afternoon light. The city buzzed around them, oblivious to the failure that weighed on John's shoulders. Mick Garrett was free, and the justice John sought seemed further away than ever.

But beneath the frustration, a steely resolve hardened. Mick thought he'd won. Thought he was untouchable. John vowed silently that he was wrong.

He slid into his car, the engine rumbling to life. Across the street, Mick climbed into a waiting vehicle, casting a final glance in John's direction.

Not by a long shot, John thought, pulling into traffic.

A sharp rap on his office door pulled John back to the present. He blinked away the memories, his eyes refocusing on the reflection in the window.

Ramirez stood in the doorway, concern etched on his face.

"You alright?" Ramirez asked softly.

John nodded, though the weight of the past still pressed heavily upon him. "Just thinking."

Ramirez stepped inside, closing the door behind him. "About the trial?"

"Can't help but wonder if we're making the same mistakes," John admitted. "Mick slipped through our fingers then. What if it's happening again?"

"We've got new evidence this time," Ramirez reminded him. "But I get it. Something feels off."

John sighed, running a hand through his hair. "Back then, I was so sure we had him. But the jury didn't see it. And now, with everything Claire's been saying..."

Ramirez leaned against the desk. "Claire's got good instincts, but so do you. We can't second-guess ourselves at every turn."

"Maybe," John conceded. "But I can't shake the feeling that we're missing something. That there's more to this than just Mick."

Ramirez regarded him thoughtfully. "Maybe it's time we look at things from a different angle. Re-examine the evidence with fresh eyes."

John met his gaze. "Agreed. We can't afford to let the past blind us."

The two men sat in contemplative silence for a moment, the hum of the city outside the only sound.

"You know," Ramirez began, choosing his words carefully, "it's not just about Mick. It's about Sam, too."

John's jaw tightened, but he didn't look away. "I know."

"Carrying this alone won't bring her back," Ramirez said gently. "Maybe it's time to let others in. Let us help you carry the weight."

John looked down at his hands, the memories of the trial still raw. "I just want justice," he whispered.

"And we'll find it," Ramirez assured him. "Together."

John took a deep breath, feeling a measure of the burden lift. "Alright. Let's get to work."

He stood, reaching for the case files spread across his desk. The past had haunted him long enough. It was time to confront it head-on, with open eyes and a clear mind.

As they delved back into the investigation, John couldn't help but glance once more at the window, where his reflection merged with the city's lights. The game wasn't over, but this time, he was determined to play it differently.

This time, he wouldn't let the past repeat itself.

CHAPTER 16
THE WEIGHT OF TRUTH

The conference room was cloaked in a heavy silence, punctuated only by the soft hum of the air conditioning and the occasional rustle of paper. Fluorescent lights cast a cold glare over the scattered files and photographs strewn across the large table. John sat at the head, his eyes fixed on a single photograph—Sam's smiling face, forever frozen in time.

He traced the edges of the photo with a calloused thumb, the familiar ache in his chest tightening. The case files surrounding him were a mosaic of pain and unanswered questions, each one a piece of a puzzle that refused to come together.

Ramirez leaned over the table, his brow furrowed as he sifted through reports. A deep crease had settled between his eyebrows—a testament to hours spent searching for connections that remained elusive. "There's got to be something we're missing," he muttered, frustration clear in the tightness of his shoulders.

Claire sat opposite John, her sharp eyes scanning over a series of crime scene photographs. She tapped a finger thoughtfully on one of the images. "The similarities are too precise to ignore," she said quietly. "The binding techniques, the positioning—they're identical across the cases."

John glanced up, shadows under his eyes betraying the weight he carried. "But Mick Garrett's never been connected to Emily Reardon's disappearance," he replied, his voice rough around the edges. "He has an alibi for the time she went missing. No overlaps, no connections."

Claire met his gaze, a hint of concern flickering across her face. "It's possible we're dealing with someone else," she suggested. "Someone who knows the details of both cases intimately."

Ramirez looked up from the files, skepticism etched into his features. "An inside man?" he asked, the words heavy with implication. "That's a hell of an accusation."

"Not necessarily an officer," Claire clarified, her tone measured. "But someone with access. The missing pages from Emily's file, the misplaced evidence—it's too much to be coincidence."

John's jaw tightened. The thought of a mole within their ranks made his skin crawl, but he couldn't deny the possibility. He leaned back in his chair, rubbing a hand over his face as he stared at the cluttered table. "So we're looking for someone with knowledge of the cases and the means to manipulate the evidence."

A heavy silence settled over them, the weight of the implications pressing down like a physical force.

Suddenly, the door swung open, and Matt Lawson stepped inside, his expression grave. "Got the DNA results back," he announced, holding up a sealed envelope.

John straightened, the tension in the room sharpening. "And?"

Matt hesitated before speaking, his eyes flickering briefly to Claire and Ramirez. "The blood on Mick Garrett's jacket—it doesn't match Sarah Thompson."

A flicker of confusion crossed Ramirez's face. "Then whose is it?" he asked, urgency creeping into his voice.

Matt's gaze shifted to John. "It's a match for Emily Reardon."

The air seemed to thicken, the gravity of the revelation sinking in. John felt a cold knot form in his stomach. "That doesn't make sense," he said slowly.

"Emily disappeared years ago. How could her blood end up on Mick's jacket?"

Claire's eyes narrowed in thought, her mind racing through possibilities. "Unless someone planted it there," she said. "To frame Mick and throw us off the real trail."

Ramirez shook his head, disbelief evident. "But who would go to such lengths? And why?"

John's mind raced, piecing together fragments of information. The missing files, the inconsistencies, the too-perfect evidence. An unsettling suspicion began to form. "Someone who's been one step ahead of us this whole time," he murmured, more to himself than to the others.

Claire leaned forward, her gaze intense. "We need to consider the possibility that the killer is manipulating the investigation from within."

Ramirez exhaled sharply, crossing his arms. "You think it's one of our own?" he asked, his tone laced with skepticism.

"Not necessarily," Claire replied, choosing her words carefully. "But someone with access to our processes, our evidence. Someone who knows how we operate and can anticipate our moves."

John clenched his fists under the table, frustration boiling beneath the surface. The thought of a traitor in their midst ignited a fierce anger. "We need to re-examine everything," he said firmly. "From the ground up. No assumptions."

Matt shifted uncomfortably by the door. "I'll start reviewing the lab records," he offered, his usual confidence wavering slightly. "See if there's any irregularities."

John nodded, appreciating the initiative. "Good. And we keep this between us," he added, his gaze sweeping over the team. "If there's a leak, we can't risk alerting them."

The others exchanged glances, a mix of determination and unease settling over them. Ramirez rubbed the back of his neck, tension evident in the set of his shoulders. "Agreed," he said finally. "We'll be careful."

As they began to gather their materials, Claire lingered, her eyes resting on John. She seemed to weigh her words before speaking. "John, are you holding up okay?"

He avoided her gaze, focusing on stacking the files into a neat pile. "I'm fine," he replied tersely.

She didn't press further, but her concern was palpable. "We're here if you need anything," she said softly, her voice barely above a whisper.

John paused, the weight of her words settling over him like a heavy blanket. He glanced up, meeting her eyes for a brief moment. "Thanks," he said quietly, the word carrying more weight than usual.

As the team dispersed, the conference room emptied, leaving John alone amidst the scattered remnants of their investigation. The fluorescent lights buzzed faintly overhead, casting harsh shadows that seemed to mirror the turmoil within him.

He reached into his pocket, pulling out the worn photograph of Sam. Her eyes sparkled with life, a stark contrast to the emptiness he felt inside. Memories flooded his mind—her laughter, the way she used to curl up on the couch with a book, the last conversation they had. Regret gnawed at him, an ever-present companion.

"I'm not going to let you down again," he whispered, his voice barely audible in the empty room. The promise hung in the air, a silent vow that he clung to desperately.

He gathered the files, determination hardening his features. The path ahead was fraught with uncertainty, but he was resolute. Whoever was behind this had made it personal, and he would stop at nothing to bring them to justice.

As he left the conference room, the corridor stretched before him, the fluorescent lights casting long shadows that danced along the walls. The precinct bustled with activity—phones ringing, voices murmuring, the distant sound of laughter—but it all felt distant, removed.

John made his way to his office, the familiar surroundings offering little comfort. He sat at his desk, opening the case files once more. His eyes scanned over reports, photographs, witness statements—each piece a potential clue, each detail a thread that might unravel the tangled web they were caught in.

A knock at the door drew his attention. Ramirez stood in the doorway, a cup of coffee in hand. "Figured you could use this," he said, offering it to John.

John accepted it with a nod. "Thanks."

Ramirez pulled up a chair, sitting across from him. He studied John's face for a moment before speaking. "Hell of a day," he remarked, his tone laden with understatement.

"That's one way to put it," John replied, a hint of wry humor in his voice.

They sat in companionable silence, the weight of the day's revelations settling between them like a dense fog.

"You really think someone on the inside is involved?" Ramirez asked finally, his gaze steady.

John took a sip of the bitter coffee, considering his response. "I think we can't rule anything out," he said. "Too many things aren't adding up. Missing evidence, misplaced files—either we're dealing with gross incompetence, or someone's manipulating us."

Ramirez nodded slowly, his expression thoughtful. "It's a hard pill to swallow," he admitted. "But if it's true, we need to root it out."

"Agreed," John said. "But we have to be careful. We don't know who we can trust."

Ramirez leaned back in his chair, crossing his arms. "You know I've got your back," he said firmly. "We'll figure this out."

John managed a faint smile. "I know. And I appreciate it."

As Ramirez left, John returned his focus to the files. The hours stretched on as he delved deeper, notes filling the margins of reports, timelines sprawling across pages pinned to the wall. He traced connections, circled inconsistencies, and highlighted anything that seemed out of place.

The night wore on, but John remained undeterred. The glow of the desk lamp cast a pool of light amidst the darkness, illuminating the determined set of his features. The precinct quieted as the night shift settled in, the bustle of the day giving way to a calmer rhythm.

A soft knock interrupted his concentration. Claire stood in the doorway, a folder tucked under her arm. "Still at it?" she asked, a hint of a smile tugging at her lips.

"Can't sleep," he admitted, leaning back in his chair.

She stepped inside, closing the door behind her. "I found something that might interest you," she said, laying the folder on his desk.

He opened it to find a detailed analysis of the binding techniques used in the murders. "What am I looking at?" he asked, scanning the pages.

"An expert in knot theory reviewed the patterns," she explained. "These knots are not just identical—they're specialized. Used primarily by a specific branch of the military."

John's eyes widened slightly. "Meaning our suspect could have a military background."

"Exactly," Claire confirmed. "It's a narrow field. We can cross-reference personnel records."

A spark of hope flickered within him. "This could be the break we need."

She nodded, her expression mirroring his resolve. "I thought you'd want to know right away."

"Thank you," he said sincerely. "Your insight is invaluable."

She gave a modest shrug. "Just doing my part."

They shared a brief moment of understanding—a silent acknowledgment of the stakes involved and the personal demons each was battling.

As she turned to leave, she paused at the door. "Don't push yourself too hard," she advised gently. "We need you sharp."

He offered a small smile. "I'll try."

When she was gone, John leaned back, exhaling slowly. The pieces were beginning to align, but the picture was still incomplete. The possibility of a military connection added a new dimension, one that could narrow their search significantly.

He pinned the new information to the wall, stepping back to survey the array of notes and photographs. Threads connected various points, forming a web of leads and theories. His eyes lingered on a photograph of Mick Garrett, then shifted to an image of Emily Reardon. The questions swirled—who was orchestrating this? And why?

A sense of determination settled over him. The path was murky, the enemy unseen, but he would not falter. Not this time.

He glanced once more at the photograph of Sam on his desk. Her eyes seemed to gaze back at him, a silent reminder of what he was fighting for.

"I won't let you down," he promised again, the words firm.

As dawn approached, John remained at his desk, the first light of morning creeping through the blinds. The city stirred to life outside, oblivious to the battles waged in quiet offices and shadowed corners.

CHAPTER 17
GAME IN MOTION

Dawn crept through the threadbare curtains of Mick Garrett's bungalow like an unwelcome intruder. Pale light revealed a living room drowning in decay—peeling wallpaper curling away from the walls, carpet worn to threads beneath years of pacing feet. The stench of stale cigarettes mingled with something more insidious, a sour note of desperation and defeat.

Outside, engines idled with predatory patience. But Mick, locked in his private panic, pressed his cell phone harder against his ear, as if it might offer escape.

"Listen to me," he hissed, his whisper carrying an edge of raw fear. "I don't care what it takes. Get over here now. They're coming." His bare feet traced silent circles on the worn floorboards as his eyes darted to the window, where the dark silhouettes of unmarked police cars lurked like waiting wolves.

The door exploded inward with a sound like thunder, showering splinters across the entry. Morning light flooded the room as tactical officers poured through the breach, their movements precise and practiced, weapons held at the ready. A red laser sight danced across dusty family photos, marking memories Mick had failed to preserve.

"Police! Search warrant!" The lead officer's voice cut through the stagnant air, sharp as broken glass.

Mick's head snapped up, his eyes wide with the wild recognition of cornered prey. His gaze locked onto Detective John DiMatteo as he stepped through the ruined doorway, badge catching the early light, face set with the grim satisfaction of a hunter closing in.

"What the hell is this?" Mick's voice cracked as he shoved his phone deep into his pocket. The tremor in his hands betrayed the bravado in his words.

John surveyed the room with cold precision, deliberately avoiding Mick's desperate stare. "Secure the perimeter," he ordered, each word clipped and final. "Search everything. We're looking for anything connecting Garrett to Sarah Thompson—clothing, fibers, personal effects. Nothing gets overlooked."

Ramirez appeared at his shoulder, a dark shadow directing officers through the house with silent gestures. The search team moved like a well-oiled machine, methodically dismantling Mick's world. Drawers crashed open, closet doors banged against walls, furniture scraped across floors. The cacophony of invasion filled the small house, drowning out the morning birds beyond the broken door.

Color flooded Mick's face, rage warring with fear beneath his skin. "You can't do this!" He lurched toward John, fists balled at his sides. "This is harassment, pure and simple!"

"Back off, Mick." John's voice dropped to a dangerous whisper, his eyes finally meeting Garrett's. "We've got the warrant. Don't make me add resisting to the charges."

"Charges?" Mick's laugh held an edge of hysteria. "Based on what—your obsession? Your personal vendetta? Everyone knows you've been gunning for me since day one, DiMatteo. Everyone."

John's jaw clenched, but his voice remained steady. "This isn't personal. This is about justice for Sarah Thompson."

"Justice?" The word dripped with venom as Mick took another step forward. "You wouldn't know justice if it—"

"Detective." Ramirez cut through the tension, positioning himself between them with practiced ease. "Mr. Garrett, take a seat. Let us do our job."

Mick retreated a half-step, pulling his phone back out. "My lawyer will bury you for this," he snarled, fingers stabbing at the keypad.

"Make your call," John replied, turning his attention to the search. But he caught the slight tremor in Mick's hands, the sweat beading at his temples. Something about Garrett's panic felt wrong—too pronounced, too performative.

The search intensified, each officer meticulously documenting their findings. Mick paced near the kitchen table, muttering threats into his phone while shooting venomous glances at the invasion of his space. The morning light strengthened, illuminating years of accumulated grime and secrets.

"Detective!" Officer Daniels' voice cut through the chaos, sharp with discovery. "Back bedroom!"

John exchanged a quick glance with Ramirez before moving down the narrow hallway. The bedroom stretched before them, a study in calculated disorder—sheets twisted into ropes on an unmade bed, clothes scattered with too-perfect randomness, a television flickering silent blue shadows across the walls. Daniels stood by a closet, holding up a dark blue canvas jacket like a trophy.

John's pulse quickened as he approached. Time seemed to slow as he took the jacket, his trained eyes immediately finding the jagged tear along the left sleeve. Dried mud caked the edges, but beneath it, something darker stained the fabric—a rusty brown that spoke of violence.

"Blood?" Ramirez breathed, leaning in close.

John pulled out his phone, fingers steady as he brought up the crime scene photos. The piece of fabric they'd found snagged on barbed wire near Sarah's body had haunted his dreams. He held the jacket's torn sleeve against the image, and the match sang out like a struck bell—the distinctive weave pattern, the unique thread count, even the angle of the tear aligned with devastating precision.

"This is it," John said, his voice tight with controlled triumph. "Get it logged and bagged. I want the lab processing this within the hour."

They returned to the living room, where Mick's phone conversation died mid-sentence at the sight of the evidence bag. "What the hell do you think you've found?" His attempt at dismissive anger couldn't mask the fear threading through his words.

John held up the sealed bag, letting the morning light illuminate their prize. "Look familiar, Mick?"

Mick's eyes darted to the jacket and away, like a guilty man unable to face his crimes. "It's just a jacket. I've got dozens. What's your point?"

"The point," Ramirez cut in, "is that this particular jacket has a tear matching fabric we found at Sarah Thompson's murder scene. Want to explain that coincidence?"

"This is insane." Sweat tracked down Mick's temple despite the morning chill. "You're trying to set me up. Again. This is all just another DiMatteo special, isn't it?"

"Mick Garrett," John's voice carried the weight of years of pursuit, "you're under arrest for the murder of Sarah Thompson."

Rage twisted Mick's face into something feral. "You think this will stick?" He backed away as Officer Daniels approached with handcuffs. "You're delusional, DiMatteo! This is exactly what happened last time—you seeing what you want to see!"

The front door burst open again, flooding the room with gray morning light. Richards, Mick's attorney, filled the doorway in his thousand-dollar suit, righteous indignation radiating from every pore. His presence changed the atmosphere instantly, turning a police raid into a chess match.

"Detective DiMatteo." Richards' voice dripped with professional disdain. "Harassing my client again? Some habits die hard, don't they?"

"Your client is being arrested based on physical evidence linking him to Sarah Thompson's murder." John met the lawyer's gaze without flinching. "He has the right to remain silent—though I see he's already exercising his right to counsel."

"Evidence?" Richards moved deeper into the room, his expensive shoes crunching over splinters from the broken door. "You mean another circumstantial witch hunt? More coincidences twisted to fit your obsession?"

"The evidence speaks for itself," John replied, his calm masking the storm beneath. "Your client can explain the blood-stained jacket to a jury."

Mick struggled as Daniels secured the handcuffs, his composure crumbling. "They're setting me up, Richards! Just like before!"

"Don't say another word, Mick." Richards' tone could have frozen hell. "Detective, I suggest you think very carefully about your next moves. False arrest, harassment, civil rights violations—I'm sure these terms are familiar to you by now."

"Very," John said, watching as his officers led Mick toward the door. "And I'm equally familiar with what constitutes solid evidence. Your client can save his performance for court."

As they passed each other, Mick leaned close to John, his voice a poisonous whisper. "This isn't over, DiMatteo. When I'm done, you'll wish you'd never heard my name."

John stood his ground, meeting Mick's gaze with steel in his own. "The evidence will speak for itself, Mick. That's what scares you, isn't it?"

Outside, gray clouds pressed down on the neighborhood like a closing fist. Curious faces peered from behind curtains, neighbors drinking in the spectacle of Mick Garrett's arrest. Whispers rippled down the quiet street, tomorrow's gossip taking root.

Ramirez joined John at the curb as they watched the patrol car pull away, Mick's silhouette growing smaller in the back seat. Rain threatened overhead, matching John's darkening mood.

"Think we finally got him?" Ramirez's question carried more weight than its simple words suggested.

John crossed his arms against the chill, watching until the patrol car disappeared around the corner. "The jacket puts him at the scene. The blood evidence, if it matches Sarah's DNA..." He let the sentence hang unfinished.

"But?" Ramirez knew his partner too well to miss the doubt in his voice.

"It feels wrong." John ran a hand through his hair, frustration evident in every movement. "Mick's smart, Ramirez. Slippery. In five years, he's never left evidence this obvious. Why start now?"

"Everyone slips eventually," Ramirez offered, though his tone suggested he shared John's unease. "Maybe the pressure got to him."

"Or maybe someone wants us to think that." John turned to survey Mick's house, its shabby exterior somehow more ominous in the growing gloom. "I want the lab to fast-track everything. Every fiber, every blood drop. If there's any chance this is staged, we need to know."

John pulled out his phone, thumb hovering over Sarah Thompson's mother's number. The weight of responsibility pressed down on him like the threatening rain clouds above. Making this call meant offering hope—hope that could shatter if his instincts about the evidence proved right.

The line rang twice before Mrs. Thompson answered, her voice thin with exhaustion. "Hello?"

"Mrs. Thompson, this is Detective DiMatteo." He softened his tone, remembering all too well how these calls felt from the other side. "We've made an arrest in Sarah's case."

The sharp intake of breath carried years of pain and desperate hope. "You... you have someone?"

"Yes, ma'am. We've found evidence linking a suspect to Sarah's murder. I wanted you to hear it from me before the news breaks."

Silence stretched across the phone line, heavy with unspoken questions. "Is it... are you sure it's him?" Mrs. Thompson's voice trembled with cautious hope.

"We're following the evidence," John replied carefully, unwilling to promise certainties he suddenly doubted. "I'll keep you informed of every development."

"Thank you," she whispered, emotion thickening her words. "For not giving up on Sarah."

The call ended, leaving John standing in the growing drizzle, the weight of her gratitude pressing against his chest like lead. Behind him, the forensics team continued documenting the scene, their cameras flashing like silent lightning in Mick's emptied house.

Ramirez approached, his footsteps squelching in the gathering puddles. "Lab's already processing the jacket. They're making it priority."

John nodded, unable to shake the creeping unease that had settled in his gut. This arrest should have felt triumphant—a victory years in the making. Instead, questions multiplied in his mind like shadows at dusk.

Later, the precinct hummed with controlled chaos. John sat at his desk, surrounded by case files and preliminary reports, searching for something he couldn't name. The jacket lay at the center of everything—too perfect a piece of evidence, too conveniently discovered.

"Initial blood typing matches Sarah's," Ramirez announced, dropping a fresh report on John's desk. "DNA results pending, but it's looking solid."

John opened the folder without enthusiasm. "Mick's alibi?"

"Holds up except for those two hours." Ramirez settled into the chair opposite John's desk. "More than enough time to do it."

"Or enough time to create reasonable doubt." John rubbed his temples, fighting a growing headache. "The jacket was sitting there in plain sight, Ramirez. Like it was waiting for us."

"You think someone planted it?"

"I think Mick's played this game before." John's phone buzzed, drawing his attention to a text from an unknown number. The message made his blood run cold:

Congratulations detective. It looks like you finally got your man.

He forwarded the message to tech, knowing they'd find no trace of its origin. The sender was too careful for that, too deliberate—just like the evidence they'd found today.

"What is it?" Ramirez asked, noting John's expression.

"Someone's watching us," John said quietly. "Someone who knows exactly what we'll find and how we'll react." He closed the folder, decision crystallizing in his mind. "We need to dig deeper. Re-interview every witness. Check every timeline. If this is a setup, we need to know before we go to trial."

Rain drummed against the windows, casting wavering shadows across the office. Somewhere out there, someone was orchestrating events with terrifying precision. The jacket might have given them Mick Garrett, but John's instincts screamed that they were missing something bigger—something darker.

As night settled over the city, John stared at the text message again, understanding dawning with chilling clarity. They hadn't caught their killer today.

They'd just become part of their game.

CHAPTER 18
INNER DARKNESS

The interrogation room's fluorescent lights cast harsh shadows across Mick Garrett's face as officers led him inside. His cuffed hands hung loose before him in an oddly casual pose, setting off warning signals in John's mind. Mick's expression—that barely concealed smirk, the calculated gleam in his eyes—spoke of someone who knew exactly how to play this game.

John straightened, muscles coiled beneath his practiced calm. The familiar sight of Mick in custody stirred something dark inside him, a rage he'd spent years trying to contain. But there was something different this time, something in Mick's expression that set John's teeth on edge. Mick didn't look like a man caught—he looked like a predator waiting for the perfect moment to strike.

Mick's gaze locked onto John, his lips twisting into a bitter smile that felt more like a challenge than surrender. "Got nothing new for me, DiMatteo?" His voice carried a mocking edge. "Same song and dance as last time? Or did you at least come up with some fresh lies to throw at me?"

John took a measured step forward, every muscle in his body screaming for action. Behind him, Ramirez cleared his throat—a quiet warning John chose to ignore. The air between them crackled with years of unfinished business.

"You want to talk about lies, Mick?" John's voice dropped to a low, dangerous tone. "Let's talk about the jacket we found in your house. The one with Sarah Thompson's blood on it. Want to explain that away?"

Mick's laugh cut through the room like broken glass. "A jacket? That's what you're hanging this frame job on?" He leaned forward, chains rattling softly. "You really think I'm stupid enough to keep evidence lying around my house? Come on, Detective. You can do better than that."

"The evidence speaks for itself," Ramirez cut in, his diplomatic tone a stark contrast to the charged atmosphere. "We've got your jacket with Sarah's blood on the sleeve, the tear matching fabric from the crime scene. This isn't just speculation anymore, Mick."

Mick settled back in his chair, something dangerous flickering behind his eyes. The overhead light caught the silver of his handcuffs as he spread his hands in a gesture of mock surrender. "You want to know what this really is?" His voice dropped lower, taking on an edge that made the air feel thick. "This is DiMatteo's obsession playing out all over again. You're so desperate to pin something on me, you can't even see when you're being played."

John's pulse thundered in his ears, his control slipping. "Being played? The only one playing games here is you, Mick. First Sam, now Sarah—"

"John." Ramirez's warning came sharp and clear, but it was too late.

"There it is." Mick's smile widened, revealing teeth. "Always comes back to Sam, doesn't it? You couldn't prove anything then, and you won't prove anything now. Because you're seeing what you want to see, Detective. Just like last time."

The muscles in John's jaw worked as he fought to contain the explosion building in his chest. Mick knew exactly which buttons to push, how to dig beneath his professional veneer to the raw wounds beneath.

The door opened, cutting through the tension. Claire entered, her presence shifting the room's dynamics. She moved with deliberate calm, her eyes taking in every detail—John's barely contained rage, Mick's calculated performance, the subtle undercurrents that threatened to pull them all under.

"I need a moment with him," she said, her voice carrying quiet authority. "Alone."

John started to protest, but something in Claire's expression made him pause. She wasn't just offering to interrogate Mick—she was throwing him a lifeline, a chance to step back before he crossed a line he couldn't uncross.

"Let her work," Ramirez murmured, already moving toward the door. "We both know where this is heading if we stay."

Reluctantly, John stepped back, though the frustration was evident in his rigid posture. He crossed his arms, eyes burning into Mick from across the room.

Claire took the seat across from Mick, her movements unhurried, precise. The room felt different with just the two of them—the rage and history that had crackled between Mick and John replaced by something more clinical, more calculating.

"I'm not here to replay old arguments, Mick." She placed her hands flat on the table, studying him with the practiced eye of someone who read killers for a living. "I want to understand something. You say you're being framed. Tell me how."

Mick's demeanor shifted subtly. The performative defiance he'd aimed at John mellowed into something more contemplative. "You're the profiler, right?" He leaned forward, lowering his voice. "Then you already know this doesn't fit. Someone's orchestrating this, making it look like me. And they're doing a damn good job."

"How so?" Claire kept her tone neutral, encouraging.

"Think about it." Mick's eyes gleamed with dark intelligence. "The jacket shows up in my house—evidence so perfect it might as well have gift wrapping. Blood, tears, all matching exactly what you need to find. Since when do killers leave breadcrumbs that convenient?"

Behind the one-way glass, John watched, his fists clenched at his sides. But even he couldn't deny the unsettling logic in Mick's words.

"The person doing this," Mick continued, "they know police procedure. They understand evidence. Hell, they probably know DiMatteo better than he knows himself—knew exactly how he'd react, exactly where to lead him." A bitter smile crossed his face. "I'm just the convenient monster you all need me to be."

Claire sat back slightly, her mind working through the implications. "You're suggesting someone with inside knowledge of law enforcement."

"I'm suggesting," Mick's voice dropped to barely above a whisper, "that while you're all focused on me, the real killer is watching. Probably laughing. Maybe even from inside this building."

Before Claire could pursue this thread, the door burst open. Mick's lawyer stormed in, face flushed with righteous indignation. But Claire barely noticed him. Her attention had caught on something in Mick's expression—not fear of prosecution, but genuine unease about something else. Someone else.

The moment shattered as an officer appeared in the doorway, holding up a report like a weapon. "Lab results on the jacket," he announced, his voice cutting through the charged atmosphere. "Tear patterns match the crime scene fabric. One hundred percent confirmation."

John moved back into the room, triumph and doubt warring in his expression. The evidence they'd been waiting for had arrived, yet something in Claire's face made his victory feel hollow.

Mick's composure cracked, just for a moment—not with fear of being caught, but with something that looked almost like resignation. "You can't do this," he muttered, more to himself than anyone else. "Not again."

"It's over, Garrett." John stepped closer, his voice hard with years of pent-up frustration. "No more games. No more manipulation."

Mick's lawyer intervened, positioning himself between his client and John. "This interview is done. If you're making an arrest, do it properly. We'll be filing for bail immediately."

But Mick's attention had fixed on Claire, his eyes carrying a message she couldn't quite decipher. "You see it, don't you?" His voice dropped low enough that only she could hear. "The pieces that don't fit. The shadows moving behind the scenes. Be careful, Dr. Harper. Some monsters wear badges."

The officers moved in to secure Mick, the routine of arrest playing out with mechanical precision. But Claire sat motionless, her mind racing through the implications of his words. The profile she'd built of Sarah's killer clashed violently with the man they were leading away in handcuffs.

"We got him," Ramirez said, relief evident in his voice. "It's finally over."

John nodded, but his eyes met Claire's across the room. Something passed between them—an unspoken understanding that this victory might be masking a deeper, darker truth.

"We'll see," John muttered, watching as Mick disappeared down the hallway. Even in defeat, Mick's final glance back carried no fear, only a knowing look that chilled Claire to her core.

The interrogation room emptied, leaving behind the heavy silence of unresolved questions. Claire gathered her notes, her fingers brushing across the profile she'd built of Sarah's killer—methodical, precise, someone who understood evidence and police procedure intimately. Someone who could orchestrate not just a murder, but an entire investigation.

As she left the room, Claire felt the weight of unseen eyes following her. Mick's words echoed in her mind: *Some monsters wear badges.* She thought of the missing pages from Emily's file, the convenient evidence, the perfect trail of breadcrumbs leading them exactly where someone wanted them to go.

They had their suspect in custody, but Claire couldn't shake the feeling that the real killer was still out there, watching their every move. And perhaps, most terrifyingly, watching from much closer than any of them realized.

The precinct buzzed around her with the energy of a case nearly closed, but Claire knew better.

This wasn't the end.

CHAPTER 19
BAD OMENS

Storm clouds gathered outside John's office window, mirroring his darkening thoughts. His fingers traced the edges of the crime scene photos spread across his desk, but his mind saw beyond them—past the clinical evidence to the pattern that had haunted him for years. Mick Garrett was in a cell downstairs, but the taste of victory was bitter, laced with doubts that refused to settle.

Ramirez's footsteps in the doorway broke the heavy silence. "Judge denied bail." His voice was flat, as if delivering news that should feel like triumph but somehow fell short. "Mick's staying put."

John's jaw tightened, the muscle working beneath his skin. "It won't be enough," he said, his voice rough with years of bitter experience. "A decent defense attorney will shred this case to pieces without something more concrete."

"I know." Ramirez settled against the doorframe, exhaustion etched in the lines around his eyes. "The jacket, the blood evidence—it's all circumstantial. Strong circumstantial, but still..."

Their shared silence carried the weight of too many similar moments. Sarah and Sam—the names blurred together in John's mind, a litany of almost-justice that kept slipping through his fingers like smoke. A nagging feeling told him they were moving according to someone else's plan, following rules they couldn't see.

The door opened again, and Claire stepped in, bringing a stack of files and a look of quiet urgency. She took in John's posture—the way he seemed to fold in on himself, shadows gathering behind his eyes—and recognized the dangerous ground he was treading. She'd seen it before in detectives when cases became too personal, when the past threatened to swallow the present whole.

"John." Her voice cut through his spiral with surgical precision. "There's something you need to see."

He forced himself to focus as Claire spread the documents across his desk. She pointed to a set of document numbers, each gap in the sequence telling its own story. "Someone's been systematically removing evidence from both cases," she said quietly. "Not random losses or misfilings—calculated deletions."

The implication hit John like a punch to the gut. He leaned forward, studying the documentation anew, his instincts flaring to life. "How deep does it go?"

"Deeper than it should be possible." Claire lowered her voice, though they were alone in the office. "I reached out to Chicago PD's evidence room. Emily Reardon's case file has been gutted. Her personal journal, security footage from the night she vanished—everything critical is gone."

John's pulse quickened. Evidence didn't just disappear like this—not without help. "The journal—what did it contain?"

"According to the original log, Emily documented her concerns about someone on campus who made her uncomfortable. But every page that might have identified that person is gone. Like they never existed."

"And the security footage?"

"Time-stamped and logged into evidence the night Emily disappeared. It showed everyone who entered or left her dorm during those hours." Claire's fingers tapped a slow rhythm on his desk. "Now it's just an empty evidence bag with a perfectly documented chain of custody that leads nowhere."

The implications churned in John's gut. This wasn't sloppy record-keeping or bureaucratic incompetence. It was surgical—precise removals by someone who knew exactly what to take and how to make it look routine.

"We're not just looking at evidence tampering," he said, pushing back from his desk, as if distance might give him clarity. "We're looking at someone who knows both departments inside and out. Someone with the access and knowledge to make things disappear without raising flags."

"Someone who's been playing a very long game," Claire agreed. "Patient enough to wait years between Emily's disappearance and Sarah's murder. Careful enough to cover their tracks at every step."

John's mind raced through the possibilities. Someone with access to both cases, someone who had moved seamlessly between them. His thoughts kept circling back to the same possibility, but he couldn't say it—not yet.

"The only people who could've tampered with that evidence would have to be—"

"Someone in law enforcement or close to it," Claire finished. "But even that doesn't narrow it down enough."

John exhaled, frustration gnawing at him. The connections were there, but the pieces refused to fall into place. Whoever had tampered with Emily's case had been meticulous and careful. And now Sarah was dead because she got too close.

"We need to focus on who had access to both of these cases," John said, his voice grim. "The missing evidence, the similarities between the murders— someone is pulling the strings here. And it's not Mick Garrett."

Claire nodded. "We'll find them, John. But we can't ignore what's in front of us. If someone's covering their tracks this well, they'll slip up eventually."

John's gaze shifted to the storm clouds outside, casting the office in a cold, muted gray. The winds had picked up, and snow and ice were beginning to fall—a warning of what was coming.

The office door opened again, and Matt Lawson stepped inside, bringing a charged tension with him. Claire's posture shifted subtly—a change so slight

John might have missed it if he hadn't been trained to notice such things. Matt held a thick manila folder, his grip precise, his face professionally neutral.

"Lab results," Matt announced, laying the folder on John's desk with careful deliberation. "We analyzed the soil and plant material from Garrett's jacket. It's a perfect match to Sarah's crime scene. The soil composition is identical, and we found burdock burrs consistent with the location where her body was discovered."

John opened the folder slowly, but the evidence that should have felt like vindication left him cold. Everything aligned with perfect precision—the soil, the plant material, the blood evidence—like puzzle pieces crafted specifically to fit.

"Everything we need to place Garrett at the scene," Matt continued, his tone matter-of-fact. "The science is conclusive."

"Is it?" John looked up, studying Matt with an intensity he usually reserved for suspects. "It seems almost too perfect, doesn't it? Every piece of evidence leads exactly where we expect it to."

Something flickered behind Matt's carefully controlled expression—a micro-expression so brief John might have imagined it. "You think there's a problem with the forensics?"

"I think," John said, weighing each word, "that we need to look deeper. At everything." He met Claire's eyes, seeing his own suspicions reflected there. "Perfect evidence makes me nervous. Especially when other evidence keeps conveniently disappearing."

The room seemed to tighten, the air thick with unspoken implications. Outside, lightning split the sky, casting harsh shadows across their faces for a brief, revealing moment.

"I can run additional tests," Matt offered, his professional mask firmly in place. "Though I doubt the results will change."

"The results might not," Claire interjected, her voice carrying an edge. "But the questions we're asking might."

"Take another look at everything," John ordered, his voice hardening with resolve. "Every sample, every test result. I want to know what we found and how it got there."

The storm outside intensified, sleet lashing against the windows. John caught the subtle interplay of expressions—Claire's controlled vigilance, Ramirez's growing unease, and Matt's studied neutrality.

"Something about this whole case feels orchestrated," John continued. "Like we're being led down a specific path, shown exactly what someone wants us to see."

Claire moved closer to his desk, positioning herself with deliberate casualness. "The evidence against Mick is perfect," she agreed, her voice pitched low. "Almost like someone knew exactly what we'd be looking for. Exactly what would convince us."

"The science is solid," Matt insisted, but his tone had shifted. "Every test, every analysis—it all points to Garrett."

"Maybe that's the problem." John's words fell like stones into still water. "Maybe it points to him too perfectly."

John looked at each person in turn, acutely aware that if someone inside the department was manipulating the investigation, trust had become a luxury they could no longer afford.

"Review it all," he said, the authority in his voice unmistakable. "Every piece of evidence, every report, every connection between Emily's case and Sarah's. No assumptions, no shortcuts."

Claire gathered her notes with careful precision. "And we keep this close," she added, the warning clear in her tone. "If someone's been orchestrating events from the inside..."

"They'll know we're looking," John finished. He met her gaze, an understanding passing between them. "Maybe they already do."

As Matt left the office, the storm reached its full fury outside. Ice gathered on the windows, distorting the view of the city beyond. Somewhere in the building, phones rang, officers moved through their routines, and life continued as normal.

But nothing was normal anymore. The hunt for Sarah's killer had transformed into something far more dangerous—a search for a predator who walked among them, who knew their procedures, who might be watching their every move.

"Be careful," Claire murmured as she prepared to leave. "All of us. We're not just looking for a killer anymore."

"We're looking for someone who knows exactly how to hide in plain sight," John agreed.

They weren't just investigating a murder anymore—they were unraveling a conspiracy that reached into the heart of their own department.

And somewhere, perhaps closer than any of them realized, their true quarry was watching, waiting, planning their next move in a game that had already claimed too many lives.

CHAPTER 20
UNFORGIVEN

At the precinct, late at night, John traced his fingers over the edges of Sarah Thompson's case file, eyes distant. Outside, a storm raged, casting lightning shadows across the walls. But John barely noticed. His mind was elsewhere, caught in a memory he couldn't shake, a night that had shaped his every step since.

It had been just like this...

The precinct settled into its evening quiet, paperwork and routine masking the violence that lurked beneath the surface of every case. John mechanically signed off on a drug bust report, his mind already drifting toward home. His phone buzzed, Sam's name lighting up the screen. Something about a biology project keeping her late at school—he barely registered the details.

"Be careful," he texted back, the words automatic, thoughtless. A father's reflexive protection, stripped of real meaning by repetition. He assumed she'd be home by the time he finished his shift.

The call came a few hours later.

The hospital's number appeared on his phone, and his world tilted before he even answered. Every cop knew that ring—the one that preceded tragedy, that heralded the moment when the job became brutally personal. His fingers felt numb as he picked up, already slipping into the professional detachment that had become his armor.

"Detective DiMatteo?"

The careful delivery of his name, wrapped in layers of practiced sympathy, told him everything he didn't want to know.

"There's been an incident involving your daughter... She's en route to the hospital. You need to come now."

The facade he'd spent years constructing—the calm, controlled detective—cracked like glass. For endless seconds, he couldn't breathe, couldn't think. The world compressed to a single, terrifying thought: Sam is hurt.

He would never remember the drive to the hospital. Just fragments: keys slipping in his trembling hands, red lights bleeding into the darkness, his white-knuckled grip on the steering wheel as he whispered desperate prayers to a God he wasn't sure he believed in anymore.

Please. Please let her be okay.

The hospital doors parted with a mechanical hiss that seemed to mock the chaos in John's mind. Fluorescent lights assaulted him, too bright, too harsh, transforming the sterile corridors into a maze of blinding white. A nurse appeared, her voice a distant hum as she led him through identical hallways. She was explaining something—about Sam, about what happened—but the words dissolved before they could reach him, lost in the roar of blood in his ears.

Then he saw Helen.

His ex-wife sat crumpled in a waiting room chair, her hands trembling as they twisted together in her lap. Tears had carved pale tracks through her makeup, her eyes red-rimmed and hollow. When she looked up and saw him, fresh grief spilled down her cheeks.

They hadn't spoken in months. Their divorce had left wounds too deep for casual conversation, anger and blame calcified into silence. But now, facing the unthinkable, none of that mattered. The barriers between them crumbled like ash.

"John..." His name escaped her like a broken thing, carrying all the fear and desperation he felt churning in his own chest.

He crossed the space between them in three strides, gathering her into his arms as her knees gave way. They clung to each other, all their past bitterness dissolving in the face of this new, devastating reality. For the first time since their marriage ended, they were truly united—bound by the terrifying possibility of losing the one thing they both loved more than anything.

"She's in trauma," Helen managed between hitching breaths, her words muffled against his shirt. "They're trying, but..." The sentence fractured, the unspoken horror too vast for words.

John held her tighter, his own tears burning unshed behind his eyes. His throat closed around prayers he couldn't voice, pleas he didn't dare speak aloud. Please, God. Not Sam. Not my little girl.

Time lost meaning as they stood there, sharing their fear in silence. The antiseptic hospital air pressed against them, carrying the weight of too many similar moments, too many families waiting for news that would shatter their worlds.

"She'll be okay," John heard himself say, the lie bitter on his tongue. "She's strong. Sam's strong." But his voice betrayed him, cracking on his daughter's name.

Helen pulled back slightly, her tear-filled eyes meeting his. In them, he saw a reflection of his own terror, his own desperate need to believe the empty words. She drew a shuddering breath, her next words barely a whisper.

"You have to find who did this, John." Her fingers dug into his arms, anchoring them both against the tide of grief. "Promise me. Promise me you'll find them."

The request hit him like a physical blow. Throughout their marriage, fixing things had been his role. When things broke, John made them right. But he'd failed at that too—failed their marriage, failed at being there, failed at everything except the job that had stolen him away. And now, facing the ultimate test of his abilities, he felt helpless, stripped of all his certainty.

"I'll find them," he swore, his voice hardening with rage and pain. "I swear to God, Helen, I'll make them pay."

She nodded, clutching that promise like a lifeline. They both knew the odds—had seen too many similar cases, too many grieving families left without answers. But in that moment, his words were all they had.

The waiting room door swung open with terrible finality. A doctor stood there, her face carrying that practiced mask of sympathy that John had seen too many times from the other side. His heart seized in his chest before she even spoke.

"Mr. DiMatteo, Mrs. DiMatteo," she began, the old titles falling like stones between them. "I'm sorry. We did everything we could..."

The rest of her words disappeared into a roar of static. John felt Helen's legs give way and caught her automatically, but his own strength was failing. The world tilted sideways, reality splintering around a truth too horrible to comprehend.

Sam was gone.

Their daughter—their beautiful, bright, fierce Sam—had been taken from them. The doctor's voice continued, explaining medical terms that meant nothing, offering condolences that couldn't touch their pain. None of it mattered. Nothing would ever matter again.

When they finally let them see her, it felt like stepping into a nightmare.

They led them to her room—a sterile chamber where machines stood silent, their screens dark and accusing. Sam lay motionless on the bed, stripped of all her vitality, all her light. Her face bore the pallor of marble, eyes closed as if in sleep, but the violent truth was written in purple and black around her neck— the brutal signature of her killer.

John moved forward on legs that didn't feel like his own. His hand trembled as he reached out to touch her cheek, the cold of her skin shattering something fundamental inside him. Where there should have been warmth, life, the endless energy that was Sam, there was only emptiness.

"Sam..." The word broke in his throat, vision blurring as tears finally came. He collapsed to his knees beside the bed, clutching her lifeless hand, his body wracked with silent sobs. The weight of his failure crashed over him—every missed call, every canceled dinner, every moment he'd put the job before his daughter. He'd sworn to protect her, and instead, he'd let her slip away, let someone steal her future while he chased other people's monsters.

This wasn't supposed to happen. John was supposed to protect her. He was supposed to keep her safe. But he'd failed. His mind flashed to the missed calls, the late nights, the times he wasn't there when she needed him.

But it wasn't the world's cruelty that haunted him. It was his own failure. He'd failed Sam, and now she was gone.

Back in the present, John's fingers curled around the edges of Sarah's case file, knuckles white. The storm outside had intensified, matching the fury and doubt brewing inside him.

Had he been wrong about Mick Garrett?

CHAPTER 21
THE WEIGHT WE CARRY

Evening shadows gathered around John like old friends, lingering in the corners of his office as he pored over the case files. From her own office, Claire watched him, noting his hunched posture and the way his hands clenched every few minutes, as if fighting something only he could see. She'd seen this before—the obsessive drive, the need to solve what others might consider unsolvable. But tonight felt different. Tonight, something was about to break.

The city sprawled beneath her window, a tapestry of lights and shadows. Each streetlamp created its own island of clarity, but between them lurked darker spaces where truth could hide. Claire pressed her palm against the cool glass, remembering other nights when she'd stood at different windows, wrestling with her demons. Different cities, different windows, and always the same restless search for answers in the darkness.

A soft knock drew her attention. John stood in her doorway, the harsh fluorescent lights casting deep shadows under his eyes. His usual armor of professional detachment had cracked, revealing something raw underneath. She'd never seen him look so uncertain, so close to the edge.

"Got a minute?" His voice carried a vulnerability she'd never heard before.

"Of course." She gestured to the chair across from her desk, noting how heavily he sank into it, how his hands clasped together so tightly his knuckles whitened.

The silence between them felt charged with unspoken confessions. Outside, a siren wailed in the distance—someone else's tragedy unfolding in the night. Finally, John spoke, his eyes fixed on some point beyond her shoulder.

"I can't stop seeing the patterns," he said, his voice just above a whisper. "Mick, Sarah, Emily—it's all connected, but not how I thought. I keep seeing things I've been trying not to see."

Claire studied him carefully, recognizing the moment for what it was—a detective on the edge of a revelation he wasn't sure he could face. She'd been there herself and knew how it felt when certainties began to crumble.

"You've been pushing hard," she said, choosing each word precisely. "But this isn't just about Sarah's case anymore, is it? Something else is driving you."

His eyes met hers for a brief moment, and in that flash of contact, she saw years of buried pain threatening to surface. He looked away quickly, jaw tightening, but not before she caught the raw vulnerability.

"I've walked this road before," he admitted, the words seeming to cost him something vital. "It's too familiar. And where it's leading…" He shook his head, unable to finish.

Claire leaned forward, her voice steady. "I understand. More than you know."

The weight of those words hung between them like a physical presence. John's gaze sharpened, questioning but hesitant, as if afraid to ask what she meant. Claire drew a deep breath, knowing that if she wanted him to open up, she'd have to go first. Some wounds had to be shared to be understood.

"I don't talk about this often," she began slowly, each word a step closer to memories she hadn't revisited in years. "But you need to know you're not alone in this, John. I lost someone, too. To violence." She paused, steeling herself. "My sister, Megan."

The name felt strange on her tongue, like speaking a language she hadn't used in years. John's posture shifted, his defensive walls lowering as he sensed the truth in her words.

"She was everything to me," Claire continued, allowing herself to remember. "Not just a sister—a best friend. The kind of person who lit up rooms just by walking into them. Who could make you laugh even on your worst days." Her voice caught slightly, but she pressed on. "She had this way of seeing the best in people, even when they couldn't see it themselves."

John listened intently, his rigid shoulders easing, as if sharing her burden somehow lightened his own.

"One night, she didn't come home," Claire said, her voice tightening with remembered fear. "I thought maybe she was just out with friends, being careless like we all were at that age. But by morning..." She swallowed hard. "I knew. Deep down, I knew something was wrong. We found her in an alley half a mile from our apartment two days later."

The words fell between them like stones, each carrying the weight of years of grief. John didn't interrupt, but his eyes never left her face, understanding dawning in their depths.

"The police never caught who did it," she continued, her voice rougher now. "They had suspects, they said, but nothing ever stuck. The case went cold, and I... I couldn't handle it. I spent years chasing answers, trying to understand why it happened, why someone could just take her and walk away like she meant nothing."

Claire met John's gaze directly, letting him see past her professional facade to the scars beneath. "That's why I do what I do now. Criminal psychology and profiling were the only ways I could make sense of it. The only way I could understand how someone could commit such violence and just disappear. But even with everything I know now, even with all the tools and training, some questions will never have answers."

John sat silent for a long moment, his eyes locked on hers. Claire saw something shift in him for the first time since they'd started working together— a wall crumbling, revealing the wounded man behind the detective's badge.

"You've been carrying that for a long time," he said, recognition coloring his words.

Claire nodded, feeling the familiar ache in her chest. "Yeah. And it doesn't get easier, not really. But it does get clearer. The pain is always there, like a scar that never quite heals, but it doesn't have to control you. That's what I had to learn." She leaned forward. "And what you need to figure out too, John. Because if you let it drive you, it'll destroy you from the inside."

John looked away, his jaw working silently. It wasn't resistance this time—she could see him processing her words, letting them sink past his defenses.

"You think I'm letting my past control this investigation," he said after a moment, his voice low and rough.

"I think you're too close," Claire replied. "And that's not a judgment, John. It's a reality that I understand better than most. You lost someone, didn't you? Someone who meant everything."

John's hands flexed on the armrests, his knuckles white with tension. A muscle jumped in his jaw as he fought against years of practiced silence.

"It's not about me," he said, but the words rang hollow, lacking conviction.

Claire offered him a sad smile. "It's always about us, whether we admit it or not. The cases we choose, the ones that keep us up at night—they're always connected to the wounds we carry."

John's shoulders slumped, the weight of her words breaking through his carefully constructed walls. She could see the struggle in his eyes—the need to maintain control warring with the desperate desire to unburden himself.

"You have to separate it," Claire said. "For your sake. For everyone's sake. Sarah's case isn't Sam's case."

The name fell between them like a thunderclap. John went completely still, the air seeming to crystallize around them. Claire could almost see the memories hitting him, years of buried grief threatening to surface.

"I didn't mean to pry," she added, her voice gentle. "I just... I see it, John. The way you carry it with you. I recognize it because I carried my own grief the same way for years."

For a long moment, John didn't move, didn't speak. His gaze remained fixed on the floor, but Claire could see the storm behind his eyes. When he broke the silence, his voice was barely audible.

"It never goes away," he whispered, more to himself than to her.

"No," Claire agreed. "It doesn't. But you can choose how you live with it. Whether it defines you or drives you to help others—that's our daily choice."

John straightened slowly in his chair, some tension leaving his frame. When he met her gaze again, the walls were down. For the first time, she saw him completely—not just the dedicated detective, but the grieving father underneath.

"I appreciate what you're saying," he said, his voice steadier. "And maybe... maybe I have been pushing too hard. Seeing shadows where there aren't any." He paused, drawing a deep breath. "But I need to see this through. I need to know the truth."

Claire nodded, understanding the determination in his voice. "I know. Just... be careful, John. You're good at what you do. Don't let your past blind you to what's right in front of you."

They sat in companionable silence for a moment, the shared weight of their confessions creating a bond stronger than mere partnership. They were no longer just colleagues—they were survivors, each carrying their own scars while trying to prevent others from bearing similar wounds.

John stood, his movements more deliberate than before. "Thank you," he said, "for trusting me. With Megan."

"Thank you for listening," Claire replied with a gentle smile. "Sometimes sharing the weight makes it easier to bear."

He walked toward the door, pausing just before he reached it. "You're right, you know," he admitted. "About not letting it control me. I'll work on that."

"I'll hold you to it," she said, and they shared a moment of understanding before he nodded and stepped out, closing the door quietly behind him.

Claire sat in the darkness of her office for a long moment, feeling the weight of her past settle around her like a familiar shadow. She had opened up more than she'd intended, but sometimes, that's what healing requires—sharing your wounds so others can begin to heal their own.

She glanced at the files spread across her desk, her mind returning to the case. They were getting closer to something—something big. And now, with John beginning to see things more clearly, they had a real chance of finding the truth.

But as she reached for the next file, Claire couldn't shake the feeling that the darkness they were facing wasn't just external. It lived inside them, too, in the scars they carried and the choices they made. And sometimes, that internal darkness could be the most dangerous of all.

When John returned to his desk, the precinct was eerily quiet. Claire's words echoed in his mind, a strange mixture of comfort and warning. She had walked through hell, too. That realization changed something in him, making him see her—and himself—in a different light.

He opened a file, but his thoughts kept drifting back to Sam. He'd never talked about her, not with anyone at the precinct, not in years. But Claire had seen the weight he carried without him having to say a word. She had recognized the signs because she carried her own burden.

"Don't let it control you." The advice hung over him, competing with the memories that had driven him for so long. And for the first time in years, John thought maybe—just maybe—he could start listening.

But not yet. Not until he found the answers he was looking for. Not until Sarah, Emily, and Sam got the justice they deserved.

The night stretched ahead, full of shadows and secrets waiting to be uncovered. But for the first time in longer than he could remember, John didn't feel entirely alone in the darkness.

CHAPTER 22
THE PUPPET'S STRINGS

John had barely taken a bite of his sandwich when his phone buzzed, vibrating ominously on his cluttered desk. The number was unfamiliar—a long string of digits that sent a shiver down his spine. Against his better judgment, he picked it up.

"DiMatteo," he answered, masking his fatigue with a veneer of professionalism.

"Detective DiMatteo, this is Alan Richards, Mick Garrett's attorney." The voice was smooth and rehearsed, carrying none of its usual adversarial edge. Something in his tone made John sit straighter. "I have something you need to see."

John felt a muscle twitch in his jaw. "If this is another attempt to—"

"It's not what you think," Richards cut in. "One of Mick's neighbors came forward with security footage from the day you first brought Mick in for questioning. The timestamp shows someone breaking into his house while he was in custody."

John's fingers tightened around the phone. "Breaking in?"

"Through the back door. Professional job—they knew what they were doing." Richards paused, letting the implication sink in. "Nothing was taken, Detective. But two days later, you found that jacket with Sarah Thompson's blood on it."

The weight of those words settled in John's gut like lead. He thought back to that search, how perfectly placed the evidence had been, how convenient it had all seemed. "You're suggesting someone planted it."

"I'm not suggesting anything. I'm telling you what's on the video." Richards' voice hardened. "Look, I know our history. I know you've had it out for Mick since day one. But this footage... you need to see it for yourself."

John exhaled slowly, glancing at the chaotic pile of case files threatening to spill off his desk. Every instinct screamed at him to dismiss this as another of Mick's manipulations, but something in Richards' tone gave him pause. "Send it over."

"Already did. Check your email."

The video file loaded slowly—agonizingly so—but when it finally played, the grainy footage stopped his breath.

The timestamp showed 2:47 PM, during Mick's first interrogation. A figure moved with practiced efficiency, their movements suggesting familiarity with avoiding detection. No hesitation, no fumbling—just smooth, practiced motions that spoke of experience.

"Jesus," John muttered, rewinding the footage. Something about the way the person moved...

He grabbed his phone, dialing Ramirez. "Get up here. Now."

Ramirez arrived minutes later, slightly out of breath. "What's so urgent?"

Without a word, John played the video. He watched Ramirez's expression shift from skepticism to focused intensity as the scene unfolded.

"That's not some random break-in," Ramirez said finally. "That's someone who knows what they're doing. Someone with training."

"Someone who knew exactly when Mick would be in custody," John added. "Someone with access to our investigation timeline."

They shared a look, the implications hanging heavy between them. John ran a hand over his face, his mind racing. If the jacket had been planted... if someone had orchestrated this...

"We need to keep this quiet," Ramirez said, his voice low. "If this person really did plant evidence—"

"Then they're probably still watching us," John finished. The thought sent ice through his veins. Everyone looked exactly where they were supposed to look.

But someone had been looking elsewhere. Someone who knew their procedures, who understood chain of custody, who could move through their world without raising suspicion.

"Pull the security logs," John told Ramirez. "I want to know everyone who had access to evidence processing during Mick's interrogation. And get me the original lab reports on that jacket—all of them."

As Ramirez left, John played the video one more time. The figure moved with such confidence, such precision. Like they belonged there. Like they knew no one would question their presence.

Across the precinct, Claire sat alone in her office, surrounded by stacks of security logs and timeline data. She'd been reviewing footage from the weeks leading up to Sarah's murder, trying to establish patterns they might have missed. The work was tedious, but something about the case wouldn't let her rest.

Her eyes burned from staring at the screen, but she forced herself to focus. The security logs showed card key access to various departments, timestamped and catalogued. Most followed predictable patterns—day shift arrivals, evening departures, the occasional weekend warrior putting in extra hours.

Then she saw it.

Matt Lawson's key card accessing the forensics lab at 3:17 AM. Not once, but repeatedly, in the weeks before Sarah's death. She sat up straighter, scrolling through the data. The pattern was clear: late-night entries, always between 2 and 4 AM, always when the lab should have been empty.

Claire pulled up the corresponding security footage. Most cameras showed only darkness, but the lab's internal feeds captured Matt moving through the space with practiced familiarity. He wasn't running tests or processing evidence—he was accessing the secure storage areas, places where critical evidence was kept.

Her training kicked in, years of studying predatory behavior patterns suddenly snapping into focus. This wasn't just unusual activity—this was methodical. Calculated. The kind of pattern that spoke of someone manipulating the system from within.

Something else caught her eye. On the day of Mick's interrogation—the day John had nearly hit Matt with his car after Harrison's reprimand—there was a gap in Matt's lab presence. His card showed no activity between 2:15 PM and 3:30 PM.

Claire's pulse quickened as she dug deeper into the logs. Every piece of evidence in Sarah's case had passed through Matt's hands. He'd had access to everything—physical evidence, DNA analysis, chain of custody records. If someone wanted to manipulate the investigation...

She thought of Sarah Thompson, of how precisely her murder had been staged. The forensic evidence, the blood patterns, everything had been perfect. Too perfect. Like it had been orchestrated by someone who knew exactly how evidence would be processed and analyzed.

Someone who knew their procedures inside and out.

Her hands trembled slightly as she pulled up Matt's personnel file. Transfer from Chicago PD forensics division. Multiple commendations for his attention to detail. A perfect record—almost suspiciously so.

Claire closed the file, her mind racing. She needed to be careful. If she was right about this, if Matt really was involved...

She reached for her phone, then hesitated. She couldn't go to John with just suspicions. She needed more—concrete evidence, historical patterns, something that would prove Matt was more than just a diligent lab tech working odd hours.

But first, she needed to check one more thing.

She pulled up the investigation timeline for Sarah's case. Every major break, every piece of evidence that pointed to Mick Garrett—it all connected back to the forensics lab. To Matt.

Her computer pinged with a new email. John, sending over the security footage from Mick's neighbor. She opened it, her breath catching as she watched. The figure moved with a familiar precision, each movement controlled and deliberate.

The timestamp made her blood run cold: 2:47 PM. Right in the middle of Matt's unaccounted time.

Claire sat back in her chair, her mind racing. The coincidence was too perfect. Matt's lab absences, his late-night access patterns, the precise way evidence kept appearing exactly when needed—it all suggested someone working from inside the investigation.

Her finger hovered over John's number in her phone, but she stopped herself. She couldn't go to him with just suspicions and coincidences. John was too invested in Mick's guilt to accept a theory this radical without solid proof.

No, she needed more. She needed to understand who Matt Lawson really was, where he came from, what patterns he might have left behind. If he really was manipulating evidence, this wouldn't be the first time.

Claire pulled up the database for cold cases. She had a long night ahead of her.

The precinct grew quiet around her as night fell, but Claire barely noticed. She had learned long ago that the most dangerous predators were the ones who hid in plain sight, who used respectability as their camouflage.

And she was beginning to suspect they had one working right beside them.

CHAPTER 23
BEHIND BLUE LINES

Claire waited until the precinct had quieted for the evening before pulling Matt Lawson's employment file from her drawer. She'd already memorized most of it, but something about his career progression kept nagging at her. The path from evidence room clerk to forensic technician wasn't typical—especially not with such a rapid advancement.

According to his file, Matt had started in Chicago PD's evidence room in 2018, shortly before Emily Reardon's disappearance. Within six months of her case going cold, he'd transferred to the forensics lab training program. By the time he applied to Columbus PD, his recommendations were glowing, his technical skills exemplary.

Too exemplary, perhaps.

Claire made notes on her legal pad, drawing connections. Evidence room clerk during Emily's case. Access to all physical evidence and documentation. Then a swift transition to forensics, building the exact expertise needed to manipulate evidence at a technical level.

She needed to see his office. Not just the professional facade he presented during work hours, but the personal space he thought was private. The place where he might let his guard down.

Claire gathered several old case files—ones unrelated to their current investigation—and made her way to the forensics lab. She'd noticed Matt always took his break at the same time, another example of his rigidly controlled patterns. She had about fifteen minutes.

"Matt?" She knocked on his door, adopting the slightly frazzled demeanor of someone caught up in bureaucratic frustration. "Sorry to bother you, but I'm hitting a wall with these cold cases. The chief wants a review of our evidence storage protocols, and I could really use your expertise."

Matt looked up, his face showing just the right amount of professional interest. "What kind of protocols?"

"Chain of custody documentation, mainly." Claire held up the files. "These cases from the '90s seem to follow a different system. I know you handled similar reviews in Chicago..."

"Let me take a look." Matt stood, ever helpful, ever precise. "The filing system changed around '98. We should check the archive room."

As they walked to the evidence archives, Claire kept him engaged with questions about documentation procedures. The moment they entered the archive room, Matt went straight to the relevant section, his need for order making him predictable.

"I'll pull the original intake forms," he said, disappearing into the rows of shelves.

She waited until Matt's footsteps faded into the archive room before slipping back into his office. The air felt different now—colder, charged with unseen threat. Everything about the space spoke of obsessive control: files aligned with military precision, equipment placed at exact angles, even the dust motes seemed to hang suspended, afraid to settle out of place.

Claire's pulse thrummed in her ears as she began her search. She had maybe three minutes before Matt would return. Four if she was lucky. Her hands moved with practiced efficiency, disturbing nothing, leaving no trace of her presence.

The desk drawers were locked, but a framed photograph caught her attention. It sat partially concealed behind his monitor, as if meant to be private yet positioned where he could always see it. A college party scene—Matt in the center, wearing that same controlled smile she'd come to recognize. A Loyola Chicago banner hung in the background.

Then her heart stopped.

Emily Reardon stood in the background, her face caught in mid-laugh. She was slightly blurred, but Claire had studied her case file photos too many times to mistake those features. Emily looked happy, unaware—a ghost captured in the moment before her life intersected with a predator's path.

A sound from the hallway made Claire freeze. Footsteps? No—just the building's heating system cycling on. Still, sweat prickled at her neck. Every second she remained felt like tempting fate.

She reached for her phone to photograph the picture, but movement in the hallway caught her eye. A shadow passed the frosted glass of Matt's door. Claire's breath caught. Someone was coming.

In three silent steps, she reached the doorway, pressing herself against the wall beside it. The shadow grew larger. Through the glass, she could make out a figure approaching—tall, deliberate movements.

Matt.

He was coming back sooner then expected.

Claire's mind raced. If he caught her here, if he realized what she'd found... The hallway to her right offered escape, but movement would draw attention through the glass. The alternative was to stay hidden, pressed against the wall, and pray he didn't enter his office.

The footsteps drew closer. She could hear the soft squeak of his shoes on the linoleum, the subtle rhythm of his breathing. The handle of the door was less than two feet from her face.

The footsteps stopped.

Claire didn't breathe. Her heart pounded so hard she was sure it would give her away. Through the frosted glass, Matt's silhouette remained motionless, as if listening. Sensing.

One second stretched into three. Into five.

Then the shadow moved, continuing down the hallway. The footsteps grew fainter until they disappeared around the corner.

Claire released her breath in a silent shudder. Her legs felt weak with relief, but she couldn't stay. She had to move. Now.

With one last glance at the photograph—Emily's frozen smile now seeming more like a warning—she slipped out of the office. Her heels made no sound on the carpet as she forced herself to walk, not run, back to her office.

She was in position, examining an evidence box, when Matt returned moments later.

"Found those original intake forms," he said, his voice carrying that same measured calm. But something in his eyes made her skin crawl—a flickering attention that suggested he was cataloging her every movement, every micro-expression.

Did he know? Had she disturbed something in his perfectly ordered space? With Matt, even dust motes could tell tales.

Claire forced a smile, casually sliding Emily's file under other papers. "Thanks, Matt. Just leave them there—I'm a bit swamped at the moment."

He placed the files on her desk with precise movements. His eyes flickered briefly to her computer screen, then to the papers she'd tried to hide. Something shifted in his expression—so subtle she almost missed it.

"Emily Reardon," he said, his tone perfectly neutral. "That's an old case."

Claire's pulse quickened, but she kept her voice steady. "Just reviewing cold cases. Looking for patterns in evidence processing."

"Interesting choice." Matt lingered a moment too long. "Let me know if you need anything else."

After he left, Claire sat perfectly still, her heart pounding. That wasn't just professional interest in his voice—it was warning. Her chair had been slightly repositioned during their conversation, angled away from her desk. Her coffee mug wasn't quite where she'd left it.

Small changes. Subtle messages.

She was being watched.

Claire forced herself to breathe normally, to maintain her routines. She'd studied predators like Matt for years—men who lived for control, who turned stalking into an art form. They wanted their victims to know they were being watched, to feel powerless.

But Matt had made a mistake. His need for precision, for perfect evidence trails, was becoming his tell. Like the photograph he kept hidden yet displayed, or the way he'd subtly marked his presence in her office—he wanted to be noticed, even as he tried to remain invisible.

She began documenting everything: the exact position of items on her desk, the angle of her chair, timestamps of Matt's appearances. She installed a small camera in her office plant, angled to capture anyone entering when she was away.

Two could play at this game of observation.

As evening settled over the precinct, Claire reviewed her notes. She had enough to be certain—Matt's connection to Emily, his evidence room access, his too-perfect career progression. But certainty wasn't proof. She needed something concrete, something that would convince John that their trusted forensics expert was actually a calculating predator.

Her computer chimed with an incoming email. Security logs she'd requested from Chicago PD, showing access patterns from their evidence room during Emily's investigation. As she scrolled through the data, a familiar pattern emerged—late-night entries, missing documentation, evidence logged and then mysteriously "misplaced."

The same pattern they were seeing now with Sarah's case.

Claire saved the files to an encrypted drive. She wasn't ready to take this to John—not yet. She needed to understand the full scope of Matt's operation, to anticipate his next moves. Because she was certain of one thing: if Matt realized she was connecting these dots, she wouldn't just be observing his patterns.

She would become part of them.

The precinct had grown quiet, most officers gone for the day. Through her office window, she could see Matt in his lab, methodically processing evidence. To anyone else, he looked like the perfect professional—dedicated, precise, trustworthy.

But Claire knew better now. She saw the predator behind the facade, the calculated movements of someone who had turned murder into a science.

She thought of Sarah Thompson, of Emily Reardon, of all the other potential victims whose cases might have crossed Matt's path. He thought his position made him untouchable, that his carefully constructed identity would protect him.

Claire closed Emily's file, a cold determination settling over her. Matt Lawson might be watching her, might be playing his games of control and intimidation. But he didn't realize what he was dealing with.

She wasn't just another investigator to manipulate. She was someone who understood his kind all too well.

And she was done being watched.

CHAPTER 24
CONNECTING THE DOTS

A half-eaten sandwich rested in front of Ramirez, ignored. The precinct had settled into the quiet hum of late afternoon. Across the room, John was following up on witness leads, while Claire was buried in research on Emily Reardon's case. Ramirez sensed that, although they were each tugging at different threads, they were all leading to the same tangled knot.

The missing documents in Emily's file gnawed at him. Something vital had been deliberately removed, erased by someone who didn't want the truth to surface. But who—and why?

His phone buzzed, jolting him out of his thoughts. He glanced down to see the name Mike Halpern—a retired Chicago detective who'd worked the Reardon case. Ramirez had reached out on a long shot, hoping Halpern might remember something.

"Halpern," Ramirez greeted, sitting up a bit straighter.

"Yeah, it's me," the man's voice crackled through the line, sounding older, rougher than Ramirez remembered. "You're looking into the Reardon case again?"

"That's right. We think it might connect to a recent homicide, and… well, we've noticed some gaps in the original file."

A low whistle sounded over the line. "No kidding. Been years since I thought about that one. Damn shame we never found her."

"Do you remember anything unusual about the case?" Ramirez pressed. "Anything that might explain the missing information?"

There was a long pause, the kind that stretched too far. Finally, Halpern spoke, his tone hesitant. "Funny you ask that. A couple of pages went missing before I handed the file off to evidence. I chalked it up to a clerical error back then, but looking back… I'm not so sure."

Ramirez's pulse quickened. "What was in those pages?"

"It was notes on a student from one of the nearby colleges—a person of interest, though nothing solid. Just speculation. I couldn't get much traction with it." He paused again, as if weighing his words. "Kid was sharp. Kept his nose clean, but something about him didn't sit right with me. I always thought he knew more than he let on."

Ramirez scribbled down the details, though his mind was already racing. "You're sure those notes were missing?"

"Positive," Halpern replied, his voice edged with regret. "I reported it, but nobody seemed eager to follow up. It was like the whole thing got swept under the rug."

Ramirez thanked him and hung up, the weight of this new revelation settling on his shoulders. This wasn't a mistake or poor filing—it was deliberate. Someone had intentionally removed those pages, erased the name of a student who might have known more about Emily's disappearance than he ever admitted. A student who had become a meticulous forensic technician in their own precinct.

Ramirez's phone buzzed again as he sat back, piecing together what Halpern had told him. A message from Claire: Meet me in John's office. Found something.

He was out of his seat and heading down the hall before he even hit reply.

When he stepped into John's office, he could feel the tension like static in the air. Claire had spread photographs and documents across John's desk, building a timeline of Matt's movements between Chicago and Columbus.

"Finally," Ramirez muttered, closing the door behind him. "What've we got?"

Claire looked up, her expression focused and grim. "I've confirmed Matt worked in Chicago PD's evidence room shortly after Emily's disappearance. He had direct access to everything - physical evidence, documentation, chain of custody records. Then, six months after her case went cold, he suddenly transfers to forensics training."

"Convenient timing," John said, his voice tight.

"That's not all," Claire continued, pulling out a photograph. "I found this in Matt's office - hidden behind his monitor, but positioned where he could see it. It's from a basketball watch party at Loyola." She pointed to the background of the image. "That's Emily Reardon, the night she disappeared."

Ramirez felt a chill creep down his spine. "And now my conversation with Halpern makes even more sense. He remembers pages going missing from Emily's file - pages about a person of interest they could never fully investigate."

"Because someone was erasing the trail," Claire said, her voice hardening. "The same way evidence keeps disappearing now. The same way the jacket showed up perfectly placed in Mick's house."

John leaned forward, his eyes fixed on the photograph. "Matt's been playing us from the start. Using his position in the lab to manipulate evidence, to guide our investigation exactly where he wanted it to go."

"Think about it," Claire said, laying out security logs. "The late-night lab access, the missing documentation, the way evidence appears exactly when needed - it's all controlled. Calculated. He's not just hiding his involvement; he's orchestrating the entire investigation."

Ramirez sank into a chair, the weight of their discovery pressing down on him. "So what's our next move? We can't confront him directly."

"No," John agreed, his voice cold with determination. "We build this carefully. Document everything. Track his movements, his access patterns, every piece of evidence he touches."

"And we keep this between us," Claire added. "If Matt realizes we're onto him..."

The implications hung heavy in the air. They were dealing with someone who had spent years perfecting his methodology, who knew their procedures intimately enough to stay one step ahead.

"I'll start reviewing old cases," Ramirez said. "If this is his pattern, Emily and Sarah can't be the only ones."

John nodded, but his eyes never left the photograph of Emily. "We do this right. No mistakes. No loose ends. Matt's been watching us all along - now it's our turn to watch him."

They shared a moment of grim understanding. The monster they'd been hunting hadn't been hiding in shadows - he'd been walking among them, wearing a badge, processing their evidence, playing his part to perfection.

And if they weren't careful, if they made one wrong move, he would disappear again, leaving nothing but questions and cold cases in his wake.

CHAPTER 25
THE WATCHER

Ramirez's reflection stared back at him from the laptop screen, the Zoom logo spinning in an endless loop. The laptop's glow cast shadows across his face, deepening the lines of tension that had settled there. His fingers tapped a restless rhythm against the desk, but his gaze drifted to John and Claire. They were across the room, heads bent over case files, working with practiced synchronicity. Yet all he could focus on was the call about to start—the conversation with Mark Lewis. Every instinct honed by years on the force told him this call would change everything they thought they knew about Matt Lawson.

A chime broke the silence, and Mark Lewis's face appeared on the screen. His features, washed out in the cold light of his apartment, looked younger than Ramirez had expected, yet something haunted lingered in his eyes. His hands shook slightly as he adjusted his headphones, a visible nervousness setting Ramirez's instincts on edge.

"Can you hear me okay?" Mark's voice crackled through the speakers, threaded with apprehension.

"Coming through clear," Ramirez replied, keeping his tone even, coaxing. He'd interviewed hundreds of witnesses and knew better than to come on strong. "Thanks for taking the time, Mark. I know revisiting this stuff isn't easy, but we're looking into some cases that might connect to Emily Reardon's disappearance. I understand you knew her?"

Mark's expression tightened, a flash of regret flickering in his eyes, as if he'd already started second-guessing his decision to speak. "Knew her? Not really. I just… saw her around. Campus, mostly. Parties sometimes. We weren't close."

Ramirez nodded, watching Mark's face closely, noticing how he avoided looking directly at the screen. "We're trying to piece together her final days. Anything you can remember might help."

Mark's hand rose to rake through his hair, a nervous gesture. "She was… quiet, mostly. Friendly, but the kind of person who keeps to herself." His voice softened. "Except at parties. That's when she really came alive. But she was always careful, you know? Not reckless. At least, not in a way that felt dangerous."

Ramirez's gaze narrowed slightly. "You were at a party the night she disappeared, right? One of the Loyola houses?"

The question made Mark stiffen. He cast a quick glance off-screen as if gathering his thoughts. "Yeah, I was there," he murmured. "It was just a regular Friday night—drinks, music, nothing out of the ordinary. She was there, too, early on. I don't remember talking to her. Then… at some point, she just wasn't there anymore. We figured she left with friends."

Ramirez leaned forward, focusing on Mark's every twitch, every flicker of discomfort. "Were you usually with the same group of people at these parties?"

"Yeah," Mark said, though his hesitation was noticeable. "Some Loyola guys, some friends from back home."

"Like Matt Lawson?"

The name dropped into the silence like a stone, the tension thickening in the room. Mark's whole demeanor shifted—shoulders hunched, gaze darting as if Matt might appear behind him at any moment.

"Matt… yeah. I knew him from high school," he said, his voice quieter. "But we weren't exactly close. Not the kind of guy you get close to."

Ramirez kept his tone gentle, leading him forward. "Different, how?"

Mark's voice wavered, his discomfort palpable even through the screen. "He was intense. Quiet, sure, but not the way Emily was quiet. With her, it was natural. With Matt… it was like he was always watching. Studying everyone like we were specimens."

A chill crawled down Ramirez's spine. "Tell me more about how he'd watch people."

Mark shuddered, glancing over his shoulder as if expecting to see someone there. "He didn't socialize, not really. He'd stand in corners or doorways, somewhere he could see everything. He'd just watch, for hours, like he was cataloging us." Mark paused, swallowing hard. "And he'd say weird things sometimes about how people are predictable or how easy it is to make someone disappear in a city like Chicago. We all thought he was trying to be edgy. But after Emily disappeared… it didn't seem like a joke anymore."

Ramirez waited, letting the silence coax more from him.

"Was Matt there that night?" he asked, though he suspected he already knew the answer.

Mark nodded, his expression darkening. "Yeah. Same as always, standing in a corner, watching everyone. But he left early, which was strange. Usually, he was the last to leave, but that night…" He stopped, running a hand over his face. "He just disappeared. And then, after that night, he was gone. Like he'd never been there at all."

Ramirez leaned closer, lowering his voice. "Did you ever see him again?"

Mark shook his head, his hands twisting together like he was trying to wring the memories out. "No. It was like he vanished. At the time, we didn't think much of it. Just figured he'd moved on. But looking back… the way he watched Emily, tracked her movements, almost like he knew where she'd be." His voice shook, barely a whisper now. "He knew too much. Too much about her habits and her schedule. It wasn't just creepy; it was preparation."

Ramirez's pen paused over his notepad, pressing into the paper until it nearly tore. "Did he ever mention Emily directly? Any conversations that stand out?"

Mark's gaze dropped to his hands, fingers still twisted. "Not directly, but… there was one time, maybe a week before she vanished. A couple of us talked about how she'd seemed different—quieter, maybe a little jumpy. And Matt just… smiled. Said something about how people never notice the important changes in others until it's too late. Like he was enjoying a joke, none of us got."

A cold certainty settled over Ramirez, the pieces aligning with chilling clarity. "And after she disappeared? Did Matt seem affected?"

"That's the part I can't get out of my head," Mark replied, his voice shaking. "Everyone else was panicking. Calling hospitals, organizing searches, and passing out missing person flyers. But Matt… he never asked a single question. Didn't help search, didn't seem to care at all. It was like…" His voice cracked. "Like he already knew exactly where she was."

The silence that followed was deafening. Mark's face had paled, haunted by a realization he couldn't escape, his hindsight bringing clarity to a horror he hadn't seen in time.

"Thank you, Mark," Ramirez said gently. "If you remember anything else,"

"Just find him," Mark interrupted, his voice raw. "Find him and find out what he did to her."

The screen went dark, leaving Ramirez staring at his reflection, the weight of Mark's words sinking deep. Everything about Matt Lawson had fit neatly into place, revealing a pattern Ramirez knew was there, though he hadn't wanted to see it.

He found John and Claire still poring over case files, their faces tight with focus. They looked up as he entered, and his expression made them tense.

"I just talked to Mark Lewis," he said, sitting across from John. "It's worse than we thought."

Claire sat up, her expression sharpening. "What did he say?"

Ramirez's voice was low, each word heavy with conviction. "Matt was at that party the night Emily disappeared. But this wasn't a coincidence. Mark says

Matt had been watching her for weeks, maybe months. He embedded himself in her social circle and tracked her every move. Just like he did with Sarah."

John's jaw clenched, his face hardening. "So he stalked her, learning her patterns, waiting for the right moment to strike."

"Exactly," Ramirez nodded. "Mark said Matt would come to parties, stand in corners, and watch. Not talking, just observing. He even commented about disappearances, how easy it would be to make someone vanish in Chicago. Mark said they thought he was being weird, but now…"

"He was studying them," Claire finished coldly. "Learning their patterns, vulnerabilities. That fits his profile perfectly. It's more than just stalking—this is a methodical process, a careful preparation."

John rose abruptly, his pacing heavy with the weight of realization. "So he embedded himself in Emily's life, waiting for the perfect moment to act. And once she was gone, he moved on, just like that."

Ramirez nodded grimly. "Mark said Matt completely disappeared after Emily went missing. No goodbye, no follow-up, nothing. He had no more use for them once she was gone."

"Because they were just props in his performance," Claire said, her tone steely. "Matt wanted access to Emily's world. The rest of them were expendable once he'd taken what he needed."

The silence in the room was charged. Each of them confronted the darkness they'd missed, the monster that had walked so comfortably among them, hidden in plain sight.

John turned, his gaze fierce, determined. "We have to move on this. Mark's testimony and the other evidence—we're close to building a solid case. But we have to be careful. Matt's smart, and if he's watching us, he'll know the moment we make a wrong move."

"He's still out there, probably already scouting his next target," Ramirez said, his voice tight with urgency.

"Then we stop him," Claire replied, her voice as hard as steel. "We know his methods, his patterns. Now, it's time to use that against him. We find him before he has the chance to disappear again."

The precinct hummed around them, oblivious to the dark realization within its walls. Outside, the city's nightlife cast long shadows across the streets. Somewhere among those shadows, Matt Lawson lurked, watching, waiting.

But they were ready now. They'd seen the pattern and understood the twisted performance Matt had been orchestrating. And this time, they wouldn't be chasing shadows. They would be one step ahead, waiting for him in the shadows he thought were his.

CHAPTER 26
UNDER SUSPICION

The forensics lab buzzed with artificial life—the soft whir of machines and the flickering fluorescent lights that cast harsh shadows across Matt Lawson's face as he hunched over his desk. Beyond his closed door, the precinct's familiar symphony played on—phones ringing, papers shuffling, detectives' voices rising and falling like a distant tide. But today, those sounds felt different. No longer comforting, they pressed down on him like accusations.

Matt's fingers moved mechanically across his keyboard, clicking through test results with practiced precision. The screen's cold glow illuminated columns of data—evidence logs, chemical analyses, DNA markers—but the familiar patterns blurred before his eyes. His mind kept slipping from the present, drawn back to memories he'd carefully locked away.

A silver photo frame caught the harsh overhead light, demanding his attention. The image within was from another life: a college watch party, faces flushed with victory and cheap beer as Loyola Chicago celebrated their win over Tennessee. Matt stood among them, wearing a smile that now looked foreign. But it was the figure partially visible in the background that made his stomach twist—Emily, her face caught mid-laugh, unaware she was being watched. Always watched.

Claire's words from earlier echoed in his head: "I didn't know you went to Loyola." The words had been simple, but her tone carried something else—a subtle probe, testing for weakness. Her eyes had lingered too long on the photo, seeing too much.

"Just visited a friend there once," he'd replied, the lie smooth on his tongue. But Claire's arched eyebrow and the flicker of doubt in her gaze had planted a seed of unease that now grew like a cancer in his chest.

He shook his head, trying to dispel the unease coiling in his spine. It was just a photo. Just an innocent snapshot from a lifetime ago. But then why did it feel like a noose tightening around his neck?

Matt forced his attention back to the computer screen, but the data swam before his eyes, meaningless symbols that couldn't drown out the roar of memory: the press of bodies in that cramped apartment, bass-heavy music vibrating through the walls, the sharp scent of spilled beer. And Emily—always Emily—her laughter cutting through the chaos, her eyes meeting his for just a moment before looking away. She'd never suspected. None of them had.

A sharp knock shattered his reverie. Ramirez filled the doorway, his casual stance belied by the predatory focus in his eyes.

"Got a minute?" Ramirez's tone was light, but Matt recognized the hunter's patience beneath.

"Sure." Matt forced his features into a mask of normalcy, though sweat began to bead at the base of his neck. "What's up?"

Ramirez stepped inside, his gaze sweeping the room with calculated indifference. "We're revisiting some old cases." He paused, eyes landing on the photo still in Matt's hand. "Emily Reardon's name came up. Ring any bells?"

The name hit Matt like a physical blow, but years of practice kept his expression neutral. He set the photo down carefully, face-down. "Not really. Sounds familiar, but I didn't know her."

"Funny." Ramirez's finger tapped against the filing cabinet he leaned against. "Because there's a photo of you two at a party. College days, wasn't it?"

Matt's throat constricted, but his voice remained steady. "I went to UIC, not Loyola. Must be thinking of someone else."

Ramirez's eyes bore into him. "Maybe. But that's definitely you and her in the picture. Clear as day. Thought you might be able to help fill in some blanks."

"Sorry," Matt said, the strain in his voice barely noticeable. "It was a long time ago."

Ramirez studied him a moment longer before pushing off the cabinet. "Right. Well, if anything comes back to you..." He left the threat unspoken as he turned and walked away.

The door clicked shut with the finality of a coffin lid. Matt released a shaky breath, his carefully constructed world beginning to crack at the edges. His hands trembled as he ran them through his hair, mind racing with implications.

They know. Or they suspect. The thought circled like a vulture in his mind.

He moved abruptly, knocking over a forgotten coffee mug. Dark liquid spread across his desk like blood, soaking into papers and evidence logs, dissolving them into meaningless pulp. As he scrambled for napkins, his eyes caught Emily's face again, peeking from beneath a sodden file. Her frozen smile seemed to mock him now.

He stood, grabbing a handful of napkins to mop up the mess. "Damn it," he muttered, voice trembling as he wiped up the spill. But Emily's face remained, smiling up from the soaked photograph, taunting him with memories he couldn't bury.

"Just a coincidence," he whispered, but the words rang hollow in the sterile lab. He knew better. Coincidences didn't bring that look to Ramirez's eyes. They circled closer, like sharks that had caught the first taste of blood.

With a sudden, desperate movement, he yanked open his desk drawer, shoving the photo inside and slamming it shut. The metallic click of the lock felt inadequate against the walls that seemed to be closing in. The lab's familiar comfort had transformed into a trap, every shadow concealing potential witnesses, every whisper carrying accusations.

He sat back down, forcing himself to focus. Pulling up the latest autopsy reports, he immersed himself in the clinical details—precise measurements and sterile observations. Normally, the detachment brought comfort, but today, it felt hollow.

Through the thin walls, he caught fragments of John DiMatteo's voice, the detective's tone edged with obsession. Probably still fixated on Mick Garrett, Matt thought, a bitter smile twisting his lips. Poor Mick—perfect patsy with a history of violence. Matt had counted on John's tunnel vision, feeding it carefully over months of subtle manipulation.

But now…

A sharp knock interrupted his spiral of thoughts, and before he could respond, Kate Whitman pushed into the lab. She carried a folder like a shield, but her eyes swept the room with clinical precision, taking in details Matt suddenly wished he could hide.

"Need those tox screens, Matt," she said, her gaze settling on him with uncomfortable intensity.

"Working on them now." He turned to his computer, feeling her continued scrutiny like a physical weight. The cursor blinked accusingly on his screen, the data meaningless under her watchful eyes.

"Everything okay?" Kate's voice carried a note of concern that made his skin crawl. "You seem distracted."

He forced a laugh, the sound brittle in his ears. "Just swamped. You know how it gets."

"Right." She nodded slowly, unconvinced. "Let me know if you need help."

"Appreciate it," he said, offering a tight smile.

As she turned to leave, her eyes caught on the mess of wet papers still spreading across his desk. "Spill something?"

"Coffee." The lie came automatically. "Just being clumsy."

Kate lingered in the doorway, her expression unreadable. "Get those screens to me by the end of the day."

The moment she left, Matt's carefully maintained facade crumbled. Panic clawed at his chest, each breath coming shorter than the last. The walls pressed in, years of careful planning and meticulous control threatening to unravel in an instant.

He needed air. Space to think.

Grabbing his jacket, Matt fled the lab, navigating the precinct's corridors like a rat in a maze. Each face he passed seemed to watch him, each conversation dying as he approached. Or was that just paranoia? He couldn't tell anymore where reality ended and his fears began.

The January air hit him like a slap as he burst outside, the Central Ohio cold finding every gap in his clothing. Above him, the sky hung low and colorless— that familiar Columbus gray that trapped the city under a lid. Fine snowflakes drifted lazily through the air, harbingers of the heavier snow the meteorologists had warned about all morning.

The city sprawled before him, indifferent to his inner turmoil. Along High Street, traffic moved in its endless dance, brake lights glowing dully in the gray afternoon light. Students from Ohio State hurried past in huddled groups, shoulders hunched against the cold. A child's laugh rang out from a shop doorway, pure and innocent against the city's winter drone. The normalcy of it all felt obscene.

He wandered, the sounds of the precinct fading behind him. His breath came in visible puffs, dissipating into the steel-colored sky. His mind raced, thoughts tumbling over one another in a chaotic spiral as scattered as the snowflakes swirling around him.

They suspect me. How much do they know? How long before they find something?

Images flashed in his mind—Emily's laughing face, Sarah's lifeless body, the countless nights spent blending into the background, watching, waiting. The wet sidewalks reflected the gray sky, making it seem like he was walking through a world turned upside down.

He stopped at a crosswalk, the light flashing red. The wind picked up, carrying the sharp bite of approaching snow. More flurries filled the air, dancing in the beams of headlights. Pedestrians brushed past him, lost in their worlds of glowing phone screens. Matt felt a sudden disconnect, as if he were watching himself from a distance.

A child laughed nearby, tugging at his mother's hand, trying to catch snowflakes on his tongue. The sound was pure, untainted. Matt's eyes followed them, a pang of something—regret? Longing?—twisting in his chest.

The light changed, and he moved with the crowd, carried along by the tide of humanity. His phone buzzed, and his cold-numbed fingers fumbled as he pulled it from his pocket. Kate Whitman's number flashed on the screen: "Where are you? We need to meet."

Matt's heart hammered against his ribs. Does she know? What does she know? His fingers trembled as he typed back: "Just stepped out, on my way back."

Three dots appeared, pulsed, and then vanished. The silence that followed screamed with possibilities.

Matt's grip tightened on the phone, his palms slick with sweat despite the biting cold. Every instinct screamed at him to run, to disappear. But where would he go? Cincinnati? Cleveland? How far could he get before they caught up? The approaching snow would make travel difficult, and highways would be the first place they'd look.

He turned down a narrow alley off High Street, the buildings rising like frozen prison walls on either side. Old snow lay in the shadows where the sun never reached, gray and dirty against the brick. Leaning against the rough wall, Matt forced himself to think past the panic. He needed a plan. Options. A way to redirect attention back to Mick Garrett, to blur the trail that led to him.

But John wasn't stupid. And Claire—she saw too much and understood the shadows where monsters like him lived. The wind whistled through the alley, carrying the sharp scent of approaching snow and the distant rumble of salt trucks preparing for the storm.

A stray cat darted past, its dark shape stark against a patch of old snow, before disappearing behind a dumpster. The sudden movement jolted Matt back to reality. He couldn't stay here. The temperature was dropping—he could feel it in his bones—and the increasing flurries meant the storm was moving in faster than predicted. Lingering only made him more conspicuous.

Squaring his shoulders, he pushed off the wall and made his way back toward the precinct. Each step felt heavier than the last as if wading through invisible drifts. The snow was falling harder now, the flakes fat and wet, clinging to his hair and shoulders. By morning, Columbus would be transformed into a white landscape that might hide many sins—but not his. Never his.

He passed the Statehouse, its limestone facade looming gray against the grayer sky. The columns cast long shadows across the snow-dusted lawn like prison bars stretched across white sheets. How many times had he walked this route, believing himself invisible, believing his secrets were safe? Now, each familiar landmark felt like an accusation.

His phone buzzed again in his pocket, but he didn't check it. Whatever message waited, there wouldn't change what was coming. He could feel it as surely as he could feel the storm rolling in from the west—the inevitable collapse of his carefully constructed world.

The precinct came into view through the thickening snow, its windows glowing warm against the gathering darkness. Inside, he knew they were piecing it together, finding the patterns he'd worked so hard to disguise. Soon, they would see him for what he was.

Matt brushed the snow from his jacket before entering, careful to maintain appearances even now. The blast of warm air in the lobby felt suffocating and artificial. Like everything else, it was just another facade, another lie.

He returned to his lab, boots squeaking against the polished floor, leaving wet prints that marked his path like evidence at a crime scene. Each step brought him closer to a decision he knew he would have to make.

Run. Stay. Fight. Surrender.

The options tumbled through his mind like the snowflakes outside, each carrying its own weight and consequences. Beyond his window, Columbus disappeared into the swirling white of the gathering storm, as if the city was trying to erase all trace of what had happened here.

But some things couldn't be erased. Once laid, some tracks remained visible no matter how deep the snow.

And Matt's tracks led straight to a truth he could no longer outrun.

A knock at the door made him freeze. John DiMatteo stood in the doorway, snow melting on his shoulders, his expression unreadable in the lab's fluorescent light.

"Matt," John's voice carried an edge that hadn't been there before. "Got a minute?"

"Of course." Matt minimized his screen with practiced casualness, turning to face the detective. "What do you need?"

John stepped inside, closing the door behind him. Snow had soaked the cuffs of his pants, and his shoes left wet marks on the pristine floor. He pulled out a small evidence bag containing a fragment of dark fabric. "Found this at a secondary scene. Doesn't match any known samples. Think you can run it through the system?"

Matt accepted the bag, studying the material while his mind raced. The fabric was familiar—too familiar. His stomach clenched as he recognized the weave and the particular shade of blue. "No problem," he managed, his voice steady despite the panic clawing at his chest. I'll get on it right away."

"Appreciate it." John didn't move, his gaze steady and penetrating. "Everything alright? You seem a bit... off."

"Just tired," Matt lied, the words tasting bitter. "I've had a busy day."

"Haven't we all," John agreed, though his eyes remained fixed on Matt. "Let me know as soon as you find anything."

After John left, Matt exhaled shakily. Through his window, the snow had transformed into a proper squall, the flakes now thick and heavy, obscuring everything beyond the immediate parking lot. The snowstorm was finally arriving, and it was right on schedule.

Matt's hands shook as he reached for the evidence bag, his mind racing. The fabric was damning—too specific, too obviously connected. He had been so careful, planned for every contingency, but somehow, he'd missed this. Or had he? Maybe this was John testing him, watching his reaction, waiting for him to make a mistake.

His gaze drifted to the supply closet, where solvent bottles waited like silent conspirators. A plan began forming in his mind—desperate perhaps, but necessary. The storm outside grew fiercer, the wind now driving the snow sideways past his window. It was perfect weather for accidents, evidence destruction, and trail obscurement.

Moving quickly, he retrieved a canister of solvent. The harsh chemical smell filled the air as he worked, his movements precise despite the trembling in his hands. The evidence would have to go—all of it. Let them blame it on an accident, a tragic combination of circumstances. By the time they sorted through the ashes, he would be gone.

As he prepared, a memory surfaced—Emily standing in the snow outside that party in Chicago, her breath visible in the winter air as she laughed at something someone had said. She looked so alive at that moment, with snowflakes catching in her dark hair. He had watched her from the shadows, already knowing how it would end.

Then Sarah, her investigative instincts finally led her too close to the truth. She had been clever, but not clever enough—not in the end.

The jazz music played on, incongruously smooth and calm, as Matt set his plan in motion. Outside, Columbus disappeared into the storm's white fury, nature conspiring to cover his escape. Soon, the lab would join the chaos—another scene in the performance he had orchestrated for years.

He pulled the lighter from his pocket—an old habit he'd never entirely kicked. The metal was cold against his palm but warmed quickly as he held it. One last act in a play that had run far longer than anyone suspected.

CHAPTER 27
THE VANISHING

The party pulsed around Emily Reardon like a living thing, bass-heavy music vibrating through the floorboards of the cramped Loyola apartment. Red cups dotted every surface, and the crisp March air slipped through open windows, carrying with it the faint promise of spring. Emily wove through the crowd, accepting congratulations on the basketball team's win, though her mind was elsewhere. Something felt off tonight. Had felt off for weeks now.

She caught her reflection in a window—dark hair falling in waves past her shoulders, cheeks flushed from the heat. The girl staring back at her looked normal enough: junior at Loyola, dean's list student, the kind of person who always had a smile ready and never met a stranger. But beneath that carefully curated exterior, exhaustion lurked in the shadows under her eyes, worry creasing her forehead.

Behind her reflection, she saw him again. Matt Lawson.

He stood in his usual corner, nursing a beer he'd barely touched all night, watching. Always watching.

A chill ran down her spine despite the apartment's stifling warmth. He wasn't even supposed to be here. Matt didn't go to Loyola. He just knew some guys who did—Mark Lewis and his crowd. But lately, he seemed to be everywhere she turned. At parties like this one, his presence a constant weight. In the campus library where she studied, always choosing a table with a clear view of her usual spot. Crossing the quad when she walked to class, his path somehow intersecting with hers, though he had no reason to be there.

At first, she'd told herself it was just coincidence. Chicago was a big city, but the campus community was small. Running into the same faces wasn't unusual. But this felt different. Calculated. Like she'd wandered into a play where everyone else knew the script but her.

Two weeks ago, she'd been at the library late, working on a paper for her American Literature class. Around midnight, she'd glanced out the window and seen him standing in the snow across the street, staring up at her study room. He hadn't moved for nearly an hour, completely still, like he was waiting for something. When she finally packed up her things and left through a side exit, she'd felt his eyes on her all the way back to her dorm.

"Emily!" Mark Lewis's voice broke through her thoughts. He appeared at her elbow, grinning, his face flushed from alcohol and victory. "Where've you been hiding? We're heading to Murphy's to keep celebrating. You coming?"

She forced a smile, though her stomach churned. Mark was one of the first friends she'd made at Loyola—a genuinely good guy. He didn't know about the growing unease that had consumed her thoughts, about the way Matt's constant presence made her feel like she was suffocating. How could she explain it without sounding paranoid?

"Think I'm going to head home actually," she said, trying to keep her voice light. "Got an early class tomorrow, and Dr. Matthews isn't exactly forgiving about tardiness."

Mark's face fell slightly. "Come on, it's not even midnight. One drink?"

"Rain check?" She touched his arm apologetically. "I'm just tired. It's been a long week."

He hesitated but nodded, already distracted by someone calling his name from across the room. Emily watched him disappear into the crowd, then glanced back at Matt's corner.

Empty.

Her pulse quickened.

The night air hit her like a slap as she stepped outside, cutting through her light jacket. The street was quieter than she'd expected, most students either still at parties or already moved on to the bars. Streetlights cast pools of yellow light on the pavement, and somewhere in the distance, a car alarm wailed.

Emily pulled her jacket tighter and started walking, her boots clicking against the concrete. The sound seemed unnaturally loud in the stillness, like a beacon announcing her presence. She quickened her pace.

Don't be paranoid, she told herself. You're fine. Everything's fine.

But she couldn't shake the feeling of eyes on her back. Every shadow seemed to shift, every rustle of the wind made her jump. She'd felt this way for weeks now—watched, studied, like prey being stalked. Her friends had brushed it off, told her she was overthinking. Even her mother hadn't taken her concerns seriously when she'd called home last weekend.

"You're working too hard," her mom had said. "Taking too many classes. Of course you're stressed."

Maybe they were right. Maybe midterms and maintaining her scholarship were just getting to her. Maybe—

Footsteps behind her. Steady. Unhurried.

Emily's heart slammed against her ribs. She didn't turn around, just walked faster, her keys clutched between her fingers like makeshift brass knuckles. Her dorm was still three blocks away. Too far.

The footsteps matched her pace. Getting closer.

Her breathing quickened as she fumbled for her phone, trying to pull up her contacts without dropping it. The screen was too bright in the darkness, her trembling fingers missing the keys. Behind her, the footsteps grew louder. Closer.

Run, her instincts screamed. *Run now.*

But before she could move, something sharp pressed against her neck. A hand clamped over her mouth, stifling her scream. The phone slipped from her grasp, clattering to the sidewalk.

"Shh." Matt's voice was soft in her ear, almost gentle. "Don't fight it. It'll only make things worse."

The needle slid into her skin, and ice spread through her veins. Emily tried to struggle, but her limbs wouldn't respond. Her vision blurred, the streetlights stretching into long, distorted trails of light. The last thing she saw was Matt's face, his expression calm and focused as he lowered her to the ground.

"You brought this on yourself," he whispered, his words fading as darkness crept in. "You're not better than me. None of you are."

The world tilted sideways, then disappeared completely.

Emily Reardon vanished that night. Her absence left a hole in the world that would echo through years and lives she'd never know. But in that final moment, as consciousness slipped away, she understood with terrible clarity what her friends and family had missed: sometimes the monsters didn't hide under the bed or in the shadows.

Sometimes, they smiled at you from across the room.

And Matt Lawson had been smiling for a very long time.

CHAPTER 28
HIDDEN IN PLAN SIGHT

The precinct was unusually quiet; the drone of computers and the occasional ring of a phone were the only sounds breaking the stillness. Claire Harper sat at her desk, a mountain of files spread before her. For hours, she'd combed through every scrap of information that might connect Emily Reardon, Sarah Thompson, and Matt Lawson. She was close—she could feel it—but something still eluded her. A piece of the puzzle remained maddeningly out of reach.

Leaning back in her chair, she rubbed her temples and stared at the computer screen, her thoughts racing. Matt Lawson. The Loyola connection. His suspicious behavior. Everything pointed to him, yet she needed something concrete, something that would break the case wide open.

Her eyes wandered across the mess of files, landing on a yearbook buried at the edge of the pile. She pulled it closer, frowning. It had come from Sam DiMatteo's high school records—a detail she'd overlooked until now. Claire flipped it open, scanning the glossy black-and-white pages. Sam's smiling freshman photo stared back at her, her youthful energy leaping off the page.

Claire's breath caught as she turned another page.

Matt Lawson.

His senior photo was just a few pages before Sam's entry. A younger version of him, but unmistakable—the same reserved expression, the same unnerving smile. She froze, staring at the image. Matt had attended the same high school as Sam. He had been a senior while Sam was a freshman.

Her pulse quickened. Matt hadn't just crossed paths with Emily Reardon in college—he'd known Sam, too. And now both were dead.

The coincidence snapped under the weight of what she'd just discovered. This was deliberate. Matt had been connected to all three victims, and it had been right there in front of them the whole time.

Grabbing her phone, Claire texted Ramirez with trembling hands: Get to John's office now. Urgent.

She didn't wait for a reply. Snatching the yearbook, she shot up from her chair and began weaving through the maze of desks. Her strides were purposeful, her heart pounding as the pieces finally started clicking into place.

Then, the silence shattered.

A blaring alarm pierced the air, and red emergency lights strobed along the walls. Over the intercom, a calm but urgent voice echoed: "Attention all personnel: Evacuate the building immediately. This is not a drill."

Claire stopped in her tracks, her grip on the yearbook tightening. The acrid smell of smoke reached her nostrils, faint but unmistakable. A knot of dread coiled in her stomach as she turned toward the source—the forensics lab.

Matt's domain.

Chaos erupted around her as officers and staff scrambled for the exits, their faces a mix of confusion and rising panic. Shouts and hurried footsteps echoed through the precinct, a cacophony of alarm and fear.

Claire spun against the tide of bodies, pushing her way toward the smoke. Her thoughts raced, colliding in jumbled fragments. If this was Matt's doing, she couldn't ignore it. Not now.

A firm hand grabbed her arm, stopping her in her tracks. She turned to see Ramirez, his expression a mix of concern and frustration.

"Claire, what are you doing?" he demanded, his voice raised over the commotion. "We need to get out!"

"Something's wrong," she said, her tone resolute. "I need to check the lab."

Ramirez hesitated, studying her face. Then, with a sharp nod, he let go. "Let's go."

They moved against the stream of evacuating personnel, the smoke growing thicker with each step. The acrid haze clawed at their throats, and the heat became oppressive. By the time they reached the lab, the doorway was engulfed in black smoke, the flicker of flames visible through the glass panel.

They skidded to a stop as a loud crack sounded from inside, followed by a cascade of sparks and debris. The fire raged, consuming everything in its path. It wasn't just a fire—it was an inferno.

Ramirez pulled Claire back, shielding her from the heat. "We can't go in there!" he shouted, barely audible over the roar of the flames.

Claire's eyes remained locked on the blaze, frustration burning almost as fiercely in her chest. She knew he was right. The lab was a lost cause. Whatever evidence Matt had destroyed in there was gone for good.

With a reluctant nod, she turned away, allowing Ramirez to guide her back through the smoke-filled corridor. Overhead, the sprinkler system activated, dousing them in cold water as they navigated the chaos. The sharp scent of wet smoke clung to them as they finally emerged into the crisp night air.

Outside, the parking lot was a storm of activity. Officers and staff huddled in small groups, their faces illuminated by the flashing lights of fire trucks pulling onto the scene. Firefighters jumped into action, their commands blending with the wail of sirens.

Claire scanned the crowd, spotting John DiMatteo pushing his way toward them. His face was a storm of worry and barely restrained urgency.

"What the hell happened?" John demanded, his eyes darting between Claire and Ramirez.

Claire held up the yearbook, her expression grim. "We need to talk. It's about Matt."

John's brow furrowed as she thrust the yearbook into his hands. He flipped it open, his gaze landing on the photographs—Sam's youthful, smiling face and, just pages away, Matt Lawson's reserved senior portrait. His features darkened, the weight of realization hitting him like a freight train.

"He knew her," Claire said softly. "Matt went to high school with Sam."

John stared at the images, his grip on the yearbook tightening. He looked like a man who'd just been told he'd been fighting a ghost all along.

Ramirez stepped closer, his voice low. "If Matt started the fire, he knew exactly what he was doing. He's covering his tracks."

John exhaled sharply, snapping the yearbook shut. For years, he'd been certain Mick Garrett had killed his daughter. He'd chased that certainty to the ends of the earth, throwing everything he had into building a case. But now, it was all unraveling. Matt's connection to Sam, the missing evidence, the fire—it changed everything.

Claire watched him carefully. "John. What do we do?"

John didn't answer immediately. His jaw clenched, his thoughts spiraling through years of grief and anger, all of it tainted by the possibility that he'd been wrong. That he'd spent years chasing the wrong man while the real killer had been hiding in plain sight.

Finally, his gaze snapped to Claire and Ramirez. "Has anyone seen Matt?"

Claire shook her head. "No. Not since the alarm."

Ramirez frowned. "With the evacuation, he could've slipped out. He might already be gone."

John turned, raising his voice to address the cluster of officers nearby. "Listen up! Matt Lawson is now a person of interest. Spread out and find him. Now!"

The officers scattered, mobilizing quickly. The fire still raged behind them, flames consuming the lab with relentless ferocity. The scent of burning chemicals filled the air, mixing with the bitter cold of the night.

Claire stepped closer to John, her voice cautious. "Do we have enough evidence to go after him? We need to be sure."

John's jaw tightened as he stared at the blazing building. They had the high school connection, the missing documents, the suspicious behavior, and now the fire. But was it enough? Or were they risking another mistake?

His voice was low, almost a growl. "If we wait, we lose him. I won't let that happen."

Claire nodded, but unease gnawed at her. The fire wasn't just destroying evidence—it was forcing their hand. Whatever Matt's next move was, she knew it would be calculated. They weren't just chasing a suspect now. They were hunting someone who had spent years perfecting the art of staying one step ahead.

And somewhere in the darkness, Matt Lawson was already moving.

CHAPTER 29
BEHIND THE FAÇADE

The envelope landed on Claire Harper's desk at 11:47 PM, delivered by a tired-looking officer who'd found it during a secondary search of Matt's workspace. Inside were dozens of photos—surveillance shots of Sarah, Emily, and others they hadn't identified yet. The careful organization and methodical annotations made Claire's blood run cold. Each photo was labeled in Matt's precise handwriting: dates, times, behavioral observations.

The evidence board on the wall, already crowded with photos and notes, felt suffocating now. It told the story of a predator who had turned their entire system into his playground. But for the first time, Claire could see the cracks in his façade—the weak points in Matt's psychological fortress.

Her eyes drifted to the photos spread across her desk. Each image was a testament to Matt's patience and his unsettling, methodical nature. The patterns of his stalking reminded her of something—a familiar, old wound she had spent years trying to bury. Her hand moved to the bottom drawer of her desk, hovering over it.

The sound of footsteps in the hallway broke her thoughts. Most of the precinct had emptied hours ago, leaving only the skeleton crew of the night shift. But these footsteps were familiar—the steady, measured pace of someone who carried the same weight she did.

She looked up as John DiMatteo appeared in her doorway. His expression was as heavy as her own. "You're here late," he said, leaning against the frame.

"So are you." Claire managed a tired smile, though her eyes flicked back to the photos on her desk. The weight of them seemed to press harder on her chest, and the connection she'd been feeling—the reason this case haunted her so deeply—finally clicked into place. She hesitated, then made a decision. "Come in. There's something I want to show you."

John stepped inside, settling into the chair across from her desk. Claire pulled out her key ring, selecting a small silver key she rarely used. With a soft click, she opened the bottom drawer and withdrew a worn manila folder, different from the department's standard files.

"Twenty years ago," she began, her voice steady despite the tremor in her hands, "my sister Megan disappeared from her college campus in Michigan. She was brilliant—studying psychology, just like I would later. She had this way of understanding people that felt almost magical to me." Claire smiled faintly at the memory, the kind of smile that held both warmth and pain. "I was sixteen when it happened."

John leaned forward, the grief in his own life recognizing hers. Claire opened the folder and revealed a photograph of a young woman with Claire's eyes and smile.

"The investigation was thorough, but they never found her killer. He was careful and methodical—just like Matt. He knew how to hide his tracks, how to blend in." Her voice faltered, but she pressed on. "What really haunts me is that Megan knew something was wrong. She told me about feeling watched, about little things in her room being moved. At the time, we all thought she was just being paranoid. But now…"

"Now you see the pattern," John finished softly.

Claire nodded, her fingers lightly brushing the edge of the photograph. "That's why Matt's case feels so familiar. The way he stalked his victims, made them doubt their instincts—it's the same playbook. When I started studying criminal psychology, it wasn't just about understanding predators. It was about understanding what happened to Megan."

She pulled out another document—a psychological profile she'd created during her early training. "I've spent years analyzing cases like this, trying to learn how these men think, how they choose their victims. Every case teaches me something new—something I hope might help prevent another family from going through what mine did."

John was silent for a moment, absorbing her words. "Is that why you pushed so hard to be on this case?"

"Partly," Claire admitted, meeting his gaze. "But it's more than that. When I saw the patterns in Matt's behavior—how he targeted women who reminded him of his own inadequacies—I knew we couldn't let him slip away. Not like Megan's killer did."

She stood and moved to the window, looking out over the city. The lights twinkled below, each one representing countless lives and stories, each one a potential victim. "Sometimes I wonder if Megan would be proud of me. If all this—the studying, the understanding of darkness—would make sense to her."

John joined her at the window, his presence steady and grounding. "She would be," he said quietly, with certainty. "You're not just studying these cases, Claire. You're giving voices to the victims. You're making sure they're not forgotten."

Claire turned to him, seeing her own pain reflected in his eyes. "Like you do for Sam?"

His breath caught, but he nodded. "Yeah. Exactly like that."

For a moment, they stood in silence, two people bound by the weight of loss and purpose. Finally, Claire broke the quiet, her voice stronger now. "Matt's different from Megan's killer in one crucial way—we know who he is. We can stop him."

"We will," John assured her. And for the first time, Claire believed it.

She returned the folder to its drawer, locking away the physical remnants of her past. But the strength it gave her—the drive to understand and prevent such crimes—remained. She and John had both been forged in the fire of personal tragedy, and they were stronger for it.

"Thank you," John said, his voice low but sincere. "For sharing that with me."

Claire met his gaze, seeing not just understanding but a deep connection—a shared pain that had forged them into who they were now. "Thank you for listening."

She turned back to the evidence board, her eyes scanning it with renewed focus. The weight of her past, of Megan's loss, had always been a part of her work. But now, after sharing it with John, she felt lighter. Stronger.

They weren't just hunting a predator anymore—they were standing against everything Matt represented. Every life he had tried to destroy.

"We should get back to it," Claire said, determination hardening her tone. "Matt's not going to stop unless we stop him."

John nodded, his expression resolute. Their connection deepened, forged in shared pain and purpose. Together, they returned to the case, ready to face whatever came next.

The hunt for Matt Lawson wasn't just about justice anymore. It was about ensuring that what happened to Megan, to Sam, and to all their victims—past and potential—never happened again.

And this time, they wouldn't let him slip through their fingers.

CHAPTER 30
BROKEN FOCUS

John knew this drill. He'd been doing the cop-at-the-window routine for twenty minutes now, staring at Columbus's skyline like it might cough up answers. Or maybe Matt Lawson's head on a platter. Either would do.

The sky matched his mood—the kind of oppressive gray that makes undertakers smile. His reflection in the glass told the whole sorry story: bloodshot eyes, jaw clenched so tight it might snap, that thousand-yard stare you don't need a badge to recognize.

Especially when the dead kid in question was your own.

Sam.

Funny how one word could feel like a knife to the gut.

He slammed a fist against the windowsill, his knuckles going white. Mick Garrett. He'd chased that bastard for five years, convinced Mick had murdered his daughter. Mick had the motive, the violent past, the temper. Everything pointed to him. Until it didn't.

Now Mick Garrett was walking free somewhere, probably laughing his ass off. But Mick wasn't the one keeping John awake at night anymore.

No, that honor belonged to Matt Lawson—the quiet, unassuming forensics tech who had processed evidence from Sam's case with steady hands and just enough detachment to seem professional. The same Matt who smiled at office parties, brought donuts to the bullpen, and nodded along at crime scenes like he wasn't planning his next move.

And now Matt Lawson was gone. Vanished.

John's fists tightened until his nails bit into his palms. He'd spent years hunting monsters in the shadows, only to miss the one wearing a lab coat, hiding in plain sight. The signs had been there—bright as neon, obvious as a bloody footprint. But he'd been too busy playing Ahab, chasing Mick Garrett's white whale, to notice the shark swimming circles around him.

And Sam?

The thought hit harder than any suspect's right hook. His little girl, his Sam, had been there at the end. Alone. Scared, maybe. While he'd been playing detective, chasing bad guys across the city, she'd been in the crosshairs of a predator who had probably smiled at her in the school hallway.

She never said a word. Never dropped a hint. Never mentioned the name Matt Lawson.

But then again, when was the last time he'd really listened?

John shoved off from the window like it had burned him. No time for the daddy-guilt Olympics now. Matt Lawson was out there somewhere, watching, waiting, playing whatever sick game got his rocks off.

The hunt was on.

And this time, John wasn't just hunting a killer.

He was hunting the man who'd murdered his daughter.

The office door creaked open, cutting through the silence. Claire Harper entered, her expression steely with determination. Ramirez followed, clutching a stack of reports, his phone buzzing incessantly.

"The APB is out," Ramirez said without preamble. "Every unit's been alerted. Surrounding counties are on board, state police are mobilizing.

Roadblocks are up on all major highways."

"Any leads on his movements?" John asked, his voice sharp enough to cut steel.

Claire nodded grimly. "Last known location was his apartment. He cleared out sometime last night, probably after we started piecing things together. We're pulling security footage, but all we have are a few grainy clips of him heading west."

John exhaled sharply, raking a hand through his hair. "He's not stupid. He knows our playbook. He knows how to disappear."

"We've compiled a list of his known associates and hangouts," Ramirez added. "Teams are canvassing. If he tries to hide, we'll flush him out."

John wanted to believe that, but he couldn't shake the feeling that Matt was always two steps ahead. Matt wasn't just fleeing—he was evading. Mick Garrett had been reckless, impulsive. Matt was methodical, calculated. Every move would be deliberate, planned.

Claire stepped closer, her voice firm. "We'll find him. But we need to stay focused. Matt's not infallible. Everyone slips up."

John nodded, but the suffocating weight of guilt pressed down on him. He'd failed Sam once. With Matt on the loose, it felt like he was failing her again.

"Find me a lead," he said, his voice low and controlled, a storm simmering beneath the surface. "Anything that tells us where he's headed."

Ramirez nodded, his phone buzzing again as he stepped out. Claire lingered, studying John with narrowed eyes.

"We'll get him," she said softly. "But you need to stay clear-headed. This is about Matt now. Not Sam."

John's jaw tightened, but he didn't respond. He knew she was right, but the line between the two blurred in his mind. Sam's death was why he became a detective, why he spent five years chasing justice. And now Matt's face haunted his every waking moment.

Hours passed, each one heavier than the last. Tips flooded the precinct—dozens of Matt Lawson sightings, none panning out.

John paced the bullpen, surrounded by the chaos of ringing phones and hurried voices, but his mind drifted. He couldn't stop thinking about Sam—those final weeks of her life. He'd been distant, buried in another case. Had she known something was wrong? Felt scared?

Had she stayed silent to avoid burdening her detective father?

"John."

Claire's voice snapped him back. She stood in front of him, her expression serious.

"We've been reviewing the files again—Sam, Emily, Sarah. Ramirez thinks he found something."

In John's office, Ramirez was poring over a spread of crime scene photos and timelines. His brow furrowed as he pointed to the evidence.

"I've been cross-referencing Sam's case with Emily's and Sarah's," Ramirez said. "There's a pattern in how the scenes were staged. But what's interesting is the timeline."

John's stomach tightened. "What about it?"

Ramirez hesitated, glancing at Claire before answering. "Matt was experimenting. Sam's case—it was messier. Sloppier. The knots, the staging—it wasn't as precise. But by the time he got to Sarah, everything was calculated. Almost... perfected."

Claire leaned in, her voice steady but urgent. "He's escalating, John. From Sam to Emily to Sarah—each time refining his methods. He's not done."

John's fists clenched at his sides, his nails biting into his palms. "We need to find him before he strikes again."

The hours dragged on. The precinct buzzed with activity, but each lead felt like a dead end. Every passing minute tightened the noose around John's chest.

Finally, his phone buzzed. A text from Claire.

We might have something. Briefing room. Now.

John entered to find Claire and Ramirez standing before a map, red lines and pins tracking Matt's movements.

"He's heading west," Claire said, pointing to the map. "But he's avoiding the highways. Moving deeper into the state."

"Why?" John asked, frowning.

Ramirez exchanged a glance with Claire. "We think he's heading to a cabin. Remote, off the grid. He could lay low there for weeks."

John's heart pounded. "Do we have a location?"

"General area," Ramirez replied. "It's secluded, but we're narrowing it down."

John's jaw tightened. "Assemble a team. We're going after him."

The drive was long, tension thick in the car. John sat in the passenger seat, fists clenched, his mind racing. Every mile brought them closer to Matt—or further from him.

When they reached the cabin, shadows stretched long over the forest. The air was still, the woods silent.

John's hand hovered over his gun as they approached. His heart hammered in his chest. Was this it?

They kicked in the door.

The cabin was empty.

No Matt.

But on the table was a map, red lines connecting the locations of the murders: Sam, Emily, Sarah.

John's blood ran cold. Matt wasn't done.

He was just getting started.

CHAPTER 31
SEEDS OF EVIL

Matt Lawson had always been good at blending in.

As a kid, he was the quiet one in the back of the classroom, invisible by design. Teachers called him "polite," "reserved," "mature beyond his years," but none of them really knew him. His classmates didn't notice him either. And that was exactly how he liked it. Being invisible meant freedom. It meant he could observe, learn, and plan without anyone suspecting a thing.

By high school, Matt had turned the art of invisibility into a science. While his peers obsessed over popularity, grades, or sports, Matt studied them. He learned what they feared, what they hid, what made them tick. Their insecurities were open books, and Matt read every page.

There was power in knowing people's secrets—even the ones they didn't know they had.

But in his senior year, one person disrupted the quiet, controlled world Matt had built: Sam DiMatteo.

At first, Sam was just another face in the hallways. A freshman. Quiet, reserved—like him. But where Matt's invisibility was intentional, Sam's seemed effortless, like she lived in a world apart from everyone else. She didn't play the social games. She didn't crave approval. She didn't even seem to notice the hierarchies everyone else was trapped in.

It was her indifference that intrigued him.

At first, it was curiosity. During lunch, he watched her sit alone by choice. In study hall, she buried herself in books, oblivious to the noise around her. She moved through the world untouched, self-contained. Unreachable. It was the kind of calm Matt envied.

And it was the kind of calm he wanted to break.

The idea began as a flicker—an experiment. He wanted to see if he could crack that armor. What would it take for her to notice him? To let him in? The thought of unraveling her self-possession consumed him.

It wasn't love. It wasn't even lust. It was control.

Soon, Sam became an obsession. He mapped her routines: which halls she walked between classes, how she lingered by her locker, the way she chewed her pen during chemistry. He imagined scenarios—conversations, encounters, moments where he could force her to see him. In his mind, it became a game of power. Sam was the challenge. And he never lost.

But Sam never gave him the opportunity. She was untouchable in a way that frustrated and fascinated him. Even when he saw her with her father— Detective John DiMatteo, the famous cop everyone whispered about—Matt felt the same thrill of invisibility. The man who could read criminals like open books had no idea who was watching his daughter.

Matt graduated before he could act. He told himself it didn't matter. It wasn't real, just a passing fixation. But the game felt unfinished. Unresolved.

And then, years later, there was Emily Reardon.

Emily was nothing like Sam. Where Sam was quiet, Emily was vibrant— magnetic. People gravitated toward her without her trying. She moved through the world with an ease that made her untouchable in a different way. She wasn't just admired; she was adored.

Matt saw her for the first time at a Loyola party. He'd only gone because Mark Lewis, an old high school acquaintance, invited him. Matt had no intention of staying—he hated crowds—but then he saw Emily.

She wasn't like the others. She stood out effortlessly, surrounded by friends and admirers. Untouchable. Safe.

And that's why Matt couldn't look away.

He began attending more parties, blending into the background like he always did. No one noticed him, least of all Emily. But Matt studied her, learning her patterns: where she went, who she trusted, when she let her guard down. It was a new game, and this time, he wouldn't leave it unfinished.

Mark became his in. People like Mark were easy to manipulate—desperate for validation, eager to trust. Matt slipped back into his life with little effort, using him as a cover to stay close to Emily without raising suspicion.

The night Emily disappeared had been carefully planned. Matt knew her habits, her vulnerabilities. He'd waited months for the right moment. When she left the party alone, vulnerable and isolated, Matt knew it was time.

Taking her wasn't just an act of power. It was proof that he could make someone untouchable vanish.

The news broke the next day: Emily Reardon was missing.

And for the first time, Matt felt the rush of real power.

But after Emily disappeared, the investigation that followed was too close for comfort. Matt hadn't anticipated how relentless people would be in looking for her, how her disappearance would dominate headlines and spark a citywide search. The police were everywhere, and for the first time, Matt felt the pressure of his actions closing in around him.

He hadn't planned for what came after. The rush of taking her had blinded him to the reality of what came next—the consequences.

That's when the opportunity with Chicago PD came along. He had just graduated with his degree in criminal justice and was looking for a way to escape the growing scrutiny in his personal life. When the position in the evidence room opened up, it seemed perfect. A low-profile job, far from the public eye, but with access to all the information flowing through the department.

The timing was ideal. The police were still chasing leads on Emily's case, but they were getting nowhere. Matt saw his opportunity. He used his new position to slowly erase any trace of his connection to her disappearance. He made sure that critical pieces of evidence—witness statements, security footage, small but important details—never made it to the right hands. Files were misplaced, evidence was mislabeled, and what had been an active investigation slowly turned cold

.

It was easier than he'd imagined.

At first, he had felt nervous—waiting for someone to catch on, for someone to notice the missing files. But Chicago PD was overwhelmed with cases, their attention spread thin. No one suspected that one of their own was tampering with evidence right under their noses. And as time passed, Matt's confidence grew. He realized just how much control he could exert from the inside. Not only had he made Emily disappear, but he had also made sure her case would never be solved.

For Matt, it wasn't just about escaping punishment—it was about the thrill of getting away with it.

Working in the evidence room gave him access to more than just the files on Emily's case. It was a treasure trove of information, a way to learn the ins and outs of police procedure. He read through old case files, studied the mistakes detectives made, and began to see patterns—how cases fell apart due to small, seemingly insignificant details. It was all there, laid out for him to see, and he became an expert in manipulating those weaknesses.

When he learned that the forensic technician position with Columbus PD was available, it felt like a new beginning. A fresh start in a new city, where no one knew his past, and where he could continue perfecting his craft. He applied, and with his clean record and experience in the evidence room, he got the job easily.

But Matt wasn't just leaving Chicago behind. He was leaving the weight of Emily's disappearance behind, knowing he had buried any chance of the truth coming to light. He had done it—he had outsmarted the system.

When he moved to Columbus, he carried with him the confidence that he could do it again. He could find new victims, exert his power, and still stay one step ahead of the police. And he knew, with his new role as a forensic technician, he would have even more access, more control over the investigations that followed.

When Matt met Sarah Thompson, he knew he had found someone different. Sarah wasn't like Sam or Emily—she wasn't untouchable. She was kind and warm and saw the good in people, even when they didn't deserve it.

That kindness made her vulnerable.

Matt didn't take long to work his way into her life. At first, it had been easy—just casual conversations at work, small talk that gradually turned into friendship. But as he got closer to her, he noticed the same patterns he had seen in Sam and Emily. Sarah was too trusting and willing to help others, even when it put her at risk.

And then she started asking questions.

Sarah had found something—something that connected Matt to Emily's disappearance. She had reached out to him, trying to be subtle, but Matt wasn't stupid. He knew what she was getting at. He could see the doubt in her eyes, the suspicion creeping in.

That's when he knew he had to act.

Sarah had been so close to uncovering the truth, exposing him for what he was. But Matt wasn't going to let that happen. He had been careful, planning every move, just like he had with Emily. He knew how to cover his tracks, how to stay invisible.

But this time, something had gone wrong. John DiMatteo had gotten involved.

Matt had always known about DiMatteo. Everyone had. The detective whose daughter had been murdered, whose life had been consumed by the case. Matt had watched from a distance as DiMatteo chased Mick Garrett, convinced he was the killer. It had been easy for Matt to hide behind Garrett's shadow, letting DiMatteo's obsession with Garrett blind him to the real threat.

But now, with Sarah's death, DiMatteo was getting too close.

Matt knew he had to be careful. He had made it this far by staying invisible, by blending in with the crowd. But DiMatteo was different. He wasn't like the others. He was relentless, driven by a need for justice that bordered on obsession.

For the first time, Matt felt like he was being hunted.

But he wasn't worried. Not yet. He had been careful. He had covered his tracks. And even if DiMatteo was closing in, Matt knew how to stay one step ahead. He always had.

Because, in the end, control was everything.

It always had been.

CHAPTER 32
BEHIND CLOSED DOORS

Silence enveloped the precinct like a living thing, the usual cacophony of ringing phones and hurried voices reduced to murmurs. John DiMatteo stood rigid at the window, his reflection a ghost in the rain-streaked glass. Outside, the parking lot blurred beneath sheets of water, the storm matching the one brewing inside him. They were so close—so close to the truth he could almost taste it. And yet, he'd never felt more powerless.

"You know why it has to be this way." Ramirez's voice, firm but measured, cut through the heavy stillness. He stood in the doorway, his usual easy demeanor replaced by something harder, more urgent.

John's jaw tightened, but he didn't turn. "I can handle it," he said, though the hollowness in his tone betrayed him.

"Can you?" Ramirez stepped further into the room, his boots thudding softly against the floor. "Because if you lose control for even a second—if you push too hard or too fast—Matt walks. Everything we've built falls apart."

John's hands curled into fists at his sides, his knuckles going white. The truth in Ramirez's words burned like acid. Standing down now, when they were so close, felt like surrender. But the risk was too great. He'd seen cases ruined by emotion before, and if this one unraveled, he'd never forgive himself.

Claire Harper lingered near the door, her sharp eyes catching every flicker of emotion crossing John's face: the muscle ticking in his jaw, the slight tremor in his hands, the way his shoulders hunched like he was carrying an invisible weight. This wasn't just about justice—it was about Sam. It had always been about Sam.

"We'll bring him down, John," Ramirez said, his voice softening. "But we have to do it right. By the book. No room for error."

John finally turned, and Claire caught her breath at the raw pain in his eyes. "This is it, isn't it?" he said, his voice rough and barely controlled. "If you find what we think you'll find…"

"Then it's over," Ramirez finished. "Matt Lawson goes away for good."

The silence that followed was suffocating, heavy with everything unsaid. John ran a hand through his hair, his fingers shaking slightly. He looked older, more worn, like a man who had carried grief too long.

"Keep me updated," he muttered, the words scraping like gravel in his throat.

Claire stepped forward, her voice steady but gentle. "Let them handle this part," she said. "You've carried this long enough."

The door clicked shut behind Ramirez, leaving them in a silence that felt like drowning.

Dusk bled quickly into night as Ramirez led his team down the suburban street toward Matt Lawson's house. A bitter January wind cut through their tactical gear, stinging their faces with icy snow. Beneath three inches of fresh powder, the lawns lay pristine and uniform, each one a copy of the next— perfect suburban stillness. It was the kind of scene that belonged on Christmas cards, not at the center of a monster's lair.

Matt's house stood like all the others: a two-story, cookie-cutter suburban dream. Icicles hung from the gutters like crystalline teeth, and warm light glowed in the windows, projecting a calculated normalcy. A single set of footprints led from the driveway to the front door and then vanished, as if their maker had dissolved into the house itself. Even the smoke curling lazily from the chimney felt sinister, as if mocking the brutality hidden within.

Ramirez's gut twisted. This wasn't just another warrant. This was the endgame. Years of missed clues, dead ends, and wrong turns had led to this moment. "Move in," he ordered, his voice low but firm. "Silent and clean."

The team advanced, boots crunching softly in the snow. The stillness of winter made stealth nearly impossible, every sound amplified in the freezing air. But Ramirez didn't care. If Matt was inside, he was likely watching them now, savoring the tableau they created against the night—the hunters closing in, ready to bring the curtain down on his carefully crafted performance.

A single kick sent the door crashing inward. The team poured into the house, flashlights cutting through the darkness.

The sterility hit first.

Everything gleamed under the beams of their lights—polished floors, furniture dusted to perfection, surfaces so clean they reflected like mirrors. The air was thick with the sharp tang of cleaning products, sterile and artificial.

"Clear the rooms," Ramirez barked, forcing back the unease creeping up his spine. "Every corner. Every closet. Leave nothing unchecked."

The officers fanned out, their boots echoing in the unnaturally spotless space. At first, the house revealed nothing unusual—just the meticulous neatness of a man obsessed with control. But as they moved deeper, the facade began to crack.

Claire, who had insisted on joining the search, moved with precision. Her sharp eyes swept every corner, every shadow. This house—it told her more about Matt than words ever could. The obsessive neatness wasn't just control; it was concealment. A mask to hide the chaos underneath.

Then they reached the back of the house. Matt's workspace.

The door creaked open, revealing a room that stopped Ramirez in his tracks.

Unlike the artificial perfection of the rest of the house, this space felt raw and exposed—a glimpse behind Matt's carefully crafted mask. Shelves lined the walls, each filled with labeled boxes and neatly arranged tools. Everything had its place, its purpose.

And then Claire noticed it: a drawer slightly ajar, disrupting the perfect symmetry.

"Here," she murmured, moving toward it. She pulled it open, revealing its grotesque contents: coils of paracord, identical to the type that had bound Sarah Thompson, each arranged with the care of a jeweler displaying priceless artifacts.

"Jesus Christ," someone whispered behind Ramirez.

He reached for one coil with gloved hands, bile rising in his throat as he recognized the pattern. It wasn't just similar—it was identical. The same manufacturer, the same gauge. A perfect match.

And that was only the beginning.

Beneath a false panel in the floor, they found vials of Dexmedetomidine, the same sedative found in Sarah's system. The syringes lay neatly in a padded case, cleaned to surgical precision.

"He's been building this for years," Ramirez said, his voice hollow. "Perfecting it."

But the discovery that chilled Claire most was the scrapbook.

Hidden behind a locked cabinet panel, it was bound in dark leather, the edges worn smooth from handling. Inside, pages of newspaper clippings chronicled Matt's twisted legacy—Emily Reardon's disappearance, Sam DiMatteo's murder, Sarah Thompson's final days. Each article was annotated in Matt's precise handwriting, the margins filled with observations, calculations, and chillingly methodical plans.

"Look at this," Claire said, her voice tight. She turned a page, revealing candid photos of Sam, taken without her knowledge. "He's been tracking them all. Studying them."

Ramirez's face darkened. "Sarah must have found something. Got too close."

"And that threatened his control," Claire finished, her voice shaking. "So he silenced her."

Claire flipped through the pages, her hands shaking slightly. Each note, each scribbled thought, was a window into Matt's mind. And what she saw terrified her.

Back at the precinct, John paced his office like a caged animal. The silence from his phone was deafening. He should be there, leading the search, not trapped here waiting for news. Every second felt like an eternity.

When his phone finally buzzed, he nearly dropped it to answer.

"Tell me," he demanded, not bothering with pleasantries.

"We found it all." Ramirez's voice was grim but triumphant. "The paracord, the sedatives, a goddamn trophy collection. Everything we need to nail him, John. It's over."

The words should have brought relief. Instead, they hit John like physical blows, each piece of evidence a reminder of his failure. Matt had been there all along—working alongside them, processing evidence, playing his role to perfection. While John had been focused on Mick Garrett, the real monster had walked among them, wearing a badge and a friendly smile.

How many chances had he missed? How many clues had he overlooked? Sarah was dead. Sam had been dead for years. And he'd failed to stop it.

"John?" Ramirez's voice cut through his spiral. "You still there?"

"Yeah," he managed, sinking into his chair. "I'm here."

"Listen to me—we got him. The case is solid. Matt Lawson isn't walking away from this."

But John barely heard him. His eyes had fixed on Sam's photo on his desk— her smile frozen in time, forever young, forever lost. The evidence they'd found might convict Matt, but it wouldn't bring her back. Nothing would.

Ramirez appeared in his doorway an hour later, his face etched with exhaustion but determined. "Time to finish this," he said. "We're bringing him in."

John stood slowly, years of grief and rage coalescing into cold purpose. "He won't come quietly."

"No," Ramirez agreed. "But this time, we're ready for him."

As they prepared for the final confrontation, John felt something shift inside him—a quiet certainty replacing the chaos of emotions. Matt Lawson had played his game for years, manipulating them all like pieces on a board, but the game was ending.

And this time, Matt wasn't writing the rules.

The storm outside intensified, rain hammering against the windows like nature was trying to wash away the horrors they'd uncovered. But some stains, John knew, ran too deep for rain to cleanse. Some wounds never truly healed.

They could arrest Matt, convict him, and lock him away until time forgot his name.

But the echoes of what he'd done would linger—in the empty chairs at family dinners, in the birthdays never celebrated, in the futures stolen from young women who had dared to trust the wrong person.

John squared his shoulders, checking his weapon with practiced hands. They had their proof now. They had their killer.

All that remained was bringing him to justice.

And God help anyone who stood in their way.

CHAPTER 33
SILENT CONFESSIONS

John sat at his desk, staring at Sam's case file, the edges worn and frayed from years of handling. The office felt colder tonight, the air heavier, pressing against his skin like a tangible weight. Everything felt wrong as if the world had shifted just enough to leave him off balance. His thoughts swirled in a mess of anger, frustration, and regret. He had once convinced himself that solving the case would bring peace, but now, the truth felt like a knife twisting deeper. Mick Garrett hadn't killed Sam. Matt Lawson had been hiding in plain sight the whole time, and John had missed it.

He flipped through the pages slowly, each turn feeling like a punch to the gut. The photographs of the crime scene, once a blur of procedural necessity, now felt personal—too personal. Sam's smiling face stared back at him from a school photo, her eyes full of life—eyes he would never see again. He clenched his fist, fighting the urge to crumple the photo. His guilt weighed heavy, an anchor pulling him down into the darkness he'd been running from.

A wave of nausea hit him as he reached the autopsy report, the cold, clinical language a stark contrast to the vibrant girl he had raised. Lividity patterns suggest... No evidence of sexual assault... Cause of death: ligature strangulation... The words blurred together, and he slammed the file shut, pushing it away as if the act could distance him from the truth. But the truth was always there, gnawing at him, relentless.

He stood abruptly, pacing the room, hands running through his hair in frustration. The case had consumed him, but worse than that—he had let it. He had let the job take over his life, and in doing so, he had lost Sam. Not just to the killer but long before that. To his own distractions. His phone calls had grown shorter, his visits less frequent. He was too busy chasing ghosts and solving other people's problems while ignoring the one before him.

His mind returned to their last conversation, which now haunted him like a specter.

It was late afternoon, the sun casting long shadows through his kitchen window. The golden light filtered through the blinds, splintering across the countertops and illuminating the tiny dust particles in the air. John stood at the sink, rinsing off a plate, his movements methodical, automatic, his mind already on the next task. The house was quiet, the quiet that only existed when he was alone—something he had grown used to in recent years. The refrigerator's hum was the only sound breaking the silence, the steady thrum a reminder of the life that kept moving even when everything else felt like it had paused.

His phone buzzed on the counter, a short vibration against the cool granite surface. He wiped his hands on a dishtowel and glanced at the screen, seeing Sam's name light up. A smile tugged at his lips. It had been a few days since they last spoke; her voice had become an anchor in the chaos of his life. He grabbed the phone, answering before the third ring.

"Hey, Dad," Sam's voice came through, bright but carrying an undertone that he couldn't quite place at the time. It was a tone he'd brushed off at the moment but one that would later haunt him, a subtle signal that everything wasn't quite right.

"Hey, kiddo," he replied, leaning back against the counter, the dishtowel forgotten in his hand. "How's school?"

There was a slight pause, just long enough for him to register that something was off. Sam always answered quickly, eager to fill him in on her day, even during the usual mundane routine of classes and homework. But today, her response came slower, like she was searching for the right words.

"Fine, I guess," she said, her tone suddenly flat, the shift so subtle that it barely registered with him. "Same old stuff. I'm just... I don't know. I'm feeling kind of... weird lately."

John frowned, his concern flickering to life. The words were vague, but something about them stirred an unease in him. He straightened up, his focus sharpening on the conversation, the usual background noise of his thoughts falling away. "Weird? How so?"

There was another pause, this one longer. He could hear the faint rustling of paper on the other end of the line, the small sounds that filled the spaces between conversations but said so much. She was hesitating, and that wasn't like her. Sam was never one to hold back when something was on her mind.

"It's nothing," she finally said, her voice dismissive. Still, there was something forced in her tone, like she was trying too hard to convince herself—and him—that whatever it was didn't matter. "I'm probably just being paranoid."

John chuckled lightly, trying to inject some levity into the moment. "You've been watching too many horror movies again, haven't you?" he teased, hoping to coax a laugh out of her, pulling her back into the usual easy rhythm. He wanted her to brush it off, to say she was okay with him overreacting.

And she did laugh, but it was a hollow sound, thin and distant, not the warm, full laugh he was used to. At the time, he hadn't noticed the difference. He hadn't wanted to see. "Yeah, maybe," she said, her voice softer now. "It's probably nothing."

Probably nothing. John had let those words slide by, too caught up in his own world to recognize that she was reaching out, that her "probably nothing" was really a desperate something. In hindsight, the signs were there—small, almost invisible to someone not paying attention—but John hadn't been paying attention. He'd been distracted, his mind already drifting back to work, to the cases piling up on his desk, to the endless list of things that always seemed more pressing at the time.

"Well, don't hesitate to tell me if something's bothering you," he said, his tone light but detached, as if he was offering her an out, a way to end the conversation and move on. He hadn't pressed, hadn't asked her what was really going on, hadn't told her that he would always make time for her no matter what. It was a mistake, a missed opportunity that gnawed at him now, a regret that sat like a stone in his chest.

"I won't," she replied softly, the words hanging between them like a fragile thread. There was another pause, longer this time, as if she wanted to say something more as if she was searching for the courage to tell John what was on her mind. But then, in that soft, almost whispering voice, she said, "I love you, Dad."

The simplicity of the words hit him, but not as hard as they should have. "Love you too, kiddo," he'd replied, glancing at the clock and thinking about his next meeting, the next case, the next everything. His mind was always one step ahead, always moving forward, and in doing so, he hadn't noticed what was happening right in front of him.

The conversation ended, the click of the phone cutting through the quiet of the kitchen. John placed the phone back on the counter, the moment slipping away as quickly as it had come. He hadn't realized then that it would be the last time he heard her voice, that those would be the last words they ever exchanged.

Now, standing alone in his office, the weight of that realization hit him like a freight train. The last conversation he had with his daughter—the last time he could have done something—he had been distracted, distant. He had let her slip away, one small moment at a time, until she was gone.

The guilt was overwhelming, a crushing force that threatened to consume him. He had spent his life chasing criminals, hunting down killers, and bringing justice to other families. But when it came to his daughter, he missed the signs. He hadn't been there when it mattered.

John sank into his chair, his hands shaking as he ran them through his hair. The memory of that conversation echoed in his mind, looping repeatedly, each time more painful than the last. He wanted to go back, shake himself, and tell him to pay attention and listen. But it was too late.

John rubbed his temples, the memory like a dull hammer beating against his skull. He should have known. John should have asked more questions. The signs had been there, but he'd missed them. Now, he was chasing a killer, the same way he'd always chased answers, hoping it would somehow absolve him of his guilt. But it never would.

The door creaked open, and Claire Harper stepped in, quiet but steady. She'd been his rock these past few weeks, the one thing that kept him from unraveling completely.

"John," she said softly, her eyes scanning the mess of papers on his desk. "You're still here."

"I couldn't sleep," he admitted, his voice hoarse. He gestured toward the files. "Thought I'd go over Sam's case again."

Claire's gaze softened as she moved closer, pulling out a chair beside him. "You've gone over it a thousand times. There's nothing you missed."

John shook his head. "I missed everything, Claire. I ignored the evidence that pointed away from Mick because I wanted it to be him. I was so damn desperate to put a face to the pain... and I got it wrong."

Claire watched him for a moment, her eyes full of understanding. "You didn't get it wrong. You followed the leads that were in front of you. Nobody saw Matt coming."

"I should have," John snapped, standing abruptly and pacing the room again. "He was right under my nose the whole time. And now Sam's gone, and I was too busy playing detective to notice she needed help."

"You couldn't have known," Claire said firmly, standing and touching his arm. "No one could have. Don't do this to yourself."

John pulled away, the anger bubbling just beneath the surface. "I was her father! It was my job to protect her, and I failed."

The silence between them stretched out, heavy and suffocating. Claire stepped closer again, her voice softer this time. "John, we all have regrets. We all wish we could go back and change things, but that's not how it works. What you're doing now... this isn't about fixing the past. This is about finding Matt and ensuring he never hurts anyone else."

John's jaw clenched, the muscles tight as he struggled to control his emotions. "What's the point? Catching Matt isn't going to bring Sam back."

"No," Claire agreed, her eyes locked on his. "But it'll stop him from taking another life. It'll stop him from destroying another family. And that's something. It's all we can do."

He sank back into his chair, rubbing his face with both hands. The exhaustion was overwhelming, pulling at him from every direction. He wanted to believe Claire and find solace in the idea that stopping Matt would mean something. But the hole in his chest was too wide, too deep.

"I can't stop thinking about how I wasn't there," John said quietly, almost to himself. "Not just the day she died... but all the days before that. I wasn't there for her. I was always at work, always chasing something. I missed the signs."

Claire knelt down beside him, her hand resting on his knee. "You did the best you could with what you knew. We can't change the past, but we can decide what we do next."

John stared down at her, her words sinking in slowly, like water seeping through cracks in a dam. He wasn't ready to forgive himself, maybe not ever, but Claire was right. Matt was still out there, and every second they wasted was another second he could be planning his next move.

"We still have a chance to stop him," Claire said, her voice steady. "And when we do, you'll be honoring Sam's memory. You'll be doing what you've always done—protecting people."

John nodded, though the weight in his chest didn't lessen. "I just don't know if I have anything left to give."

Claire stood, her eyes unwavering. "You do. You're not alone in this, John. We'll find Matt together."

For a moment, the room was silent, the only sound the steady ticking of the clock on the wall. John took a deep breath, steadying himself, pulling the pieces of his resolve back together. It wasn't much, but it was enough.

"Okay," he said quietly. "Let's finish this."

Claire gave him a slight, encouraging nod. "We'll get him."

John glanced at the case files one last time before standing, his legs feeling heavy but his mind clearer than it had been in days. Matt Lawson had taken so much from him, but he wouldn't take any more.

They left the office together, and the hallway felt less oppressive than before. There was still a long way to go, but John felt like he was moving in the right direction for the first time in a long time.

The hunt for Matt wasn't over—not yet. But it would be soon.

And this time, John wouldn't miss a thing.

CHAPTER 34
ONE STEP BEHIND

John's eyes were locked on the phone, waiting for the call that might break everything wide open. His hands itched for action, for something to make all the waiting worth it. The lead they'd been chasing—the one that might finally bring Matt Lawson to justice—was still a vague promise in the air. John felt the tension gnawing at him, pulling him apart.

A movement caught his attention, and he looked up as Ramirez walked in, a sense of purpose in his stride that John hadn't seen in days. He was holding a slip of paper, his expression a mixture of excitement and the familiar edge of caution they'd learned to adapt after so many dead ends.

"We've got something," Ramirez said, dropping the paper onto John's desk. "A local resident just called in a tip. Says they saw someone matching Matt's description hiding out at an old property on the outskirts of town. It's secluded, falling apart—a perfect place for someone to lay low."

John didn't need to be told twice. He was already grabbing his jacket, his heart racing, adrenaline kicking in. "How credible is it?"

Ramirez shrugged. "The caller seemed pretty sure. It's the best lead we've had in a week, and frankly, it's the only one that's felt this solid."

John's jaw clenched as he processed the information. The moment felt fragile as if one wrong move could send it crashing into a million pieces. But he couldn't afford to hesitate. Not now. Not with Matt still out there, still planning, a threat to anyone who crossed his path. This time, John vowed, they wouldn't let him slip through their fingers.

Claire appeared in the doorway, her brow furrowed as she surveyed the scene. "You heading out?" she asked, though it wasn't a question. She could already see the tension in John's stance, the readiness to charge.

"We've got a tip," John explained. "Matt might be hiding at an old property outside of town. We're gearing up to head out there."

Claire nodded, moving closer, her presence calmingly contrasting John's barely contained fury. "We need to be careful," she said, her voice steady but carrying the weight of warning. "Matt's dangerous, but more than that, he's calculating. If he knows we're coming, he'll be prepared. We need to assume that he's already got a plan in place."

John shot her a look, frustration simmering beneath the surface. "I won't let him get away again, Claire."

"I know," she replied, her gaze softening. "But we need to do this smart, not just fast. Matt's cornered now, and that makes him even more dangerous. He's not going to surrender easily."

Ramirez cleared his throat, sensing the rising tension. "The teams are ready, John. We've got backup on standby, and state police are involved. We're not going in blind."

John nodded, but the storm inside him hadn't abated. Every second Matt was still free felt like a failure, a reminder that Sam's killer was out there, living, breathing, while his daughter was gone. He couldn't shake the image of Matt's smug face, how he'd taunted them in that last encounter, slipping through their grasp like smoke. Not this time.

"Let's move," John said, his voice hardening with resolve.

The drive to the outskirts of town was tense. John gripped the steering wheel with white knuckles, his mind racing as the cityscape faded into rural stretches. Ramirez sat beside him, eyes focused ahead, while Claire was in the backseat, quiet but thoughtful. The team followed close behind, a convoy of police vehicles cutting through the calm evening as they approached the old property where Matt was supposedly hiding.

"We need to consider how Matt's going to react when we close in on him," Claire said, breaking the silence. John glanced at her in the rearview mirror. She was staring out the window, her face a mask of concentration.

"He's not the type to go down without a fight," she continued. "He craves control. That's been his driving force all along—controlling the narrative, investigation, and people around him. Now that he's on the run, he's lost some of that control, and he'll lash out because of it."

"So, what are you saying?" Ramirez asked, turning slightly to face her.

"I'm saying that if we corner him, he will react violently. He'll try to take back control in whatever way he can, which means he's dangerous—not just to us, but to anyone nearby. We need to be prepared for him to fight back hard. This won't be a simple arrest."

John gritted his teeth, her words only adding to the tension twisting in his gut. "He's not getting away this time," he muttered. "Whatever it takes."

The landscape grew more desolate as they approached the outskirts of town, the roads narrowing, trees closing in on either side. The property they were heading to was isolated. It was a crumbling relic of a once-grand estate that had long since been abandoned to the elements. The perfect place for someone like Matt to disappear.

John's eyes scanned the perimeter as they pulled up to the property. The house stood at the end of a gravel driveway, partially obscured by overgrown trees and ivy that snaked its way up the stone facade. It was precisely where you could disappear, where no one would come looking unless they had a reason.

John killed the engine, and the team quickly gathered around him. "Ramirez, take your squad around the back," he ordered, keeping his voice low but authoritative. "Claire and I will head in from the front. No one moves in until we're sure he's here."

Ramirez nodded and signaled to the other officers. John could see the tension in their faces and how their hands hovered near their weapons. No one was taking chances.

"You ready for this?" Claire asked, her voice low as she moved beside him.

"Ready as I'll ever be," John replied, though he could feel the pulse of his anger still throbbing beneath the surface. Every part of him wanted to charge in, to find Matt and end this nightmare. But Claire was right. They had to be smart.

They approached the front of the house, moving quietly, their footsteps muffled by the overgrown grass that had swallowed the driveway. The house loomed ahead, its windows dark, the air thick with the scent of decay. John's heart pounded in his chest, every instinct telling him that Matt was inside, watching, waiting.

"Hold," John whispered, raising a hand. They paused just outside the front door, listening for any sound indicating movement inside. But there was nothing—just the eerie silence of abandonment.

He exchanged a glance with Claire, who nodded. Slowly, John reached for the door, hovering over the handle before pushing it open.

The door creaked as it swung inward, the darkness beyond it almost tangible. John led the way, his gun drawn, senses on high alert. The house smelled of mildew and dust, the floorboards creaking underfoot as they stepped inside. Claire followed close behind, her eyes scanning every corner of the room.

The place was a shell of its former self. Furniture had been overturned, and the walls were stripped of any semblance of life. The only sound was the occasional rustle of leaves from the broken windows and the wind whistling through the cracks.

They moved through the house cautiously, checking each room as they passed. There were signs that someone had been here recently—footprints in the dust, a half-empty water bottle on the floor—but no sign of Matt.

"Looks like he's been here," Claire whispered, her brow furrowing as she examined the remnants of the makeshift camp Matt had likely set up. "But he's gone now."

John's frustration spiked. How had Matt known to leave before they arrived? They'd moved fast, but Matt was clearly one step ahead.

"Damn it," John muttered under his breath. "He's still out there."

"Look," Claire said, pointing toward a small desk in the corner of the room. Papers were scattered across the surface as if someone had hurriedly left. John moved closer, scanning the documents. There were maps, notes—plans that made his blood run cold.

"He's planning something," John said, his voice low. "He's not done."

Claire's eyes darkened as she read over the notes. "This wasn't just a place to hide. He's been preparing for something bigger."

John's stomach turned as he realized what they were looking at. Matt wasn't running. He was still playing his game, and they were still pieces on his board.

Before John could respond, something on the wall caught his attention. A glint of light reflected off a piece of paper pinned near the doorway. His blood ran cold as he recognized the handwriting—Matt's handwriting.

John ripped the note off the wall, scanning it quickly. His hands shook as he read the words, each sentence a stab to his gut:

"You're too late, John. Always one step behind. You couldn't save her and won't save the next one. You'll always be chasing shadows, and I'll always be just out of reach."

The message was taunting and chilling, but the final sentence made John's blood turn to ice.

"I've already picked the next one. You'll know her name soon enough."

John stared at the note, his mind racing. Matt wasn't just toying with them— he was planning his next move. Another victim. Another life that could be taken before they had the chance to stop him.

Claire was at his side in an instant, reading over his shoulder. Her face paled as she absorbed the message. "He's taunting you," she said quietly, though her voice carried the weight of dread. "He wants you to know he's still in control."

John's fists clenched around the note, crumpling it in his grip. "Not for long," he growled. "We're going to find him, and we're going to stop him before he hurts anyone else."

But even as he said the words, a sinking feeling settled in his gut. Matt was still one step ahead, and whoever his next target was—they were running out of time.

The air in the house felt stifling now, the walls closing in as the weight of Matt's message bore down on them. John turned toward the door, his mind already racing through the possibilities. There was no time to waste. Matt was out there, planning his next move, and every second they spent standing still was a second closer to another tragedy.

"Let's go," John said, his voice hard and determined.

Claire nodded, her eyes filled with the same grim resolve. Together, they moved out of the house and into the growing darkness, the weight of Matt's words hanging over them like a storm cloud.

The ride back to the precinct was silent, each of them lost in their thoughts. John gripped the steering wheel tightly, his mind racing through the files, names, and connections—trying to figure out who Matt's next target could be. The sense of urgency weighed on him like a lead blanket.

He glanced at Claire in the rearview mirror, her face illuminated by the passing streetlights. She was staring out the window, her brow furrowed in deep thought.

"Who do you think he's targeting?" John finally asked, his voice breaking the heavy silence.

Claire turned to him, her expression dark. "It could be anyone connected to the case—anyone who might have been close to Sam, Emily, or Sarah. Someone Matt sees as part of the pattern he's created in his head."

John's stomach churned. The list of possibilities was endless, and with Matt's twisted sense of control, it could be anyone. But whoever it was, John knew one thing for sure.

They didn't have much time.

As they pulled into the precinct, the weight of the task ahead pressed down on them. Matt was out there, still playing his game. And now, it was a race against the clock to stop him before he struck again.

John stepped out of the car, his heart pounding with renewed urgency.

The hunt wasn't over. It was only just beginning.

CHAPTER 35
UNDER SURVEILLANCE

Claire pressed her key into the lock of her apartment, pausing as the faint metallic click echoed louder than usual in the silence of the hallway. She pushed the door open, hesitating in the threshold, her pulse quickening. The hinges creaked—a noise she'd heard a hundred times before—but tonight it seemed amplified, ominous.

She stepped inside, the familiar thud of the door shutting behind her grounding her for a moment. Automatically, her hand flicked the deadbolt into place, and she leaned against the cool wood. Her breath hitched as she stood there, listening.

The building was silent. Too silent.

Her eyes swept the room, every detail illuminated in the dim glow of the streetlights filtering through the curtains. The small plant by the window was still tipped over, soil spilled onto the sill—a mess she'd made in her rush this morning. That detail brought a flicker of reassurance. Nothing had been disturbed. Nothing had been moved.

But the feeling in her gut wouldn't go away.

A cold draft brushed against her skin, and she froze. Turning slowly, she saw the curtains by the living room window billowing gently. The window was open.

Her stomach tightened. Had she left it like that? Claire racked her brain, trying to remember. She was meticulous about keeping things secure, especially since the investigation had taken its darker turns.

She crossed the room cautiously, each step making her skin prickle. Her fingers trembled as she gripped the edge of the window and slid it closed. The lock clicked into place with a metallic finality, but it didn't settle her nerves. She stood there for a moment, staring out at the fog-covered street below. The darkness stretched endlessly, the faint glow of streetlights barely cutting through the haze.

Claire's reflection in the glass stared back at her, pale and tense. Behind her, the room loomed in shadow, every corner a potential hiding place.

Stop it, she told herself. You're letting him get to you.

She turned back to the apartment, her gaze sweeping the space again. Her eyes landed on the table—and her keys.

Her heart lurched.

She always left her keys on the kitchen counter by the door. Always. Had she dropped them there when she came in? Or had someone moved them?

The question lodged itself in her throat like a shard of glass. She replayed the moment she'd entered, trying to recall her movements, but her memory was muddled. The adrenaline coursing through her veins made it impossible to think clearly.

Claire crossed the room in quick, deliberate strides, grabbing the keys and clutching them tightly in her hand. She scanned the apartment, searching for anything else that felt out of place. The clock on the wall ticked too loudly, the refrigerator hummed, and the weight of the silence pressed in on her.

Was she imagining it? Or had someone been here?

Her thoughts spiraled, dragging her back to the precinct earlier that day. She'd told John she couldn't shake the feeling that Matt was still in control, even now. "You're letting him get in your head," he'd said, his voice edged with concern but laced with dismissal. "Focus on the facts. Stay grounded."

But this wasn't just paranoia. She knew men like Matt. They didn't just disappear when cornered. They lingered. They studied. They waited.

And she had gotten too close. She was sure of it.

She sat down at her desk, her hands trembling as she flipped open her laptop. The screen glowed, casting the room in cold light. She wanted to dive into the case, to immerse herself in the safety of work, but her focus kept slipping. Every creak of the floorboards, every faint sound, made her pulse spike.

Her phone buzzed on the desk, snapping her out of her thoughts. She picked it up, her thumb hovering over the screen.

One new email.

The subject line made her blood run cold: "We're closer than you think."

Her breath hitched as she opened it.

The message was short, just a few words: "You think you're safe? You're not."

Claire's hand flew to her mouth, stifling a gasp. The room seemed to shrink around her, the shadows pressing closer. Was this Matt? Was he watching her?

Her gaze darted toward the window, the curtains now drawn tight, and then to the door, where the lock remained firmly in place. But that didn't matter. He didn't have to be inside to know exactly how to rattle her.

Her mind raced. Was this just another mind game? Or was it a warning?

Her phone was still in her hand, her fingers trembling as she dialed. John picked up on the second ring.

"Claire?" His voice was sharp, instantly alert.

"I think…" She swallowed hard, trying to steady her voice. "I think Matt's trying to mess with me. I just got an email. It feels like him."

There was a pause, and she heard him exhale sharply. "I'll be there in ten. Don't open the door for anyone."

The call ended, leaving Claire alone with the suffocating silence. She clutched her phone tightly, her other hand gripping the edge of the desk to ground herself.

Her eyes flicked back to the keys on the table, and the question gnawed at her again: Had she put them there? Or had someone else?

* * *

Matt stood in the shadows outside Kate Whitman's house, his figure blending seamlessly into the overgrown bushes. The night was quiet, the silence only broken by the occasional rustle of wind through the trees or the distant hum of traffic. He crouched low, his breath steady, his eyes locked on the softly lit windows of the house in front of him.

He had been watching her for weeks now, ever since she had first appeared in his world. At first, Kate hadn't stood out—just another expert in a field full of them, someone the police called on when they needed her forensic expertise. But as the investigation into Sarah Thompson's murder had progressed, Matt had become aware of just how involved Kate was. And that bothered him.

Kate was smart—too smart for her own good. She had started to connect dots that others hadn't, asking questions that made Matt's skin crawl. But it wasn't just her intelligence that got under his skin—it was her arrogance. Her confidence. She carried herself as if she was untouchable, as if her mind put her above the rest of them.

Matt hated that.

He'd seen it before. He'd seen it in Emily, Sarah, and Sam. That quiet arrogance, that belief that they were somehow better than him, that their intelligence, beauty, or popularity made them invincible. And every time, he had been the one to show them just how wrong they were.

But Kate was different. With Emily and Sarah, it had been about control—taking something from them, making them powerless. With Kate, it was more personal. It wasn't just about silencing her. It was about proving that her intelligence was nothing compared to his. She thought she could outsmart him, that she could uncover the truth. But Matt was always one step ahead.

Kate had no idea he was watching her, and that gave him the upper hand. He had studied her every move, learned her routines, understood the way her mind worked. And the more he watched her, the more he saw the cracks in her armor. She wasn't as flawless as she pretended to be. Beneath that cool, professional exterior, she was just another vulnerable, weak woman.

Matt's grip tightened around the syringe in his pocket, the same one he had used on Sarah. He had the power here. He had always had it. And tonight, he would prove it.

As Kate moved through her house, her silhouette visible through the window, Matt's thoughts drifted back to the moment he had first become aware of her. It had been during one of the many briefings at the precinct, where Kate had presented her forensic findings to the team. At first, he had dismissed her—a typical forensic examiner, methodical and detached. But as she spoke, her confidence radiating, something inside him shifted. She wasn't just doing her job; she was asserting her dominance. Her intellect, her certainty—it was all a challenge.

He had felt it instantly, a surge of resentment that he hadn't been able to shake. It wasn't enough that she was good at what she did. She had to be the best. The smartest person in the room. And as she had gone through the evidence with the team, pointing out details that others had missed, making connections that no one else had thought of, Matt had felt his hatred grow.

She thought she was better than him. She thought her intelligence made her superior. But Matt knew better. He had seen it in all of them—the same self-assured belief that they couldn't be touched. And every time, he had been the one to bring them down.

It was the same with Kate. She thought she was in control, but Matt was the one pulling the strings. He had been there, watching her, listening to her, learning her habits. He knew when she worked late, when she left her house, when she returned. He knew how she moved, how she thought, and tonight, he would make sure she understood that her intelligence was meaningless in the face of his control.

Kate was the key. She had become the embodiment of everything he despised—her arrogance, her belief in her superiority, her professional dominance. She had to be taken down. She had to be made powerless.

But he had to be patient. He couldn't afford any mistakes.

Not this time.

Kate was more than just another target. She was a statement. The chief medical examiner—the woman who stood between him and freedom. Killing her would send a message to anyone who thought they could control him. No one was safe. Not even those in positions of power.

Matt's mind raced back to Sarah's death and the precision with which he'd planned it. Every detail had been meticulously crafted, just like Emily before her. He'd stalked, manipulated, and waited. And now, he was waiting again— watching Kate, knowing her time was running out.

The cold vial pressed against his palm, grounding him in the moment. Tonight, she would learn what it meant to be powerless. What it meant to be entirely at his mercy. He reveled in the thought, a slow smile spreading across his face.

Just like Sarah. Just like Emily.

Kate would go down in the same way, another perfectly executed plan. And when the police found her, they'd be no closer to catching him than before. Matt knew how to cover his tracks. He'd been doing it for years, hiding in plain sight, playing the role of the invisible man.

He shifted his weight, watching as Kate moved through the back hallway, the soft glow of light still illuminating her figure. She paused by the back door, her hand hovering over the lock. For a brief moment, Matt wondered if Kate sensed him. If she could feel his presence like a whisper against her skin. But then she locked the door and turned off the light, her shadow disappearing up the stairs.

He exhaled slowly, the thrill of anticipation humming through his veins.

Tomorrow, he would strike. But tonight? Tonight, he would wait. Watch. Let the tension build until the moment was just right.

This wasn't just about silencing her. This was about proving that no matter how intelligent, how successful, or how confident she was, he was still better. He was still the one in control.

And when she realized that—when she looked into his eyes and saw that he had outsmarted her—it would be the greatest victory of all.

CHAPTER 36
INTO THE WOODS

The tension in the precinct was thick and heavy, the air practically crackling with urgency. Every officer was moving fast, grabbing gear, checking radios, and exchanging glances that carried the weight of months of pursuit. This was the moment they'd been waiting for, and no one wanted to miss their shot at Matt Lawson.

Ramirez stood at the head of the table in the cramped briefing room, his posture rigid. His hands gripped the edges of a map spread across the table like it held the key to the entire case. It was a detailed layout of the North Creek hiking trail, marked with red lines and circles, showing the paths they would cover and the zones they'd already searched.

"We've got Lawson in a corner," Ramirez said, his voice stern with certainty. "His vehicle was found abandoned near the North Creek trail. He's on foot and hiding somewhere in those woods. We've got to flush him out."

The officers around the table leaned in, their faces set with determination, but in the back of the room, John DiMatteo stood with his arms crossed, his eyes dark with suspicion. Something gnawed at him. The whole situation felt too easy.

Matt had evaded them for too long and had been too clever in how he covered his tracks. Abandoning his car at a trailhead? It didn't sit right with John. He couldn't shake the feeling that they were being led into something. But he kept his thoughts to himself. The team needed to believe this was it. They needed the momentum.

Ramirez continued, "We'll split into two teams. Alpha will cover the eastern edge, Bravo the western. Keep your radios hot, and don't hesitate—Lawson is armed and dangerous." His tone was clipped and controlled, but John noticed the faint tension in the captain's jaw. Even Ramirez felt it—that something was off.

The officers murmured a low agreement as they dispersed, adrenaline buzzing through the room. Everyone wanted to be the one who brought Matt Lawson in, the hero who stopped the monster.

John joined Ramirez outside, where the cool night air bit at his skin, starkly contrasting with the precinct's heated atmosphere. He zipped up his jacket as he watched officers file into their vehicles, the low rumble of engines breaking the silence of the night. Claire lingered by one of the SUVs, her face pale but focused, her phone gripped tightly.

"You good?" John asked, his voice softer than usual but laced with concern.

Claire glanced up, her eyes shadowed with exhaustion. "I don't know. Something feels wrong. It's like he's... playing with us."

John stiffened, the knot in his gut tightening. Claire was the profiler; she had a sixth sense about these things, how Matt operated, his psychology. If she felt it too... "We can't second-guess every lead," John said, but the words felt hollow, even as he told them. He didn't believe it. Not really.

"Let's just get him," he added, his jaw tightening with determination. "We can't let him slip away again."

Claire nodded, but her eyes stayed troubled, lingering on the trees beyond the lot. She hadn't said it outright but was fighting the same creeping doubt. This didn't feel like Matt's endgame. It felt like the beginning of something else they hadn't yet seen.

The convoy of vehicles rolled out, their tires crunching on gravel as they headed toward North Creek. The night closed around them, and the trees loomed large and menacing under the dim moonlight, casting long shadows that twisted and danced across the road. It felt like the woods themselves were watching and waiting.

The hiking trail was darker than expected, the moon obscured by thick clouds, leaving the officers to rely on their flashlights to guide them. John and Ramirez led the Alpha team down a narrow path, the dense foliage brushing against them as they moved deeper into the forest. The woods were too silent, and every rustle of a branch, every snap of a twig, sent tension rippling through the group.

"He's close," Ramirez said quietly, gripping his flashlight like a lifeline. "I can feel it."

John nodded, his jaw clenched. But the knot in his gut kept tightening. The car was too obvious, too much like bait. Matt was smarter than this. He'd always been one step ahead, always out of reach, and John couldn't shake the feeling that this time wasn't different.

"Alpha Team, report in," Ramirez barked into his radio. A crackle of static followed.

"Nothing yet, sir," came the reply, breathless. "Just more footprints leading deeper into the trail."

"Keep pushing forward," Ramirez ordered. "We'll cover the perimeter."

John's flashlight cut through the trees, the beam bouncing off the underbrush as they pressed deeper into the woods. The branches scraped at their jackets, the crunch of leaves underfoot the only sound breaking the stillness. Every breath felt heavier, the silence pressing in on them like a vice.

John's instincts were screaming at him now. This wasn't right. The trail of footprints—they were too perfect, too easy to follow. Matt was leading them somewhere, but it wasn't to him.

Back at the precinct, Claire was pacing her office, her nerves fraying with every second. The glow from her laptop bathed the room in a faint blue light as she pored over the satellite view of the hiking trail. Her fingers tapped restlessly on the keys, her mind racing.

There was something they were missing. Matt's profile was meticulous and obsessive. He didn't make mistakes. He wouldn't leave his car out in the open, practically handing them a lead. This wasn't how he operated. He was too careful, too controlled. He always had a plan, always.

Her phone buzzed on the desk beside her, and Claire's hand hovered over it for a second. She wanted to call John and tell him that they were being played. But she knew how John thought—he needed to be on the ground, chasing leads, not second-guessing himself. Still, the feeling gnawed at her, tugging at the edges of her mind.

"We're missing something," she whispered to herself. And the worst part? Matt was always two steps ahead, and she was terrified that it would already be too late by the time they realized it.

Ramirez's radio crackled to life. "Sir, we've found something," came the breathless voice on the other end. "It's fresh—looks like Lawson's been here recently. A campsite. Footprints leading west."

John felt a flicker of hope rise in his chest. Maybe they were getting closer. Perhaps this time, they really had him.

"Copy that," Ramirez responded, his tone sharp with renewed determination. "Keep pushing. Don't let him slip."

John quickened his pace, his flashlight cutting through the trees. They were getting closer—he could feel the adrenaline rush from the hunt. Maybe Matt had finally made a mistake. Perhaps the pressure had finally gotten to him.

But even as they pushed forward, that gnawing doubt still clung to the edges of John's mind. This felt too easy, too perfect. They were being led somewhere, walking right into something they couldn't see.

Miles away, Matt Lawson crouched in the shadows outside Kate's house, his eyes cold and calculating as he watched the house before him. It was just past midnight, the street eerily quiet. The police were out in the woods, combing through the trails, searching for him where he had left his car.

That had been the plan all along. Leave them a trail. Make them think they were closing in. And while they were out there, wasting their time chasing ghosts in the forest, Matt would be here, finishing what he had started.

Kate was the key. She was the one who could destroy everything if she got too close if she figured out the truth. And Matt couldn't let that happen.

He watched as the lights in her living room flickered off, casting the house into darkness. She had no idea. None of them did. They thought they knew him, thought they could predict his next move. But they didn't know him. Not really.

His hand closed around the syringe in his pocket, which he had prepared for tonight. The same one he had used on Sarah. It was time to retake control.

In the woods, the search party pressed on, the cold night air clinging to their skin as they followed the trail of footprints. John moved with purpose, his mind racing as they neared the edge of a clearing. The campsite was abandoned, the fire long cold. The footprints led west, but the more John looked, the more the trail seemed... wrong.

"Hold up," John said, his voice cutting through the tense silence.

Ramirez turned to him, his brow furrowing. "What is it?"

John's eyes scanned the ground, his mind working furiously. "This doesn't feel right. He's leading us."

"What do you mean?" Ramirez asked, frustration seeping into his voice. "We've got a trail. We've got his footprints."

John shook his head, stepping back from the clearing. "He wanted us to find this. We're in the wrong place."

Matt moved with cold precision outside Kate's house, slipping through the side gate and crouching by the back door. The syringe in his pocket felt heavy, a reminder of the control he was about to take back.

Tonight was different. This time, there would be no mistakes.

A small smile crept across his lips as he reached for the door handle. The police were miles away in the woods, convinced they were closing in on him.

But Matt Lawson was always one step ahead.

And tonight, he was going to prove it.

CHAPTER 37
BAD FEELINGS

Bad feelings don't knock politely; they kick down your door and settle deep in your gut.

Claire Harper felt that familiar unease now—the kind that makes cops rest their hands on their service weapons even when everything seems normal. The precinct buzzed with its usual symphony: clattering keyboards, ringing phones, and the lingering scent of takeout food from a break room fridge that hadn't been deep cleaned since Obama's first term.

She stared at Matt Lawson's case file until the words blurred together. Psychological profiles, victim patterns, evidence logs—she knew them inside out and could recite them in her sleep. Yet something wasn't adding up.

Just then, Officer DeLuca appeared in her doorway, wearing an expression that made seasoned detectives sit up straight.

"Hey, Claire." He shifted uneasily. "Anyone heard from Dr. Whitman today?"

Claire's fingers froze mid-page. She hadn't spoken to Kate in a few days, but that was common. Kate often got lost in her work, disappearing into her files for hours. But today felt different. Frowning, Claire looked up at DeLuca.

"No," she said slowly. "Why? Hasn't she been in the office?"

DeLuca shook his head. "Nope. Her team said she didn't show up, and she's not answering her phone. It's odd. Kate's usually glued to her phone. Thought I'd check if you'd heard from her."

Claire forced a smile, but the knot in her stomach tightened. "Maybe she's taking a day off. I'll give her a call."

DeLuca nodded and headed down the hall, leaving Claire alone in the quiet of her office. She grabbed her phone and dialed Kate's number. Each unanswered ring tightened the coil of anxiety in her gut.

No answer.

She tried again with the same result—no voicemail, no text, just silence. Her mind raced through possibilities, each more troubling than the last. Kate wasn't the type to go off the grid without a reason. And with Matt Lawson still at large, the coincidence was too strong to ignore.

Suddenly, it all clicked—Matt's obsession with control, his need to dominate those who held power over him. Claire's breath caught as realization struck: Matt wasn't hiding in the woods. He wasn't running.

He was targeting Kate.

Her heart pounded as she grabbed her phone again, dialing John. It rang once, twice, then went straight to voicemail. Panic surged. She fumbled to call Ramirez. Again, voicemail.

She remembered the search team was deep in the forest, where cell service was nonexistent. Fear gripped her. She left a message for John, her voice urgent.

"John, it's Claire. Something's wrong. I think Matt's after Kate. She didn't show up at work, and no one's heard from her. I can't reach you, but I'm heading to her house. Call me as soon as you get this."

She hung up, snatched her bag, and dashed out of the precinct. The fear gnawing at her refused to let go. If Matt targeted Kate, there was no time to wait for backup. She had to get to Kate's house now.

The cold night air hit her like a slap as she stepped outside—a biting reminder of the danger ahead. She jumped into her car and sped off, the city lights blurring past. Her hands gripped the steering wheel tightly, knuckles white. Her mind raced with terrifying possibilities. Was Kate safe? Was Matt already there? The thought of Matt reaching another victim—of Kate lying helpless—made her stomach churn.

Every red light felt like an enemy, each second a cruel tick of a clock she couldn't control. She cursed under her breath, urging the traffic to move faster, willing time to slow down. Her phone lay silent on the passenger seat, with no responses from John or Ramirez. She tried to stay calm, to focus, but her heart hammered with dread.

A familiar sensation crawled up her spine as the streets grew darker—a sense of being watched. She couldn't shake the feeling that Matt was always one step ahead, orchestrating his moves like a master puppeteer. She recalled all the times they'd underestimated him, moments when they'd been too slow or reactive. Not this time. This time, she'd reach Kate before he did. She had to.

Pulling up to Kate's house, Claire left the engine running as she stared at the darkened silhouette. The house loomed silently, with no lights or movement— nothing to suggest Kate was home or anything was amiss. But Claire's gut told her something was very wrong.

She cut the engine, the sudden quiet almost deafening. Her breath fogged the windshield as she gazed at the still house. Her mind spun through every possible scenario hidden behind those dark windows. Was Kate inside? Was Matt already with her?

Unbuckling her seatbelt, Claire stepped out into the cold night, her footsteps muffled on the pavement. The air was thick with tension, the silence unsettling. She knocked softly on the front door, then harder.

No answer.

Her stomach lurched. She knocked again, louder, her voice edged with desperation. "Kate? It's Claire. Are you in there?"

Silence. The house remained still, an eerie calm settling around her.

Hands trembling, she redialed Kate's number. The phone rang, echoing into the quiet night. Claire held her breath, hoping against hope for an answer, for Kate's voice reassuring her that everything was fine.

But the silence on the other end confirmed her worst fears. Kate wasn't answering because she couldn't.

Claire's heart raced, panic clawing at her insides. She pounded on the door, shouting Kate's name. Still nothing. Her mind reeled with dark possibilities. Was she too late? Had Matt already struck?

She peered through the windows. Everything looked untouched—the door locked, the windows secure, and there were no signs of forced entry. But she knew better than to trust appearances. Matt was meticulous; he wouldn't leave a mess unless he wanted to.

Her phone buzzed in her pocket. For a moment, hope flared. She pulled it out, expecting John's name, but it was a delayed text from him in response to her voicemail.

Got your message. We're on our way, but getting out of the woods will take time. Stay put.

Stay put? Frustration surged through her. She couldn't wait—not when every second counted and Matt could be inside with Kate. She couldn't wait for John and Ramirez; they were too far away.

Resolute, Claire pocketed her phone and made a split-second decision. She wouldn't wait. She couldn't. Moving quickly around the side of the house, she searched for another way in. The darkness pressed in, amplifying every sound.

The back of the house was as still as the front, no signs of life or of Matt. But her instincts screamed that he was close, that she was walking into his trap. She couldn't shake the feeling that he was watching, waiting for the perfect moment.

She crouched by the back door, heart pounding as she tested the lock. Solid. No signs of tampering. But she knew better than to trust that. She had to get inside and find Kate before it was too late.

Her breath fogged the glass as she peered into the dark kitchen. Everything looked normal—too normal. Her fingers hovered over the handle, nerves frayed.

She had to act. Backup was too far away.

Her grip tightened on the handle, knuckles white. The night pressed in, each sound magnified, every second heavy with anticipation.

She didn't know if Matt was inside, watching from the shadows, or if she was about to enter an empty house. But she knew one thing—she couldn't wait any longer.

Taking a deep breath, Claire made her move.

CHAPTER 38
CONFRONTATION

Claire's whispered, *"Kate?"* dropped into the suffocating silence like a stone into a well. No echo. No answer. Just the heavy, all-consuming quiet of a house that felt wrong—not the obvious wrong of a broken window or shattered glass, but the insidious wrongness of a place too still. Too deliberate. Like a trap waiting to be sprung.

The house was neat—too neat. The shoes by the door perfectly aligned. The keys on the counter at a perfect angle. The cushions on the couch just so. Her eyes swept the living room, her gut knotting tighter with each passing second. There were no signs of a struggle, no upturned furniture or scattered belongings. But the air felt heavy, suffocating, as if it had been holding its breath for hours.

Her eyes landed on the open back door. The faint night breeze stirred the edge of the curtains, moonlight streaming through the glass pane. Claire frowned. Kate wouldn't leave the door open—she was too careful for that. Every instinct screamed at Claire to call for backup, to stop and reassess. But her mind kept cycling through the same horrifying thought: What if Matt has her? What if I'm already too late?

She moved cautiously toward the stairs, each creak of the wooden floorboards beneath her boots cutting through the silence like a gunshot.

Claire took the steps slowly, her breath catching with every movement. The air grew colder as she ascended, and the hallway stretched before her, impossibly dark and quiet. Kate's bedroom door was slightly ajar at the end of the corridor, a thin sliver of light escaping from the crack beneath it.

Her heart pounded.

She pushed the door open with one hand, just enough to see inside.

What she saw stopped her cold.

Kate lay on the bed, her wrists and ankles bound with paracord so tightly that the cords dug into her skin, leaving angry, raw welts. Her arms were stretched above her head, tied to the headboard, while a loop of paracord coiled around her neck, taut and unyielding. The noose was threaded through the bedframe, tightening with every involuntary twitch of her limbs.

Kate's breaths were shallow, her movements sluggish. The muscles in her arms twitched weakly, the drug in her system sapping her strength. But every movement—no matter how small—drew the cord around her neck tighter.

"Kate..." Claire whispered, her voice trembling as she rushed to the bedside. The image of Sarah Thompson flashed in her mind, bound and lifeless, her face frozen in terror. This was too similar. Too close.

"Don't move," Claire urged, her voice tight as she assessed the knots. Kate's glassy eyes fluttered open at the sound of her voice, but she couldn't focus. Her breaths were shallow and ragged, each one stealing more of the precious slack from the noose.

Kate's eyes fluttered open, barely conscious. Her breaths were shallow, her body weak. She made small, helpless movements, her wrists flexing slightly against the cords, but every twitch made the knot around her neck tighten further. Claire's heart leaped into her throat. There wasn't time.

She needed something—anything—to cut the paracord. Without thinking, she bolted from the room, practically flying down the stairs and into the kitchen. Her hands shook as she ripped open drawers, flinging utensils and random objects aside, searching for a knife.

"Come on," she muttered, her breath coming in frantic bursts. Her fingers fumbled over spoons, tongs—everything except what she needed. Every second felt like an eternity.

Finally, she found it—a chef's knife, its blade long and sharp. Claire grabbed it, her knuckles white as she clutched the handle, sprinting back up the stairs. Her chest burned with every breath, panic rising like bile in her throat. She didn't have much time.

When the reached the bedroom, Kate's body was jerking more frequently now, her unconscious movements drawing the knot tighter and tighter around her throat. Claire knelt beside her, tears stinging her eyes as she began sawing through the paracord, whispering to Kate the entire time.

"Stay with me, Kate," Claire murmured, sliding the blade under the paracord at Kate's neck. She began sawing at the thick rope, the fibers resisting her efforts. "You're going to be okay. Just hang on."

But Kate's body spasmed again, her wrists tugging against the restraints, the cord tightening another agonizing fraction around her neck. Claire's heart pounded harder, her hands shaking as she tried to cut faster, the knife barely making a dent in the thick rope. The pressure was unbearable. Every second counted. The air felt too thin, and Claire's mind raced.

The rope began to fray under Claire's desperate sawing, but not fast enough. Kate's movements were growing weaker, her lips taking on a bluish tinge. Sweat dripped down Claire's face as she worked frantically at the cords.

"Come on, come on," she muttered, her arms burning with effort. The knife caught on a particularly stubborn section of rope, nearly slipping from her trembling hands. She readjusted her grip, trying to steady herself, but panic clawed at her chest. Kate's breathing was becoming more labored, each shallow gasp a reminder that time was running out.

A floorboard creaked behind her.

Claire froze, her blood turning to ice. The sound had come from the doorway - so faint she almost missed it. Her instincts screamed at her to turn around, but she forced herself to keep working on the ropes. If she could just free Kate's neck...

Another creak, closer now. The air seemed to thicken, making it hard to breathe. Claire's hands shook so badly she nearly cut herself. She could feel a presence behind her, watching, waiting. The hair on the back of her neck stood on end.

She caught a glimpse of movement in her peripheral vision - just a shadow, but enough to make her heart stutter. Still, she didn't turn. Kate needed her. Just a few more seconds...

"Always so focused," Matt's voice came from directly behind her, soft and almost appreciative. "That's what I liked about you, Claire. You never could leave well enough alone."

Claire whirled, bringing the knife up in a defensive arc, but Matt was ready. His hand clamped around her wrist with crushing force, twisting until her fingers went numb. The knife clattered to the floor as pain shot through her arm.

Matt slammed Claire against the wall, knocking the breath from her lungs. Stars exploded behind her eyes as her head cracked against the plaster. Through blurred vision, she saw the syringe glinting in Matt's hand, impossibly close.

"I've been watching you, Claire," Matt said, his voice unnervingly calm as he pressed his forearm against her throat. "Studying you. Just like the others. Always thinking you're so clever, so in control." His lips twisted into a cold smile. "But you never saw me coming, did you?"

Claire drove her knee up, catching him in the stomach. Matt grunted, his grip loosening just enough for her to wrench free. She lunged for the fallen knife, fingers grazing its handle, but Matt recovered too quickly. His boot came down on her hand, grinding her fingers into the floor.

"That's your problem," he hissed, pressing harder until Claire cried out in pain. "You never know when to quit."

Behind them, Kate made a choking sound, her body jerking weakly against the restraints. The movement drew the noose tighter, and Claire's heart seized. She was running out of time.

With desperate strength, Claire twisted, grabbing Matt's ankle with her free hand and yanking hard. He stumbled, losing his balance just long enough for her to roll away. She scrambled to her feet, putting the dresser between them.

Her phone lay on the floor near the door, knocked free during the initial struggle. If she could just reach it, call for help...

Matt seemed to read her thoughts. He shifted, deliberately placing himself between her and the only escape route. "No one's coming to save you," he said, advancing slowly. "Just like no one saved Sarah. Or Emily." His eyes glittered with dark amusement. "Or Sam."

The name hit Claire like a physical blow. Rage surged through her, hot and electric. She grabbed a jewelry box from the dresser and hurled it at his face. Matt ducked, but the distraction gave Claire the opening she needed. She charged forward, ramming her shoulder into his chest.

They crashed into the hallway, grappling violently. The syringe swept past Claire's face, so close she felt the air displacement. She caught Matt's wrist, fighting to keep the needle away, but he was stronger. Inch by inch, the syringe descended toward her neck.

"You should see yourself," Matt panted, his face inches from hers. "The fear in your eyes. It's beautiful. Just like the others."

Claire slammed her forehead into his nose. Blood sprayed, and Matt reeled back with a howl of pain. The syringe clattered to the floor, rolling toward the stairs. Claire dove for it, but Matt grabbed her ankle, dragging her back.

She kicked out wildly, her boot connecting with his jaw. The impact sent shockwaves up her leg, but Matt's grip didn't loosen. He yanked her closer, flipping her onto her back. His blood dripped onto her face as he pinned her down, one hand fumbling for the fallen syringe.

Claire thrashed beneath him, but exhaustion was setting in. Her muscles burned, each breath a struggle against his weight. Her fingers scrabbled against the floor, searching for anything to use as a weapon. They brushed against something sharp – a shard from the broken lamp.

Matt's fingers closed around the syringe. Triumph blazed in his eyes as he raised it high, ready to plunge it into her neck. "Time to sleep, Claire."

With the last of her strength, Claire grabbed the glass shard and slashed upward. It sliced deep into Matt's forearm, drawing a surprised cry of pain. Blood poured from the wound, hot and sticky on Claire's hands.

But even injured, Matt was relentless. He knocked the glass from her grip and grabbed her throat, squeezing until black spots danced at the edges of her vision. The syringe descended in slow motion, the needle a silver flash in the dim light.

Claire's strength was fading. Her struggles grew weaker as consciousness began to slip away. Through darkening vision, she saw the needle hovering above her skin, felt its cold kiss against her neck.

This was it. She had failed. Failed Kate. Failed John. Failed herself.

The gunshot exploded through the hallway like a thunderclap.

Matt's body jerked violently. The syringe slipped from his fingers, missing Claire's neck by millimeters. His grip on her throat loosened as he stared down at his shoulder, where blood bloomed across his shirt like a dark flower.

Claire gasped for air, rolling away from Matt's collapsing form. Through tear-blurred eyes, she saw John standing at the top of the stairs, his gun trained steadily on Matt's chest. His face was a mask of cold fury, but his hands were rock steady.

"Don't even think about moving," John growled, each word dripping with barely contained rage.

Matt slumped against the wall, clutching his wounded shoulder. The fight drained from him like blood from his wound, leaving only a hollow shell of the predator he'd been moments before.

Claire struggled to her feet, her legs shaking so badly she had to lean against the wall for support. Her throat burned where Matt had tried to strangle her, and every breath felt like swallowing glass.

"Kate," she rasped, remembering with horror that time was still against them.

John kept his gun trained on Matt as Claire staggered back into the bedroom. Together, they worked to free Kate from the remaining restraints, their movements urgent but careful. When the final cord fell away, Kate drew in a desperate, shuddering breath. The sound was the sweetest thing Claire had ever heard.

"It's okay," Claire whispered, brushing Kate's hair back from her face. "You're safe now."

John stood nearby, watching as Claire tended to Kate, his expression unreadable. There was a heaviness in the air, a shared understanding between them of just how close they had come to losing everything.

Sirens wailed in the distance, growing closer. The cavalry was finally coming, but Claire knew the real heroes were already here – in this room, in this moment. She looked at John, saw the same understanding in his eyes. They had done it. Together.

"It's over," John said softly, holstering his weapon as backup arrived to secure Matt.

Claire nodded, her hand finding John's and squeezing tight. "Yeah," she whispered. "It's finally over."

But as she watched the officers lead Matt away, Claire knew some battles left scars that never fully healed. They had won, but the cost – in fear, in pain, in innocence lost – would stay with them. A reminder that sometimes victory came with wounds that ran deeper than flesh and bone.

CHAPTER 39
HEALING WOUNDS

Claire stood in the doorway of Kate's hospital room, watching her friend's chest rise and fall in the gentle rhythm of healing sleep. The morning sun filtered through half-drawn blinds, casting warm stripes across the sterile sheets. Three days had passed since they'd found Kate bound in her own home, since they'd stopped Matt from claiming another victim. Three days, and Claire still couldn't shake the image of Kate struggling against those restraints, fighting for every breath.

"You should get some rest," a nurse said softly, pausing beside her. "You've been here since dawn."

Claire managed a tired smile but didn't move. "I will. Soon." She couldn't explain that standing guard was as much for her own peace of mind as it was for Kate's. After Megan, after losing someone she loved to a predator like Matt, she couldn't bear the thought of leaving another friend vulnerable.

Kate stirred, her eyes fluttering open. Recognition and relief flooded her face when she saw Claire. "You're still here," she whispered, voice rough from the trauma to her throat.

"Always." Claire moved to the bedside, settling into the chair that had become her second home. "How's the pain?"

"Manageable." Kate's fingers brushed unconsciously against the bandages on her neck. "The physical part, anyway."

Claire reached out, gently taking Kate's hand. As a forensic psychologist, she'd counseled countless victims, helped them process their trauma. But this was different. This was personal. "You know what I'm going to say."

"That it's normal to feel this way." Kate attempted a weak smile. "That healing takes time. That I'm safe now."

"And that you're not alone," Claire added, squeezing her hand. "I'm not just here as a professional, Kate. I'm here as your friend."

Kate's eyes welled with tears. "I keep seeing his face. The way he looked at me, like I was nothing. Just another experiment." Her voice cracked. "How do you do it, Claire? How do you look into minds like his and not lose yourself?"

The question hit Claire hard, making her think of all the darkness she'd waded through over the years. "Sometimes," she admitted, "I almost do lose myself. But then I remember why I started this work. Every victim we help, every predator we stop—it matters. It has to matter."

A knock at the door drew their attention. John stood there, his usual sharp edges softened by concern. "Sorry to interrupt," he said, his gaze meeting Claire's with quiet understanding. "Just wanted to check in."

"Come in," Kate called, managing a stronger voice.

John entered, carrying a small potted plant—a peace lily. "Thought this might help brighten things up." He set it on the windowsill, somehow making the clinical room feel more alive.

Claire watched him, noting how different he was from the hardened detective she'd first met. This case had changed them both, broken down walls neither had realized they'd built.

"The DA wants to talk to you," John said to Kate, his tone gentle. "But only when you're ready. There's no rush."

Kate nodded, but Claire felt her hand tighten. "I want to help," Kate said. "I want to make sure he never hurts anyone else."

"You will," Claire assured her. "But first, you need to focus on healing. Both the visible and invisible wounds."

John's phone buzzed, and he checked it with a frown. "I should go. The team's still processing evidence from Matt's house." He hesitated, then added, "Claire, can I talk to you for a minute?"

She squeezed Kate's hand once more before following John into the hallway. The hospital bustled around them, life continuing its relentless forward motion while they stood in this pocket of aftermath.

"How is she really doing?" John asked, his voice low.

"She's stronger than she knows," Claire replied. "But recovery isn't linear. She'll have good days and bad days."

"And you?" His question caught her off guard. "How are you doing?"

Claire leaned against the wall, suddenly exhausted. "I keep thinking about how close we came to losing her. How Matt almost—" She stopped, steadying herself. "I've spent years studying predators like him, but this time it was different. This time it was personal."

John moved closer, his presence grounding her. "That's what makes you good at what you do. You never lose sight of the human cost." He paused, then added softly, "You helped me see that too."

She looked up at him, seeing the change in his eyes. Gone was the single-minded detective who'd been consumed by vengeance. In his place stood a man who'd learned to balance justice with compassion.

"We make a good team," she said, meaning more than just their professional partnership.

"We do." His hand found hers, a brief touch that carried volumes of unspoken understanding. "I have to get back to the precinct. Will you be okay here?"

Claire nodded, drawing strength from their connection. "I'll stay with Kate a while longer. Some wounds need more than just time to heal—they need witnesses to the healing."

"I know," John said, and she knew he was thinking of Sam, of all the healing he'd finally allowed himself to do.

As John walked away, Claire took a moment to breathe deeply, centering herself. This case had changed her, had forced her to confront her own vulnerabilities while helping others face theirs. But it had also shown her that she wasn't alone in carrying the weight of others' trauma.

She returned to Kate's room, picking up the conversation they'd paused. Today was about small steps forward, about being present in the moments of fear and strength alike. Tomorrow would bring its own challenges, but for now, this was enough—two survivors sharing the space between trauma and healing, finding strength in their shared understanding.

The peace lily on the windowsill caught the morning light, its white flowers glowing like beacons of hope. Claire settled back into her chair, ready to stand guard for as long as needed. Some battles were fought with badges and evidence, but others required nothing more than the steady presence of someone who understood both the darkness and the long path back to light.

CHAPTER 40
INTO THE MIND

The interrogation room was cold, almost clinical, bathed in the harsh overhead light that cast stark shadows across the table. The only sound was the ticking of the wall clock, each click counting down the seconds until they would confront the man who had haunted their every waking moment for weeks.

John sat at the table, his jaw clenched, hands folded tightly in front of him. Claire and Ramirez observed from behind the one-way mirror, Claire's eyes trained on the empty chair across from John. She drew a breath, steeling herself. This had been the hardest part—facing Matt Lawson in the flesh and pushing past his manipulations, his psychological traps. She knew his type. He would sit in that room thinking he held all the cards, and that was where they needed to turn his confidence against him.

The door creaked open, and two officers led Matt inside. His hands were cuffed, his posture rigid yet eerily relaxed, as though this were just another performance for him, a stage on which he could exercise his charm and calculated composure. He glanced around the room, his eyes finally settling on John with a smug smile that twisted something deep inside John's chest.

Matt sat, crossing his legs with a casual arrogance that belied the shackles binding his wrists. He leaned back in the chair, meeting John's gaze with a practiced calm. The silence stretched between them, thick with unspoken threats and pent-up rage.

John broke the silence first. "Matt," he said, his voice low, barely containing his anger. "We have some more questions for you."

Matt's smile didn't waver. "Detective DiMatteo, you've come back for more," he said, his tone light, almost playful. "I never made you out to be a masochist."

John fought the urge to react. He'd spent too long watching this man slip through his fingers, too long allowing him to pull the strings, manipulate the evidence, and evade capture. But now? Now he was here. Now he was theirs.

Claire, from behind the mirror, studied Matt's posture, his tone, the faint twitch of his fingers against the table as he spoke. He was comfortable, for now. That meant he thought he still held some power. She glanced at Ramirez and nodded. It was time to enter.

The door opened, and Claire walked in, her heels clicking softly on the floor as she took the seat next to John. She set her folder down on the table, meeting Matt's gaze with a look of calm indifference, almost as if he were nothing more than another profile to analyze, another puzzle to solve. His smile faded, but the smugness in his eyes remained.

"Dr. Harper," he said, his tone respectful yet mocking. "Nice of you to join us. I assume you'll be giving me my psychiatric evaluation today?"

"Something like that," Claire replied evenly, flipping open her folder. "But I'm more interested in understanding how you think, Matt. Why don't we start there?"

Matt chuckled, glancing between her and John. "You think you can figure me out? It's cute, really. You think you're here to unravel me, but you're forgetting something." He leaned forward, his eyes glinting. "I'm the one in control."

John bristled, but Claire placed a hand on his arm under the table, a silent reminder to stay calm. Matt's words were meant to provoke, to shake their resolve. She wouldn't let him.

She leaned forward, her voice measured, as if she were simply making small talk. "We've gone over your past, Matt. We've talked about Sarah, Emily, Sam... but there's something I don't understand." She paused, watching Matt's expression closely, her voice calm and even. "Why Kate?"

Matt's eyes flickered, just for a moment. He had expected her to start with the murders, to push him on the gruesome details, but this? This threw him off-balance. His lips curled into a smirk, but Claire could see the mask slipping.

"You don't get it, do you?" he said, his voice low but smug. "You think this is about what I did to them—Sarah, Emily, Sam—but that was just the beginning."

He leaned back in his chair, trying to regain his composure, but the silence stretched between them. Claire didn't flinch. She had spent years honing her ability to read people, to know when to push and when to wait. This moment was crucial—Matt was slipping into a pattern of deflection, but she could pull him out.

"You see, Kate isn't like the others," Claire said, her tone soft but deliberate. "She was more of a challenge, wasn't she?"

Matt's smirk faltered, the faintest trace of irritation flashing in his eyes. Claire continued, her voice almost casual. "It wasn't enough that she was smart. You couldn't stand that she was smarter than you, could you?"

For the first time, Matt tensed visibly. His fingers twitched, tapping a subtle rhythm on the table. Claire knew she had hit a nerve.

"Kate was different," she pressed, her voice gaining a sharp edge. "She didn't fall into your trap as easily as the others. She saw through you, and that scared you."

Matt's expression hardened, his smirk disappearing altogether. His eyes darkened, the playfulness replaced by something colder, more dangerous.

"Scared?" he spat, his voice low and venomous. "I wasn't scared of her. She was a fraud—just like the rest of them."

Claire raised an eyebrow, her tone still calm. "A fraud?"

Matt leaned forward, his voice tightening with resentment. "Kate thought she was so brilliant, so untouchable. Everyone listened to her, respected her, but she wasn't better than me. She wasn't smarter than me. She was just another self-righteous, overconfident woman who needed to be reminded of her place."

His words dripped with contempt, the bitterness palpable in the air. Claire didn't flinch. This was what she had suspected all along. Matt's need to control his victims wasn't just about power—it was about proving that their intelligence, their strength, their very existence didn't threaten him. But deep down, it did. And Kate, with her sharp mind and unshakable composure, had pushed him further than anyone else.

"You didn't kill Kate right away because it wasn't enough to end her life," Claire said softly, her gaze unwavering. "You needed her to know that you were superior, that she couldn't outsmart you. That's why you watched her, stalked her, planned every step. It wasn't just about power, Matt—it was about proving that no one could ever be above you."

Matt clenched his jaw, his hands gripping the edge of the table. The mask was gone now, replaced by raw anger and frustration. Claire had peeled back the layers, exposing the root of his obsession. She waited, letting the silence stretch again, forcing Matt to confront the truth she had laid bare.

"I had to show her," he growled, his voice laced with venom. "She thought she could solve the case, put the pieces together, figure me out. But she was wrong. She was always wrong. They all were." His eyes flashed, dark with fury. "They all thought they were better than me, but I made sure they knew the truth."

John shifted in the corner, his body tense, his fists clenched. Hearing Matt talk about his victims—about Sam, Sarah, Emily, and now Kate—as if they were nothing more than pawns in his twisted game, made his blood boil. But Claire remained calm, her focus unbroken.

"You needed to prove that their intelligence meant nothing in the end," Claire said, her voice barely a whisper now. "Because deep down, you were afraid that maybe—just maybe—someone like Kate could see through you."

Matt's eyes blazed with fury, but Claire didn't stop.

"Kate was never afraid of you," she continued. "And that's what you couldn't stand. She challenged you, and in your mind, that made her a threat. But what you couldn't see—what you refused to see—was that Kate's intelligence didn't make her better or worse than you. It just made you feel small."

"Shut up," Matt hissed, his composure finally cracking. "You don't know anything about me. You don't know what it's like to be constantly underestimated, constantly overlooked, while everyone else is praised for things they don't deserve."

Claire leaned in, her voice steady, but with a sharpened edge. "You're right, Matt. I don't know what it's like to be you. But I do know that every one of your victims—Emily, Sarah, Sam, and Kate—was stronger than you could ever understand. They didn't need to control others to feel important. They didn't need to destroy lives to prove their worth."

Matt stared at her, his face flushed with anger, but he didn't speak. The silence between them was heavy, charged with everything unspoken. Claire held his gaze, unblinking, unwavering.

"You've lost, Matt," Claire said quietly. "You can't control this anymore. You're not smarter than everyone else. You're just a man who hides behind violence because it's the only way you know how to feel powerful."

Matt's breathing quickened, his fists clenched tightly in his lap. He wanted to say something, to lash out, but the weight of the truth held him back. Claire had exposed him, stripped away his illusions of control, and now he was left with nothing.

"You wanted to dominate Kate," Claire said, her voice soft but firm. "But in the end, she's still here. She survived. And you? You're nothing more than a man in handcuffs, sitting in a room where your control doesn't exist anymore."

The words hung in the air like a final judgment, sinking into Matt's skin. He stared at Claire, his expression cold, but the fight had drained from his eyes. There was no more power left to assert, no more games to play.

Claire stood, her movements deliberate and calm. She nodded once to John, signaling that the interrogation was over.

As she walked toward the door, she paused for just a moment, turning back to Matt. "You're not in control anymore, Matt," she said, her voice final. "You never really were."

And with that, she left him sitting alone in the sterile room, the weight of his shattered illusion pressing down on him.

CHAPTER 41
SILENT VIGIL

The interrogation had ended, but its shadow lingered in John's mind like an unshakable chill. Matt's voice, cold and dripping with cruelty, echoed in his thoughts, each word a needle pricking at his conscience. The weight of Sam's loss pressed against his chest, and for the first time in years, he didn't feel the comfort of distance or resolve. All he felt was grief, raw and suffocating.

John entered his dimly lit apartment, his shoulders heavy. He closed the door, leaning against it as though it might keep the memories at bay. But they came anyway, in flashes: Sam's smile when she was little, her laughter filling the small spaces of their old house. He saw her first day of school, a wide-eyed little girl clutching his hand with excitement and fear. And then, in a painful twist, he saw her lifeless body in the morgue, her light extinguished forever.

He moved to his desk, where he'd hidden away every reminder of her, every photograph, every memento, in the hope that maybe, with enough time, the ache would dull. But it never did.

He reached into a drawer, pulling out a small, faded picture of Sam. In it, she was laughing, her face half-turned toward the camera, her eyes full of life. She was so young—barely out of high school. She'd had her whole future ahead of her, and he'd failed to protect her from a predator who had been right in front of him the entire time.

John sank into his chair, the photograph clutched tightly in his hand. "I should have been there," he whispered to the empty room. The weight of the words felt almost unbearable. It was a confession that had been building inside him for years, finally breaking free.

In his mind, John replayed the last few weeks of Sam's life. The moments he'd missed, the calls he hadn't returned, the late nights he'd spent working cases when he could have been home. John realized the signs were all there—the unease in her voice, the subtle hints of fear she'd tried to downplay. She had reached out, and he hadn't seen it.

His mind drifted to that last voicemail from her, one he'd kept but never dared listen to until now. He knew what she had said and could recite it from memory, but hearing her voice again was something he'd never been able to face. His hands shook as he reached for his phone, his finger hovering over the play button.

Just then, a soft knock broke the silence. John glanced toward the door, half-relieved and half-annoyed by the interruption. He wiped his face and stood, taking a steadying breath before opening the door.

Claire stood on the other side, her expression gentle and understanding. "I wanted to check on you," she said softly. After everything... I thought you might not want to be alone."

John managed a slight nod, stepping back to let her in. The silence in the apartment felt heavier with her there, as though his grief was laid bare for her to see. She crept to the couch, her eyes scanning the room, taking in the scattered photos, the untouched bottle of whiskey on the table, and the shadows of a haunted man.

For a few minutes, they sat in silence. It was Claire who broke it, her voice soft but unwavering. "It's okay to feel the weight of this, John. It's okay to grieve."

He looked away, staring at the photograph of Sam in his hands. "I can't help thinking I should have seen it sooner. I should have protected her."

"You can't blame yourself for what Matt did," Claire said, her voice steady. "You did everything you could to find justice for her. And you did it. You found him, John. You didn't let him get away."

John's jaw tightened, and he clenched the photo, his fingers whitening. "But I missed the signs. I didn't see what was right in front of me. I was so focused on my job and helping other families that I... I failed my own daughter."

Claire reached out, placing a gentle hand on his shoulder. "Sam knew you loved her, John. She knew you were doing everything possible to make the world safer. And she would want you to forgive yourself."

He met her gaze, a flicker of desperation in his eyes. "But how do I do that, Claire? How do I let go of the guilt when I can still hear her voice asking me for help?"

Claire took a deep breath, gathering her thoughts. "Sometimes, we carry the weight of guilt because it keeps us connected to the people we've lost. Like it's our way of honoring them, keeping their memory alive." She paused, her gaze unwavering. "But Sam's memory isn't in your guilt, John. It's in your love for her, in the way you've fought to bring her killer to justice."

He held her gaze, the knot in his chest loosening slightly. There was a part of him that wanted to believe her and finally release the burden he'd carried all these years. But another part of him, the part that had clung to his pain as a penance, resisted.

"I don't know if I can," he admitted, his voice barely above a whisper. "It's like... if I let go of the guilt, I'm letting go of her."

Claire's expression softened, her hand still resting on his shoulder. "Letting go of guilt isn't the same as letting go of her, John. You'll never lose her. She'll always be with you—in your heart and memories. But you don't have to carry the pain to keep her close."

John looked at the photograph again, his thumb tracing Sam's smiling face. He remembered the good moments for the first time—the times they'd spent together, the laughter they'd shared. He allowed himself to feel the love he'd tried so hard to bury beneath the grief.

Emotion washed over him, and he closed his eyes, letting the tears fall. Claire remained by his side, her presence a quiet comfort, a steady anchor in the storm.

After a few moments, John spoke again, his voice thick with emotion. "Thank you, Claire. For being here, for... helping me see things clearer."

She gave him a small, understanding smile. "You've been carrying this weight alone for too long, John. It's okay to lean on someone else for a change."

He nodded, the beginnings of acceptance taking root in his heart. He knew he still had a long way to go and still had wounds that would take time to heal. But at that moment, with Claire by his side, he felt a glimmer of hope—a sense that maybe, just maybe, he could begin to move forward.

They sat in comfortable silence, the weight of their shared experiences binding them in a way neither had anticipated. It was a bond forged in pain and resilience, a connection beyond mere camaraderie.

Finally, John stood and moved to his desk, where he placed Sam's photograph in a small frame. He set it on the corner of his desk, a silent tribute to her memory, a reminder that he could hold onto her without letting the guilt consume him.

A sense of peace settled over him as he looked back at Claire. They didn't need words to convey the understanding between them, the acknowledgment of all they'd been through and endured. It was enough to know they were no longer alone in carrying the weight of the past.

In the quiet of his apartment, John felt the first stirrings of healing, the beginning of a journey toward forgiveness—not just for Sam, but for himself. And with Claire by his side, he knew he wouldn't have to face it alone.

CHAPTER 42
ECHOES FADE

The courtroom felt like a vacuum, every sound absorbed by the weight of anticipation. The air was thick with the residual warmth of too many bodies pressed into a small space despite the October chill seeping through the old building's bones. Spectators filled the benches, their faces a mosaic of curiosity, anger, and sorrow. Reporters lined the back walls, their notepads ready, eyes sharp behind lenses and pens poised to capture the climax of a story that gripped Columbus through the changing seasons.

Matt Lawson sat at the defendant's table, his hands cuffed in front of him, the metallic restraints glinting under the harsh fluorescent lights. His face was a mask, betraying nothing—no fear, remorse, or defiance. His attorney whispered something in his ear, but Matt didn't react, his gaze fixed on some indeterminate point ahead, as still as the autumn leaves pressed between the pages of old case files.

John sat toward the back, his position offering him a panoramic view of the proceedings yet somehow making him feel detached. His back was straight, shoulders squared, exuding a calm that belied the turmoil inside. His eyes were locked onto Matt, but his mind was elsewhere, lost in a labyrinth of memories and what-ifs. The relentless ticking of the courtroom clock hammered in his ears, each second stretching into eternity.

Beside him, Claire shifted subtly, her presence a steady anchor in the storm of his emotions. She glanced at him, noticing the tight set of his jaw and the way his hands clenched into fists on his knees. Gently, she reached out and let her fingers brush against his arm—a silent gesture that spoke volumes. They had navigated this treacherous path together, from summer's heat through autumn's cooling embrace, bound by shared loss and the relentless pursuit of truth.

The judge cleared her throat, and the room seemed to hold its breath. "Matthew Lawson," she began, her voice measured yet carrying the weight of authority, "you have pled guilty to all charges brought against you." She continued, detailing the counts of fraud, conspiracy, kidnapping, and, most grievously, murder. Each word fell like leaves in still air, drifting through the crowd.

As the final sentence was pronounced—life in prison with the possibility of parole after 50 years—a collective exhale swept through the courtroom. A murmur rose, a blend of relief, dissatisfaction, and muted outrage, rustling like wind through October trees. Matt was led away, still impassive, flanked by officers whose expressions revealed nothing of their thoughts about the man they escorted.

John watched him disappear through the side door, a shadow swallowed by shadows. There was no triumph in his eyes, no sense of victory. Just a hollow ache that the verdict hadn't filled. The man responsible for so much pain was going to prison, yet the closure John sought remained elusive.

Outside the courthouse, the late October sky stretched above them like hammered copper, the sun struggling to pierce through clouds the color of old pennies. The air carried the sharp scent of woodsmoke and decay—autumn's particular perfume. Dead leaves skittered across the courthouse steps, dancing in the wind like lost souls. John stood there, momentarily overwhelmed by the swirl of activity—journalists clamoring for statements, protesters shouting slogans, lawyers and clients hurrying past.

Claire appeared at his side, her dark coat pulled tight against the October chill. She said nothing and stood with him, offering silent solidarity. After a moment, she touched his shoulder lightly. "You don't have to face this alone," she said softly.

He met her gaze, appreciating the sincerity in her eyes. "I know," he replied. "But there's something I need to do."

Without further explanation, he turned and walked toward the parking lot, leaves crunching beneath his feet like brittle bones. Claire watched him go, concern etching her features, but she understood. Some journeys had to be taken alone.

The drive out of the city was a blur of red and gold, the trees lining the streets aflame with autumn's last defiant display. John navigated the familiar route almost on autopilot, his thoughts a turbulent sea. Memories of Sam flooded his mind—her laughter, her eyes crinkled at the corners when she smiled, the warmth of her hand in his. The weight of regret settled heavily on his shoulders.

When he pulled into the cemetery, the late afternoon sun had taken on that peculiar October quality—golden yet somehow distant, like a memory of warmth rather than warmth itself. The headstones cast long shadows across grounds carpeted in red and gold leaves. The world seemed to slow here, the bustle of life-giving way to autumn's quiet contemplation.

He parked and stepped out, leaves crunching beneath his feet, the sound sharp in the cemetery's hushed atmosphere. Walking toward Sam's grave, he noticed how the maples had turned brilliant crimson, their leaves drifting down in lazy spirals. The oaks still clung to their leaves, stubborn in their golden glory. Nature's last pageant before winter's long sleep.

Sam's headstone stood before him, its polished surface reflecting the late autumn light. "Samantha Renee DiMatteo," it read, followed by dates that framed a life cut too short. He traced the letters with his fingertips, the stone cold against his skin, maple leaves gathering at its base like offerings.

Kneeling on the carpet of fallen leaves, John felt the earth's October chill seeping through his clothes. Memories flooded him—Sam jumping into leaf piles as a child, her laughter rising like startled birds into the autumn air; her fierce determination in high school cross country meets, running through landscapes painted in harvest colors; her last September alive, talking about college plans while they walked through Schiller Park, red and gold leaves dancing around their feet.

She had loved autumn. "Everything changes," she'd told him once, watching leaves spiral down from the trees. "But isn't it beautiful how it changes?"

John reached into his pocket with trembling fingers, pulling out his phone. The message—the voicemail she had left him that last October night—was still there, waiting. He'd carried it with him through countless seasons, a reminder of the call he'd missed, the words he'd never heard. His thumb hovered over the play button, his chest tightening. Today, finally, he would listen. Today, under these autumn leaves, he would face the last trace of her voice.

With a steadying breath that fogged in the cooling air, he pressed play.

Sam's voice filled the sacred space between earth and sky, as warm and bright as the October sun breaking through clouds. Her words wrapped around him like a memory come to life tinged with a sweetness that broke his heart. She'd called for no other reason than to tell him she loved him. There was no fear in her voice, no hint of the darkness waiting in her future. Just a simple, pure expression of love, preserved like a perfect autumn leaf pressed between pages.

John closed his eyes, tears slipping down his cheeks. He could almost see her there, autumn light catching in her hair, leaves swirling around her like they did now around her headstone. For the first time, he let himself feel the fullness of his grief, the ache that he'd carried through so many changing seasons. She had loved him—despite his mistakes, despite the distance that had grown between them. She had called just to say it, to let him know.

"I love you too, Sam," he whispered into the October air. The words felt like falling leaves drifting away in the wind. He knew she couldn't hear him, but saying it felt like a release—a letting go of the guilt that had haunted him through countless autumns. The weight in his chest loosened, replaced by a quiet peace, a sense that she was with him still, her love woven into the fabric of his life like golden threads in autumn's tapestry.

He stayed there, kneeling in the leaves, letting the silence fill him, allowing the memory of her voice to linger. Time passed unnoticed, marked only by the slow descent of leaves around him. He knew he would always carry her memory, not as a burden now, but as part of himself—like trees carry the memory of their leaves even in winter.

A sudden gust of wind stirred the fallen leaves into a dance around the headstone, red and gold spinning in the late afternoon light. John closed his eyes, imagining her touch and her presence beside him. For the first time, he allowed himself to fully feel everything—the grief, the guilt, and the love that had been overshadowed by his quest for justice.

When he finally stood, leaves clinging to his clothes, a sense of calm settled over him like evening dew. The weight hadn't lifted entirely, but it felt more bearable now as if sharing his burden with Sam—here among the falling leaves—had somehow lightened it.

As he turned to leave, he noticed Claire standing at a respectful distance beneath a maple tree, its branches a canopy of crimson above her. She offered a tentative smile, her eyes reflecting empathy and something else—perhaps admiration for his courage to finally face this autumn afternoon with Sam.

"How did you know I'd be here?" he asked as he approached her, his footsteps hushed by the thick carpet of leaves.

She shrugged lightly, autumn light catching in her hair. "Call it intuition. Or maybe I just know you better than you think."

He nodded, accepting her presence as a gift. "Thank you."

They began walking back toward the parking lot, their steps unhurried through the tapestry of red and gold that covered the ground. The silence between them was comfortable, like the quiet of late October woods. Overhead, more leaves drifted down, nature's gentle reminder that even endings could be beautiful.

"She meant a lot to you," Claire said after a while, her breath visible in the cooling air.

"She was everything," John replied, his voice steady. "Losing her... it changed everything. Like winter coming too soon."

Claire looked ahead, her expression contemplative. "Grief has a way of reshaping us. But it doesn't have to define us. Even the deepest winter gives way to spring."

He glanced at her, appreciating the wisdom in her words. "I spent so much time chasing after Matt, thinking that bringing him to justice would make things right."

"And now?"

"Now I realize that it doesn't change what happened. But it can prevent it from happening to someone else." He took a deep breath of crisp October air. "I can live with that."

They reached their cars as the sun descended, painting the sky in hues that matched the autumn leaves—orange and gold bleeding into purple twilight. John felt a sense of closure—not complete, but a step toward healing, like the natural progression of seasons.

"Are you heading back into the city?" Claire asked, keys jingling in her hand.

"Eventually," he said. "But I think I might take the long way. Clear my head a bit. The trees along the river are beautiful this time of year."

She smiled knowingly. "Drive safe. And John—don't be a stranger. You don't have to go through any season alone."

He returned her smile. "I won't. And thank you for everything."

She gave a small wave before getting into her car and driving away. John watched her taillights fade into dusk before climbing into his own vehicle.

As he drove away from the cemetery, the radio off and the windows cracked to let in the autumn air, he felt a subtle shift within himself. The road ahead was uncertain, but for the first time in a long while, it didn't seem so daunting.

The city lights eventually came into view, a mosaic of illumination against the darkening sky. Life went on—messy and unpredictable but also filled with moments of unexpected grace, like sunlight breaking through clouds or the perfect red-gold of a maple leaf. He thought of Claire and the unlikely partnership they'd formed. He thought of Sam and the love that would always be part of him, as constant as the changing seasons.

Pulling onto a bridge that spanned the Scioto River, John allowed himself a final glance in the rearview mirror. The cemetery was just visible, its trees ablaze with autumn's glory. Turning his eyes back to the road, he felt a quiet determination settle in.

There were cases to solve, people to help, and perhaps pieces of himself to rediscover. The journey wasn't over—it was just entering a new season.

As he navigated the winding streets toward home, the first stars beginning to peek through autumn's veil of clouds, John felt a tiny ember of hope ignite. The path ahead might be strewn with fallen leaves, but he was ready to walk it.

Epilogue

The lecture hall was bathed in the soft light of a spring afternoon, sunlight streaming through tall windows to paint golden rectangles across the polished floor. Claire Harper stood at the podium, her voice steady as she addressed the packed room of criminal justice students. Behind them, John DiMatteo leaned against the back wall, watching with quiet pride as she commanded the room's attention.

"Predatory behavior isn't just about violence," Claire was saying, her words carrying clear to the back row. "It's about control. About power. Understanding this psychology isn't just academic—it's about preventing the next victim, about seeing the patterns before they culminate in tragedy."

Her eyes briefly met John's, and they shared a moment of understanding. They both knew the cost of missing those patterns, of learning too late what had been hiding in plain sight.

"Take the case of Matthew Lawson," she continued, clicking to the next slide. Sarah Thompson's photo appeared on the screen, followed by Emily Reardon's, then Sam DiMatteo's. "These weren't random acts of violence. They were calculated performances by someone who had perfected the art of invisibility."

John watched as Claire walked the students through the case, noting how she wove together the technical details with the human element. She wasn't just teaching criminology—she was sharing wisdom earned through loss and pain, through years of studying the darkness that lurked behind ordinary faces.

When the lecture ended and the students filed out, their excited chatter echoing in the hallway, Claire gathered her materials with practiced efficiency. She looked up as John approached, a soft smile warming her features.

"Didn't expect to see you here," she said, sliding her laptop into its bag. "Though I probably should have. You never could stay away from the job for long."

"Neither could you," he replied, helping her collect the scattered papers on the podium. "Nice lecture. Though you left out the part about how you knew Matt was our guy before anyone else did."

Claire's smile faltered slightly, her hands stilling on the papers. "I recognized something in him," she said quietly. "Something I'd seen before, in another case, long ago."

John studied her face, noting the shadow that crossed it. "Your sister's case," he said softly. It wasn't a question.

Claire nodded, moving to the window. Outside, students crossed the sunny quad, their lives untouched by the darkness she and John had witnessed. "Megan was so much like Sarah," she said, her voice distant with memory. "Bright, determined, studying psychology. She was fascinated by predatory behavior patterns. Wrote her thesis on how killers hide in plain sight." A bitter laugh escaped her. "Ironic, isn't it?"

John stepped closer, his presence steady and grounding. "Is that why you became a profiler?"

"Partly." Claire turned to face him, her eyes clear despite the pain in them. "After they found her body, after the police said the case had gone cold, I made myself a promise. I would understand what they couldn't—or wouldn't. I would learn to see what my sister had been trying to understand."

"And you did," John said. "You saw Matt when the rest of us were looking in the wrong direction."

"Because I'd seen it before. The careful planning, the need for control, the way he watched from the shadows." Claire's hand brushed against the window glass, her reflection overlaying the spring scene outside. "Megan's killer was never caught. He just... disappeared, like smoke. But she taught me something, even in death. She showed me that the monsters don't always hide in darkness. Sometimes they walk among us, wearing badges or lab coats, hiding behind respectability."

John was quiet for a moment, absorbing her words. "Is that why you're here?" he asked finally. "Teaching the next generation to see what others miss?"

Claire smiled, though her eyes remained serious. "Partly. But I'm also here because I have something to tell you." She turned to face him fully. "I'm coming back to active consulting. The university's agreed to let me work cases part-time while maintaining my teaching position."

John's eyebrows rose slightly. "What made you decide that?"

"The same thing that brought you here today," she said, her voice gaining strength. "We're not done, John. Matt's in prison, but there are others out there. Other predators watching, waiting. And we're good at this—at seeing what others miss, at understanding the darkness without letting it consume us."

She stepped closer, her expression softening. "Besides, I've missed working with you. We balance each other. Your instincts, my analysis. Together, we see the whole picture."

John felt a smile tugging at his lips. "Are you proposing a partnership, Dr. Harper?"

"I might be." She gathered her bag, slinging it over her shoulder. "There's a new case. Remains were found out in McConnelsville. The local police are stumped."

John straightened, recognizing the look in her eyes—the same determination he'd seen when she'd first suspected Matt. "Tell me more," he said.

Claire gestured toward the door. "Buy me a coffee and I will. The diner down the street makes a decent cup."

As they walked out into the spring afternoon, John felt something settle in his chest. The weight of Sam's loss would never fully leave him, just as Claire would always carry the memory of Megan. But their shared understanding of loss had forged something stronger—a partnership built on more than just professional respect.

"You know," he said as they crossed the sunny quad, "Sam would have liked you. She had the same drive to understand people, to make sense of the senseless."

Claire's hand found his arm, squeezing gently. "And Megan would have appreciated your dedication to finding the truth, no matter how deep it's buried."

They reached John's car, the spring breeze carrying the scent of new beginnings. The darkness they fought would always be there, lurking in the shadows of seemingly ordinary lives. But they weren't facing it alone anymore.

"So," Claire said as they pulled away from the curb, "about this case in McConnelsville..."

John smiled, feeling the familiar surge of purpose. They had work to do, monsters to hunt, victims to speak for. And this time, they would face it together, their shared wounds becoming the lens through which they saw what others missed.

The shadows might hold their secrets, but Claire and John had learned to read them. And in that knowledge lay the power to prevent the next tragedy, to honor those they'd lost by protecting those who still lived.

Spring sunlight glinted off the windshield as they drove toward their next case, toward whatever darkness awaited them. But this time, they were ready. This time, they would see it coming.

And maybe, just maybe, they would save someone else's sister, someone else's daughter, from becoming another ghost that haunted the shadows between justice and grief.

ABOUT THE AUTHOR

Morgan McDonnell is the creator and co-host of the popular Crimepedia podcast. Born and raised in Columbus, Ohio, his fascination with true crime began when Unsolved Mysteries first appeared on his television screen. A graduate of Ohio Dominican University, Morgan combines his passion for storytelling with a keen interest in uncovering the truth behind unsolved cases.

When he's not delving into the depths of criminal mysteries or working at his full-time job, Morgan enjoys life as a husband and father. An avid reader and documentary enthusiast, Morgan also loves listening to podcasts and tending to his yard.